Between Time

By Carolyn Bond

www.carolynbondwriter.com

Re-edited: 2025

Previously published under the title Eternal Souls.

Trigger Warning: Miscarriage

DEDICATION

For my family for believing in me: Mom and Dad, Jeff and the kids, for lifting me up to chase my dreams, thank you.

Also, to all the souls in my ancestry that left a legacy of love and adventure.

ACKNOWLEDGEMENTS

This book would not have been possible without the help of several people who have provided anything from encouragement to editorial services.

Thank you to my husband Jeff for listening to my endless conversations about "what to do next" whether with the storyline or with getting the book published. Thank you, Jeff, for listening as I read you the entire manuscript, out loud, as I looked for errors. You always listened patiently, and I appreciate that.

Thank you to the people who took the plunge and read my drafts and the original version (Eternal Souls) and gave me invaluable input. I can't thank you enough: Dawn Chapman, Veronica Brown, Ashley Trautner, Jane Dean, Joan Graves, Brandie Pagel, Deb Colson, and JeanEllen Melton. You are all going to be awesome Protectors one day!

Contents

PROLOGUE - BEN

The young woman shook her head resisting the truth. We watched her argue with her doctor. "You must be mistaken! I saw it on the ultrasound! It's bigger than last time. It must have grown!"

"No," the doctor said, "there's nothing we can do. It may have just been a blighted ovum. It wasn't a complete embryo." The doctor sighed and grimaced.

"But it's been 8 weeks. It was real." She mumbled barely
audible.

We watched her husband stand frozen, the sadness engulfing him. He was helpless to soothe her. The doctor made a note in his chart as the couple shuffled out of the exam room.

A few hours later, the miscarriage finished. We made a circle around the couple as they held each other crying. We pressed in to protect them. To them, loss is so frightening. They don't understand…. but then, in a blinding sweep of light, we caught him.

A young man's soul broke free. A new life burst into the community of others. He looked at us, scanning each face for answers. Standing in the in-between world that his mother could not see, he looked at her. His face inches from hers. He watched as tears fell down her cheeks, tears for him. He turned to his father, and his eyes followed his father's arm around her, seeing that his father cared deeply for her, and for him. The new soul told us he wanted to tell them he loved them, to give them peace, so we helped him. For a moment, we opened her eyes to the invisible space between reality and after-life.

Her heart was open and soft. She turned slightly, blinking as she sensed a young man standing beside her. He was tall and thin. His soft curly brown hair framed his sweet face. Green eyes looked back at her with a soft glint of joy. He said, "It'll be okay, mom. I love you. I'll see you soon," and then he vanished.

She looked cautiously around as if she had to have been mistaken. Despite knowing she had to have felt such horrible loss, we knew she had peace because the light around her glowed slightly brighter. She would miss this child of hers, but maybe now she would know he wasn't gone forever.

PART ONE

1 - MARIE

1990 - Sonora, CA

Ben watched from the forest floor, peering up the hillside, up the dorm wall, three floors up. He watched Marie taking deep breaths, closing her eyes. He wondered, if she would fall, could he catch her? Could he save her? Allen would be there with her soon, so, for now, he just watched from the forest floor.

***

Marie St. Clair sat on the narrow windowsill with her legs hanging out the window. From her dorm window on the 3rd floor, she could see straight out over the Ponderosa pine forest in the little valley next to the college. The soft breeze blowing across the Sierra Madre range whistled through the trees and made a haunting song. Her shoulder- length, brown, wavy hair lifted with the rushing sound of air. She closed her hazel eyes and breathed deep. A slight smile curled at the ends of her pink, full lips. The air temperature was slightly cool but refreshing. Her whimsical, crinkled peasant skirt lifted too, but the leggings underneath kept her warm enough.

It was so green here. She'd loved living on the

coast for several years but found a feeling of homecoming here in these foothills. Something in her stirred. It reminded her of a place familiar, but she didn't know where.

The door opened, and Allen stood in the living room. He dropped his backpack on the floor and looked at her with a slight scowl of concern. His soft blue and tan plaid shirt, rolled up to his elbows, set off his blond hair and brown eyes. He saw Marie and his eyes crinkled as a natural lop-sided smile lifted his face.

"One of these days, you're going to fall right out the window," he said. She turned and smiled and then looked back out across the trees.

"How tall do you think these trees are? The tips are level with us," she said.

The dorm was on a ridge around the valley, so the base of the trees was already a long way below the first floor. "Probably a good 100 yards," he said, and he strode toward her with long strides of his nearly six-foot frame.

The enormity the trees made her feel safe, even hidden. It seemed like nothing could get her here. The world, to her, was a place to explore and admire for its beauty.

Allen went to the window and put his arms around her and eased her back inside. "I admire the forest as well, but there's no need to fall out a window to enjoy it."

Marie and Allen had met shortly after the semester started. They soon discovered they were both from Kentucky. Marie's family had moved to Southern California when she was in 4th grade. She had grown up in a beach town on the coast. On a school trip to Yosemite, she realized the Sierra Madre mountains reminded her of forgotten childhood memories.

Allen McCracken had moved to California right after high school to study forestry. A nature lover himself, he'd always dreamed of living near Yosemite, and this 2-year college was very good and affordable. He planned to transfer to Humboldt State University to finish his degree. He was very bright, 3rd in his high school class. Geology and earth science always interested him. With his geology degree he could work for the US Geologic Survey or become a forest ranger. Neither paid a fantastic wage, but his love for the forest won out. He'd looked at various options and determined that the Sierra Madre National Forest was a great place to explore. His end goal was to be a ranger in the Yosemite back country.

Allen didn't let her go after he set Marie softly on the floor. Instead, he embraced her tenderly, looking into her eyes like it had been weeks since he saw her. The closeness overtook them, and he kissed her deeply as she yielded to his passion. His searching mouth looking for her response found it as her heart swelled with the intoxicating love she felt for him. He gently released her and smiled. They both lingered in the physical proximity: the scent of skin, the warmth of closeness, the soft breath of the other on their cheek.

Marie closed her eyes and let herself get lost in the feeling of warm safety in his embrace. She had never met anyone like him with his down-to-earth nature and no pretenses. His quick mind and sultry gaze were disarming and thrilling. What thrilled her more than anything was his passionate love for her. He couldn't get enough of her. The fire that drove him to be with her was always smoldering and ready to blaze. She loved it when he would grab her in his arms and kiss her passionately and then smile his crooked grin. His brown eyes would crinkle in the corners showing his mischievous intentions. Allen McCracken was a firecracker in plain clothes.

Getting lost in his hungry kisses, she heard the rumbling of his stomach. When he pulled away, she assumed the will to live by not starving had won out.

"So, are you hungry? Let's go into town and get something to eat," he said.

"Sure!" She replied, not surprised. She slipped on her pink Topsider sneakers, already laced, and grabbed her purse. They closed the door behind them and headed to Allen's Jeep in the parking lot.

"Hi, Allen! Oh, hi, Marie." Lydia, Marie's old roommate, said as she nearly bumped face first into Allen. Her long blond hair had flung forward and covered her face as she abruptly stopped. She reached up and tousled it back and to the side, smiling seductively and hanging onto Allen's gaze with her eyes just a bit too long.

"Hi, Lydia," Allen responded flatly. Marie looked Lydia up and down and scrunched up her nose. Lydia shifted her gaze at Marie and smirked.

"Come on, Allen," Marie nudged, looking back at Lydia

as they continued down the sidewalk to the Jeep.

After they were in the vehicle and backing up, Marie remarked, "Did you see her? Hussy! Don't talk to her. She's trouble. I always knew she was a skank!"

Allen laughed out loud. "Seriously, Marie" he looked deep in her eyes, "you know I love you."

"Hmph!" Marie's face remained snarled for another 30

seconds or so before Allen tried to distract her.

"The Dendrology field trip sounds like it will be fun. Dr. Peterson is taking us to a creek that originates as an underground river."

"Hm. I suppose so." The snarl uncurled into

just a smirk. Allen tried to sneak a peek at her to gauge her mood. "He said there are some nice ferns at the mouth of the cave. Maybe we could go back there, after the field trip, and have a picnic."

She smiled a bit now, "That sounds nice. I love you, Allen. I just don't understand why some people are so rude. Obviously, she knows we have been together for months. She doesn't listen to her shoulder angel at all!" They smiled at that, and Marie relaxed and looked out the window. The overwhelming beauty of the straight tall pines and azure blue sky above was intoxicating to her. Marie felt a surge of peace and happiness just to live in that beautiful countryside and go to college with Allen.

It was a small community college, but since it was in a remote location, the school had about 100 dorm apartments. Some students were from as far away as San Francisco or Southern California, like Marie, or they were like Allen, from as far as Kentucky. The school was about 5 miles out of town, too far to walk on the winding mountain roads. Small town life blossomed in Sonora. Most of the shops were little "mom and pop" stores. There was one major grocery store, Safeway, who's "e" and "w" had been burned out, so the students jokingly called it "Saf- ay". There was also a Kentucky Fried Chicken and a McDonalds. Other than that, the only brand name you could find was the sign in a parking lot that designated the lot as a Greyhound Bus stop. You had to buy tickets in the convenience store that shared the parking lot.

Sonora was originally a town settled by gold miners. The famous 1849 gold rush brought prospectors to the area with a fever for wealth. Most of the prospectors were regular men looking to make their fortune, but greed was rampant and caused more than one gun fight over a mine shaft or stretch of the shallow river that ran through town. It was a time of the truly Wild West, but it was also over-populated and under-policed. Just one decent nugget would be enough to make dreams come true.

It was strange to think of those miners, living in tents and wading in the riverbeds with their pans. The scenery had not changed much, so it was easy to imagine them out there as you drove along the winding road to town. Marie thought occasionally she could see someone in the water, but on closer look, realized she was imagining things.

The tall pines covered much of the high foothill land here. Underneath the high canopy of branches, Marie could look across the forest floor strewn with yellow needles. Large boulders were all around, some as big as a house. In the creek beds, piles of small, rounded stones snaked along ravines or down small valleys. It was cold and dry at this time in late February, but soon the spring rains would come. Beyond the forest, dry yellow grass, rumpled from winter snow, softened the rolling landscape around majestic oak trees.

The Jeep came around a curve where a dry creek bed crossed under the road. Marie looked up the creek as her chestnut wavy hair wafted over her shoulder in the wind. An odd feeling struck her: cold and lonely. While most of the time, it was wonderful living here, there were times when you'd have a feeling like you were trespassing. Stories of wild men, hidden in the caves in the hills, who still believed there was more gold here were well-known. When she first moved here, the staff at the college warned her not to go off into the woods alone and never trespass in an area where it looked like someone might be camping or "squatting". Some people came to the area to get away from city life and pan for gold, and they really didn't want to be found. Or worse, they might think you were going to find "their" gold. They had no compunction about shooting first and asking questions later.

Marie shook off the tingling prickles crawling up her neck. She hated that feeling she would get that someone was watching her. She thought sometimes she must be delusional, so she never told anyone when she felt it. She wondered if other people felt it but just didn't say anything either. She looked over at Allen who seemed focused on the road. He didn't seem to notice anything but the road. She liked that he was so logical, but there were times she wondered how he didn't see the intuitive parts of life. She turned her gaze back out the open window of the Jeep. As they drove, she couldn't help but stare into the darkened shadows of bushes and trees. She could almost make out a face, this time of a man with wavy brown hair, but surely not. It was just tricks of her mind trying to make something out of nothing.

Trying to distract herself, she wondered what the special was at the Europa Café today, but then decided she'd get her usual club sandwich. They were regulars at the café, always getting a club sandwich platter. It was a comfortable place to grab a bite and visit with friends.

As Allen drove through the little downtown street, Marie looked at the faces of the people walking on the sidewalk. She decided she would feel out what Allen thought of the vibes she got.

"Allen, do you think we have guardian angels that, you know, protect us from evil? Sometimes I wonder. Sometimes I feel like we aren't alone."

"No," said Allen, "I'm not really convinced there is anything else here except us animals."

"Do you believe in an afterlife?

"Oh, I don't know. I guess maybe. Sometimes I think religion and all that is just a bunch of made-up stuff to make people feel better. There is nothing scientific about it. You can't test it. No one really knows for sure."

"I guess. But miracles happen. I have heard about things that didn't make sense or should never have happened. Something had to cause them."

"I think there is a logical explanation that we just don't know about. I certainly can't go through life thinking demons are trying to get me all the time. Besides, why would they? Don't they have anything better to do than run around and scare us to death?"

"I don't know. Sometimes, I," she paused and decided to dive in even if he did think she was crazy, "I just feel something, you know? I feel creepy sensations, and I feel like I'm not alone. Sometimes I feel like my ancestors watch me to see what the current generation is up to. It's a little crazy, but it happens to me often."

"Hm., I guess. I have never felt that. I can say that I have been somewhere before where my family has lived for a long time, and I can imagine the overlapping of moments that have happened. I can imagine my dad as a boy running along a road and now, I'm on that road and there are layers of life."

"That not quite the same. They are like memories. This is a real being, a person, there, other than me, in the same moment in time."

"Yeah, I know what you are trying to say. I just don't think I have ever felt that."

Marie thought for a minute. "One time I was sitting on some swings at a playground in the middle of the night. I could swear I saw movement in the darkness, and then I felt the most frightening sense of

11

impending danger. It was like a sixth sense."

"It was probably just your subconscious putting together a string of thoughts that ended with a decision to run. You may have been in danger from a mugger."

"Maybe." She thought, slightly frustrated that he had no

idea what she was talking about.

"Anyhow, until I see it with my own eyes, I just don't think I buy it... But it does make you a fascinating person!" She rolled her eyes at him.

Allen pulled into a parking space in the lot beside the café. The dusty gravel crunched under their feet as they made their way to the sidewalk. The cool breeze softly tousled their hair as they walked holding hands. They could smell the aroma of lunch being pulled together in the café's kitchen. Marie breathed in the crisp mountain air and relished the warmth of Allen's hand in hers. She closed her eyes and breathed in all the goodness of life around her.

2 THE EUROPA CAFÉ

"So, Ben, let's see how you're coming along. Look around and tell me what you see," said Tom. They were sitting opposite each other in the same booth as Marie and Allen. Marie and Allen could not see or hear their conversation. Ben and Tom, and all the other old souls sitting amongst the living at the Europa Café, occupied a parallel space in time. You could say they were ghosts, but really, they were just people with a job to do, who happened to no longer have a physical body.

Ben looked around the Europa Cafe'. He had soft curls of brown hair that framed his face. His skin was perfect porcelain, never having endured chicken pox or acne. He'd been following Tom around until he got the hang of life as a Protector. He looked around them. There was an older couple in the booth behind Tom. He heard the woman tell her husband about a new family at church that her bridge group had been talking about. She thought that the husband may have been an ex-convict and it really concerned her that someone like that might be sitting next to them every Sunday. She wasn't sure what he had done but it must have been violent, you could tell from his eyes. The man would just say, "Huh," and continue spooning vegetable soup into his mouth.

"The man is calm, pure. I feel calmness from him. The woman, she's bitter. There are dark spots around her soul." "Good," said Tom. "She isn't a lost cause, but she could

be pulled, in such a way, that would be fatal for her and cause pain for him. Pain in itself is not dangerous; what matters is how they deal with it." Tom had a short beard of brown hair that matched the hair on his head and sideburns. His white linen shirt was ironed smooth with a collar that was flat rather than folded over. The buttons had an antique look, as though they were carved perfectly from bone. He held himself in a relaxed but composed, position of a leader.

A thin, short, middle-aged woman in a ruffled waitress uniform bustled up to the table and started taking Marie and Allen's order. She looked like you couldn't get anything past her, and she'd knock you out just as fast as she'd give you a pat on the back. The noise of the living talking, giving their orders, chatting amongst each other, moving chairs, and walking around, mixed in with the chatter of the Protectors, was nearly deafening. The living could not hear the double conversations and went right on as if they were on a movie screen for the Protectors.

The Protectors lingered around chatting. The new souls, the living , would often pass right through them. Sometimes they occupied the same place without any notice. The new souls were totally oblivious to this parallel world right beside them. Perhaps it was best this way. New souls, Tom explained to Ben, tended to let fear overtake them if they didn't understand something, or worse, completely under-estimate it.

Marie was sitting half next to and half over-lapping Tom in the booth. She and Allen were talking about where they grew up.

"We live on the coast and our family sails a lot. We have a little 23' sloop and sail to Catalina Island and stay the weekend. We anchor offshore or tie up to a mooring. One time at night all the plankton glowed an iridescent blue color in the water all around us. It was magical. I'd never seen anything like it!" Marie explained.

Allen looked at her with fascination, as though filing away her words. He smiled unconsciously and the corners of his brown eyes crinkled up.

"I've never met anyone like you. You laugh so easily and seem to enjoy everything around you. You act like life is always an adventure." She smiled bashfully at his honesty.

Marie had ordered hot tea with honey and lemon. He watched her fuss over the tea bag while she talked, wrapping the string around the spoon the little bag set upon and tugging until all the tea in the bag was squeezed out. She carefully did this ritual of measuring the honey and gently stirring until all the sweetness dissolved into the tea. "No one I know drinks hot tea. I didn't even know you could order it. Who would do that, other than British people, right?" he added.

But she did. Not in a snobby way, but because it seemed to give her pleasure. It made the moment special. Marie looked back at him coyly, but the light in her eyes danced when she lingered in his gaze. Her heart raced just being near him. She reached out and laced her fingers in his and smiled.

Tom and Ben had been talking about other new souls around them when Tom stopped, his attention caught by Marie's words. "My first name is Sarah. I'm named after my great, great grandmother, Sarah Elizabeth."

"Grandma Sarah was something else. Her family had money, tons of it! And her parents wanted her to marry well so she would be comfortable, but she fell head over heels for a farmer. A poor farmer that worked hard in the fields. Her father disowned her because she wouldn't listen to him. Isn't that funny? What's wrong with marrying a farmer? She followed her heart. What's a life without love? I admire her." Marie paused and imagined this proper Victorian lady helping to harvest a field. She was strong and beautiful because she was known for following her heart.

"I like to think that my affinity for tea is like that. Yeah, it's different but it not to be snooty or anything. It's just special. It's making the ordinary something. It's making regular life more lovely.

"You know her sisters never married. I guess they chose to be alone rather than marry someone they really had no love for, just for money." She thought of how it must have been for them. "I want to be known for following my heart. I hope my great grandkids say that about me."

Tom was smiling at Marie with pride. "You see, Ben," he said as he turned his head toward Ben, "Sarah Elizabeth was MY great, great, great granddaughter. Oftentimes family units stay together on both sides of life. The familial feelings intensify our ability to influence the new souls, so it makes sense to keep the families together."

Tom's words hung in the air as they sat in the booth listening and watching. Ben's brows creased as he leaned slightly into a conversation at the table next

16

to them. A big brown curl fell across his forehead. Allen and Marie ate club sandwiches and chit-chatted. New souls bustled around the cafe waiting tables or laughing with friends. It was always crowded here. As it was every Thursday night, the Café was filled with people in square dancing dresses and outfits. The short, ruffled dresses looked so out of place in everyday life, but also quaint. There was a group that met at a dance hall on Main Street to dance and they'd all come here afterward, hungry from the exercise and full of bubbly conversation.

They were laughing and talking and hugging each other. Joy and friendship were everywhere. You could almost feel the warm vibration of positive energy in the air.

Ben was looking at Tom's face and glancing back to Marie's. Tom and Marie both had dark brown hair that lay in soft waves. They had almond-shaped eyes and porcelain skin. They were not gorgeous people per se, but they had a stately beauty. Their eyes sparkled with light. They had the same soft smile with demure, bow-shaped full lips and straight, white teeth. Their smiles were genuine and warm, like coming home, but to a person rather than a house.

Even though the generations between Tom and Marie were many, they looked like cousins, maybe even brother and sister.

"Tom, how many years did you live?" Ben asked. "Eighty-four years," said Tom. "A long time, a full life.

Many children. A marriage filled with love from and for a woman who stole my heart. We had some hard times," at this his eyes looked down at his folded hands on the table, "but love got us through."

"How is it that I am a baby and I look like I'm 20 and you are 84 and we look the same age?" asked Ben.

"Our outward appearance is merely a projection. Obviously, we don't have bodies. There is an imprinted appearance all souls create. It's you in the prime of your adult life. It's you if there had never been anything to subtract from your potential. No scars, no malnutrition, no sickness, no bad habits. It's as if you had taken your DNA and grown it for 20 years and got a human, well, sort of like you, since you technically were never born" Tom laughed at the last point.

He went on, "The one thing that often surprises new souls when they cross over is that a person who was created differently, the doctors would have called it a congenital abnormality, is the same here. That's because they were created perfectly for their purpose in life."

Tom stopped and looked at Ben's facial expression. Ben seemed lost in thought staring at the faux wood pattern in the Formica. "Ben, do you wish you had lived in the world, outside the womb?" Ben glanced up and gazed deeply into Tom's eyes, pausing before he answered.

"I suppose so, in a way. But how can I really miss something I don't know anything about? I wonder what food tastes like. They seem to enjoy it. But, in many ways, we are the same and I relate. They have relationships and care about each other like us. I would have liked to have gotten to know my parents, yes. They seemed to love me and yet they had never met me. How can that be? And I can see how the love doesn't stop when they cross over. You obviously still care for Marie and Sarah Elizabeth. Do you often see others you loved?"

Tom sighed and smiled, "Yes. I do. And you will eventually meet your parents when their time comes. My sweet Jenny and I see each other often. She is assigned to another new soul and occasions come up where the new ones get together. I also see my son Henry often."

Tom scanned the room like a sentry. "I lived about 200 years ago when this country was in the middle of the Revolutionary War. I was a Captain in that war. It was a harder life. So different from now." He gestured to the room.

He continued, "This place here was only occupied by natives then. The Europeans hadn't even made it this far west. Jenny and I lived in Virginia and moved to what is now Kentucky. The natives there killed my Henry when he was just a boy. It broke our hearts. He'd just gone to get water at the stream. It was an awful attack on a boy. He was such a sweet little thing, too," his lower lip pushed up in a pained frown as he looked away.

"We never could understand how such bad things can happen in the world, but you must go on. In truth, three of my children died that year." He sighed. "Henry hit me the hardest, though. He was so full of life."

"How did you go on?" Ben asked.

"From one breath to the next. Now, we understand about the evil all around us and how people make choices to act on impulses. Henry was just a victim of his circumstances. Of course, when my time came to leave the world of the living, Henry was there and helped me. Funny how the boy you brought into the world ends up being more of a dad to you than a son. His kind heart gave him the skills to fight that evil on the other side. He is a true warrior and is often called on by Lorenzo, our leader. My son is my hero and mentor.

You'll meet him sooner or later. He is not assigned to a soul. He tracks certain old souls that would seek to destroy anything good and pure in this world. He is quite good at his job."

A mask of seriousness covered Ben's face as he looked around the cafe'. His eyes focused in on things he had not seen before. There were more souls around him than he'd seen at first. Of course, there were the living souls eating and talking obliviously, and there were the Protectors all around like a party of ghosts in the same room, but now something else came into focus. There were others.

In corners. Under tables. Hiding behind backs. Shapeless figures in the edges of his vision were barely perceptible, but there were cold spots in the room trying to hide unnoticed.

"Why haven't I seen them before." he whispered to
himself.

Then he noticed an odd sight that gave him a shiver. A shadow crept around the shoulders of the woman behind Tom, the woman who he had been observing earlier. Ben watched the woman now peering at a young lady at the register. The lady was largely pregnant and had no ring on. She looked very casual in a loose tee shirt and sweatpants pushed low to accommodate her large pregnant belly, and her hair was in a messy ponytail. The woman smirked and Ben heard "Tsk! Tsk!" come from her down-turned mouth. The woman's Protector was a young woman who was leaning in to whisper in her ear.

"The girl needs you; she needs a friend. She is alone in this town. She's far from her family." Ben heard her urge the woman to invite the girl to sit with them and talk to her.

However, the woman ignored the Protector. The dark shadow lay comfortably around the woman's neck. The old woman seemed to look paler and the lines in her face darkened by a degree. It was as if the darkness was drinking the life right out of her.

"Ben," said Tom, "I have some work with my son Henry that I need to do. I am going to assign you to Marie for a while. If you have an easy enough time guiding her, you will be permanently placed with her."

"Okay. Do you think I'm ready?" asked Ben.

"You're still a bit green, but you won't be all alone. I have been babysitting Allen for his Protector. He should be back any minute now." Just then a tall, dark headed man with deep brown eyes that seemed to look right into your mind appeared.

"Right on cue, Jacob!" said Tom. "This is Ben who I was telling you about. I was just telling him that he would most likely be taking over Marie's handling from now on. By the looks of how snugly lovey-dovey she and Allen are, I suggest you two get along. You may be together a while."

Jacob slid into the booth and eyed Ben to size him up.

Ben looked at Marie hanging on Allen's arm, "I see the permanency of these assignments. This could take another 60-70 years."

He turned distracted by an abrupt "Harrumph" coming from the cash register. The pregnant lady's order was ready, and the waitress was ringing her up. Apparently, the girl didn't have enough for her order and the older couple was now standing behind her waiting to be checked out. The woman rolled her eyes and tapped her foot with her arms crossed. Then to her shock, her husband reached in his wallet and pulled out a $20 and said to the girl, "Here, honey. It's ok. Use the change to get something for the baby."

The man's wife looked aghast with her jaw slack and ajar. She turned on her heel and walked outsie to wait for him.

Jacob held out his hand to shake Ben's. Ben took it and gave a pleasant, unassuming smile.

"So, you are Allen's Protector?"

"I am," Jacob said, still staring at Ben with an expression of keen interest, now punctuated with a slight upturn of the corner of his mouth as though this answer was more like admitting he was a special agent.

Ben shivered a little under the pensive gaze. Tom watched Ben shrink back into his seat and chuckled, "Jacob is a very intense person."

"So, when did you live?" Ben asked Jacob.

"Ah! Yes, I walked the earth in the Middle Ages. I was

a musician. I played at court in France."

"Oh. Wow." Ben's words trailed into the din of the room, and he looked like he was trying to grasp what Jacob what talking about. Jacob didn't seem to be offering anything else.

Tom said goodbye and flashed away. Marie and Allen finished up and began to make their way to the cash register. Jacob followed them and Ben followed him. For the first time, Ben seemed lost without Tom, biting his upper lip, and glancing around at Protectors and Shadows. A group in the corner burst out laughing and Ben jumped as he glanced back.

3- A WALK IN THE WOODS

On Saturday morning, Allen and Marie headed out to the car to find something to amuse them.

"Want to hike the flume for a while? It's not too cold out," Alan said looking around at the scenery around them.

"Sure! That sounds great," Marie said.

The flume was an engineered creek that flowed around the area and carried water to lower elevations. Parts of it were constructed as a wood chute and other parts were not more than a ditch. There was a trail beside it that was good for hiking because it was maintained. The sound of running water follows you all the way, relaxing even the worst college-induced stress. A few weeks back they started early in the morning and hiked 15 miles of it together in another section farther downstream.

Allen parked the car in a residential neighborhood with cabins. Marie opened the car door and breathed in the clean mountain air. The tall pines reached up into the sky above them. Their scent added to the freshness in the air. The sky was a steel gray that looked like at any moment would let go of mountains of snow to be sifted onto the landscape. In her long johns, wool socks and hiking boots, she knew that in no time the exercise would warm her up. Allen came around the car and held her door as she got out: always the Southern gentleman. He closed the door and put his arm around her waist, pulling her close to him.

They leaned against the car, is weight pinning her against the car, as he whispered in her ear with a husky voice,

"You're not afraid to be in the woods with me, are you, little girl?"

She giggled and kissed his neck. The heat from inside his shirt warmed her cheeks. She could smell the clean scent of his body wash. "Maybe it's you that should be worried!"

Obviously not worried, his lips covered hers and she softened like melted butter. If it wasn't for the car holding her up, her knees would have buckled. Even after five months together, she still got the zingers racing through her insides when he kissed her. His kisses were pure passion, searching and hungry. Most of the time, like now, it was all she could do to breathe and not pass out.

He released her from his embrace but held onto her hand as they set out on the trail. The water babbled and bounded along the little ravine. The soothing sound seemed to push away the world. All there was in the world at that moment was Marie and Allen, the water, the tall trees, and the sky that seemed to reach all the way down to the ground. The flume trail snaked away from the road and the houses into wilderness. It was well-maintained, and she felt like it was a little bit of civilization that safeguarded her from real wilderness.

Allen spotted some deer back in the trees. "Look there!" he whispered to her. The deer stopped to look at them and then pranced away. Such majestic beauty. Marie was captivated by the natural world. It was a place where no one played the silly games of fashion or politics. It seemed like raw majesty. The danger was understandable and expected. Animals ate and protected their young and themselves. The weather was a force to be reckoned with. Either respect it or pay the price. It was all common sense and no parlor games.

In return for knowing your place in the natural world, you could enjoy breathtaking wonders. There was nothing out there that she could see or touch that she didn't understand.

"So, what are your plans for summer, Marie?" said Allen. "It'll be here soon. Are you going back to your parents?"

"I don't know. I haven't thought that far out," she said. "Maybe I could find a summer job. Maybe something in Yosemite. I know they take on summer help and have dorms you can live in. That would be awesome. My friend, Kay and I visited some of her friends there last month and it didn't look too bad. It would be fun!"

"Yeah. That might be fun. I'll need to go back home for a few weeks and visit my family over the summer. I'm not sure I could take a summer job if I'm going to be gone a while. I'm also not too excited about not seeing you for that long. Some hippy rock climber might catch your eye, and you'd forget all about me."

"Well, I don't think that'll happen," she chuckled, "but I would die a slow death of depression from missing you. I spend every minute with you now. I don't want to imagine life without you here. You're more than a boyfriend. You're my best friend."

Allen looked down at the dirt trail strewn with little bundles of pine needles. His eyebrows creased. His warm brown eyes looked thoughtful showing his internal struggle. "Well, I have thought about it for a while and wondered if you wanted to come with me back to Kentucky. You could stay at my mom and dad's. I don't know if you have any family in Louisville you'd want to visit, but we could if you did. It would put a crunch on making any income for the summer, but you wouldn't need to worry about a place to stay or food."

She thought about it. It would sure be nice to stay with him all summer. She hadn't been back to Kentucky since her family moved away when she was nine. Frankly, she wasn't sure where Winchester, Kentucky, even was. When she was a kid, it seemed to her the whole state was either Louisville, farmland or woods. She figured Winchester must fit in the farmland category.

"Hm. Well, that would be fun. I'd love to meet your family. Do you think they would like me?"

"Sure, they would. They are pretty nice people."

"Well, would they think I'm a crazy Californian? A lot of people think Californians are kind of 'out there,' you know?"

"As long as you're nice, which you are, they will love you," he said.

"Well, I know how the farther east of Louisville you get, how people kind of have a whole other way of relating to each other. What if I said something wrong or didn't say something that they thought I should? I don't even know what normal is there," said Marie.

"They might talk about you, but only behind your

back. You know how small towns are." They both laughed at that.

They came around a curve in the trail and found themselves on the edge of a small reservoir. Mist was rising from the surface of the water. It looked so peaceful. They stopped for a minute to take in the scene. The reservoir was about 50 yards across. The far side had a shallower bank, and this side had a pile of small boulders as its edge. Marie could see little air bubbles seeping up near them in the water. She stepped to the edge to look closer and see if she could see a fish. There was some movement below the surface. It was too deep to see the bottom right there. It would have made a great fishing spot. She was sure there were some good size fish lurking down in the dark depths. A swishing of the water below caught her eye.

As she leaned in, some pebbles on the boulder she stood on slid beneath her feet, throwing her off-balance, and before she could catch herself, she was falling forward toward the icy water. Allen lurched forward to catch her arm, but before he could grasp her fingers, she was too far away from him. Horror hit them both. The water was surely frigid. They were out here alone. There would be no way to get help in an emergency. A stream of thoughts flashed in Marie's mind in an instant. Allen frantically grasped at air too late.

Marie tumbled in a near complete somersault before she splashed into the water. The icy water took her breath away, paralyzing her lungs. The cold of the water felt like a thousand tiny knives all at once. Her chest contracted and any air in her lungs escaped. Her boots filled with water and her soaked clothes felt like dead weights. She frantically tried to scramble upward, but the weight of her clothes and the ineffective movement cancelled each other out. She could see Allen on the edge looking at her, his eyes wide with terror as he stood there alone. All at once she saw him dive in after her, but then he seemed to disappear. Her lungs were screaming in pain. The depth of the water was not too deep, maybe twenty feet, but more than her ears could handle. The pressure was like being boxed in the ears. The water got darker and darker, but she could still see a few feet in the murky depths. Then she saw a dark movement in front of her. Terrified, she thought she saw a woman in the darkness with long curly hair. She couldn't make out a face. It was too dark. She knew it was what she'd seen from the surface. She felt long arms wrapping around her and closing in. Then she blacked out.

4 - SOMETHING IN THE SHADOWS

Ben was in the reservoir as fast as Marie was. He saw the shadows in the water taunting her. He knew what they were. They were not fish. He found her on the bottom in the center of the swirling shapes. He pushed her up toward the surface away from the shadows.

Allen was searching in the water, but the shock of the cold was more than his senses could override. Jacob was under Allen welling the water up around him to keep him near the surface and away from the depths.

Marie's body came close enough to the surface for Allen to see her and he used his junior lifeguard training to reach across her body to pull her next to him along his side while he did a scissor kick to get to the edge. Ben and Jacob were underneath them both giving them added buoyancy and kicking away the dark fingers trying to pull them down.

Allen reached the edge and pushed her limp body up onto the boulders. He had to scramble up and heave her over the top onto the trail. His body was screaming in protest because of the cold water. His muscles were contracting, and his breathing was fast and shallow. Ben used the force of his mind to lift Marie's body off the rocks ever so slightly to aid Allen's progress. Jacob had his arms around Allen's waist holding him, so he didn't tumble back into the water. The dark souls in the water were seething mad at losing the near gain. They swirled up through the water and up into the air. They were not ready to give up so easily. Ben looked back just in time to see a woman with loose, long curly auburn hair grasping at Marie's heels, her eyes determined and full of hate. The woman faded into dark mist, disappearing when she saw Ben and Jacob.

Jacob, seeing this, said, I'll stay and protect Marie and Allen while you find help." Ben trembled slightly as he nodded, Jacob was already in full battle mode with at least four Shadows. Ben flashed out of view and searched a perimeter of the area. The nearest help was a man who lived nearby, just minutes away. The man seemed suddenly struck with the urge to go down to the reservoir. He picked up his walkie-talkie for the forest service and his coat and set out at a brisk pace. Even on this trail, dark arms clutched at the man through the smooth trunks of the manzanita trees. Their smooth red branches contrasting with the dark, bony arms and fingers. Ben beat them away. The man could hear someone crying out near the lake and began to run. The anguished cries of, "MARIE! Can you hear me? Please MARIE! Open your eyes! BREATHE!" tore at him and he started sprinting. At last, he came around the corner and saw Allen bent over Marie, alternating crying and pleading and giving mouth to mouth resuscitation. Marie's sopping clothes clung to her young frame.

Wet, dark locks of hair stuck to her pale cheeks. She was fading.

Allen saw the man and yelled, "Help me! She's not breathing!" The man pulled out his walkie-talkie.

***

Marie woke up in Calaveras County Medical Center emergency room. She had an IV, an oxygen mask, and lots of warm blankets on her. Allen was right there looking calm on the outside, but in his wide eyes, he was near hysterical. He was the first to notice she was starting to stir. The nurse, whose back was turned, was busily writing notes on a chart on a clipboard at the foot of the bed.

"Marie! Wake up, baby!" said Allen.

The nurse turned around to look and saw the monitor showing Marie's pulse going up. She stepped over and pulled up Marie's eyelids and jotted down a note about the look of her pupils. "Looks like she's coming back among the living!"

Marie sleepily fluttered her eyes open. The room seemed to spin. She just wanted to go back to sleep. It was so peaceful and quiet before, like another world. The glaring lights and beeps of the IV intruded on her peace of mind.

"Wake up, Marie! I know you're there. Come back to me," said Allen.

She opened her eyes more and saw where they were. Allen was hovering and looking into her eyes with a pained smile. His eyes crinkled up when he smiled, and he had a dimple on one side. She smiled back at him but felt like her mouth didn't work. She looked around the room and saw the nurse, a young man with dark hair and hazel eyes smiling at her and another man that leered at her. He had a mop in the corner and was slowly backing away. He didn't seem to fit in the room and for some reason looked mad at her. She turned back to Allen who was talking to her.

"Are you ok?" he asked.

She nodded. Her body still felt cold. He offered her a sip of water from the cup with a straw. She looked around again and only Allen and the nurse were there now. She wondered who those other two men were, but they were gone now.

5   - AFTER EFFECTS

Back at the dorm room later that afternoon, Allen was making her some hot chocolate and buffeting her with several blankets. Marie was trying to figure out what happened. It was such a crazy blur. She remembered slipping and thinking she was going to die for sure. The next thing she remembered was waking up in the hospital. She had no idea how Allen managed to get her there.

"Tell me again what happened. I can't remember," she said holding her head in her hands and rubbing her temples. The whole incident was making her anxiety rise again. She had a foreboding feeling, like something important happened and she couldn't catch the thought in her mind. A shape would come to mind, and she knew it had to be important and just as she started to see it, it faded into darkness.

"Did they give me a sedative or anything in the ER? I feel like I can't think straight. Things don't seem to make sense!" said Marie.

"No, in fact you were fairly sedated from the cold water. They were trying to get your heartbeat higher and warm you up. But there was one point, at the reservoir, where you stopped breathing. I did mouth-to-mouth until the paramedics got there and they gave you oxygen. Maybe the time when you stopped breathing affected your head some? They tested your brain activity at the hospital and said you shouldn't have any lasting effects, though," Allen told her.

She thought about all that a minute. She didn't realize she'd stopped breathing. Maybe that would explain why she thought she saw crazy things in the water. It was all just a hallucination. That would make the most sense. Anything else couldn't be real.

Allen looked at her with his brows knitted together.

"So, what do you remember? What is confusing you?"

She didn't want to tell him. He'd think she was crazy. She closed her eyes and tried to remember what she could. "Let me think," she said mostly to herself. She saw herself slipping and tumbling. The water enveloped her like a freezing hug. She shuddered remembering. Then it got harder to remember. She could see Allen's face looking down at her from the bank, horror stricken, and then him jumping toward her. But then she felt alone. But no, she wasn't alone. Was there someone else there?

"Was there someone else there?" she asked.

"Well, yeah," he said. "This guy showed up out of nowhere. He just came running up. He had a walkie-talkie and contacted the forest service and helped me. We wrapped you in our coats."

"Huh. But no. I mean was someone else in the water with me? I saw you jump in before I sank so far, I couldn't see, but then I didn't see you. But there was someone else there when I was on the bottom. I thought maybe someone else jumped in." She couldn't believe what she was even saying.

"Uh, no." He just looked at her with a look of fear. She knew he was worried she was imagining things. Frankly, so was she.

"Well, who knows," she said. "Like you said. I stopped

breathing, so my mind was probably going off on a crazy tangent. That was nice of that guy to stop. So, who was he?"

"I don't know! He was just running up the path. He must have heard me yelling. After the paramedics came, I lost track of him. I ran back to the Jeep and hustled to the ER. I don't even know who he was. It was a miracle though. I was panicking. I don't think you would have made it if I'd had to run to find help or if I'd had to carry you back to the car. Without the mouth to mouth, you probably would have had brain damage from lack of oxygen."

Panicking slightly, he got up and paced the room. He clenched his fists and rubbed his arms. He glanced back at her, and she looked so small in the covers.

"Marie, I was so afraid I was going to lose you. You have become part of me, my life," he trailed off. "I've never been so afraid." He knelt down next to her. "Marie, I've daydreamed about our future. I don't ever want to be without you."

"It happened so fast. I'm so glad you got me out of there. Allen, you saved my life. The water was so cold. I was terrified." They pulled each other close for a minute before he relaxed.

He got up and asked her if she was hungry. "No, not really. In fact, I'm a little nauseous," she said. "I think I just want to sleep for a while. Is that ok? Would you mind?"

"No, not at all. I would imagine you must be tired. I'll just do some reading for class. I'll be right here," he said.

He gave her a thin-lipped half smile where just the corners of his mouth turned up. She knew that was a mask to cover his concern. She could see in his sweet eyes how much he loved her.

"I love you," she told him and hunkered down into the couch pillows and closed her eyes. Her hair was a fluffy, matted mess from drying on the hospital bed.

***

Allen watched her a minute. What on earth was she talking about? There was nothing in that lake, but muck and water plants. He was really worried about the state of her head, but maybe she was right, maybe some sleep was in order. He decided he'd just watch her closely for a while. He was also kicking himself for not catching her or for not seeing what was happening sooner. Surely there was something he could have done to prevent this from ever happening. Of course, that didn't matter now, but he still felt like part of this was his fault. What caused her to lean so far over the side anyway? That was a stupid thing to do. Fear and anger gripped him as he blamed and her and himself for this accident.

6 BEN'S DE-BRIEFING

Ben and Jacob were sitting at the kitchen table of the dorm room. Ben was nearly unhinged with despair.

"Oh my God, Jacob! She nearly died! And did you see the dark souls clamoring for her. It was all I could do to keep them away! Tom is going to kill me, well, if I wasn't already dead!" Ben said.

"Yeah, that was a close one. But you must remember that we are here to do what we can. You must remember that they are not immortal and there is a predetermined time for them. We don't know when that is, so there will come a time when no matter what we do, it won't help. We cannot override Lorenzo's decisions, and only he knows when their time has come." Jacob told him as his piercing eyes stared him down. Jacob had a very intense personality. He sat back in his chair with his ankle crossed over his knee. He rested his chin on his hand and his elbow on his other knee. He looked very controlled and relaxed even. This was in direct contrast to Ben who was sitting bolt upright biting his nails down to the quick. Jacob continued to size up Ben, staring at him.

This unnerved Ben even more.

"Why are you staring at me?" Ben spat out. He got up and started pacing around. Marie had fallen asleep on the couch, and he walked around the room looking in all the corners. As he expected, a dark soul was forming in a corner beside the end of the couch.

"Look! They are still coming for her! Good grief!" Ben put his hands out and shoved at the shadow. Oddly, it started laughing at him. A female face formed and then quicker than Ben could believe, a woman appeared. He recoiled, surprised. Her startlingly plain face would have been passable, but she had that evil grin on her face. Her curly red hair was flowing in all directions, and she had deep creases in her expression. Evil had been working on her a long time. Maybe centuries. She looked as solid as him, but somehow more fluid, less content with her existence. Her body was always in motion like an eel.

"You can't keep her safe forever, you know!" She laughed a throaty gargling laugh that made Ben's blood run cold. Her talon-like freckled fingers darted forward to mockingly caress Marie's forehead. Ben reacted just as fast and blocked her. He moved himself into the same space as Marie. The woman would have to literally go through him to get to Marie. The evil vapor of a woman vanished, her laughter fading away. She was obviously toying with Ben.

After Ben pulled his head together and the room seemed quiet again, he stood up and looked at Jacob who hadn't moved during the whole scene. In fact, he looked a little tired of the whole thing, if anything.

"How can you just sit there?" Ben yelled at Jacob. Jacob straightened, stretched, and then relaxed back into his chair again. Jacob lowered his eyes to the ground and then looked back at Ben.

"Have a seat, Ben." Jacob said. "You are doing

great. You're new at this. And really, you are doing super for a newbie. It's been, what, a couple of months?" Jacob held his hand out questioningly.

Ben softened a little. His shoulders relaxed a degree. "Yes, it's been two months. The first month I had to learn fast. I wasn't born alive. In fact, I was only about ten weeks in my mother's womb. My living body was still quite unformed. The team that caught me took care of me until I got my bearings and I've been with Tom a few weeks watching Marie.

"He never should have left me with her! I'm not ready. I still don't know what I'm doing." Ben held his face in his hand as he leaned against the wall. Marie slept soundly and Allen was reading a dendrology textbook in the chair next to the couch. Darkness had fallen and Allen reached up and turned on the lamp on the table beside him, making a barely audible clicking noise.

"Well, it's not like you're totally alone, you know. I was there, too. Both of us worked together. It worked fine. These things happen all the time. Seriously. They," Jacob nodded toward Marie and Ben, "have no idea how close they come all the time."

"The whole reason life expectancy has increased over the last one hundred years is because there are more of us now. They," he nodded Ben's way again, "think it's because of hand washing and seat belts!" He chuckled to himself. "The population on both sides is exploding."

"So, this is normal?" asked Ben incredulously. "They just come at them and trick them? You saw what happened? They teased her into leaning out over the water. They let her see them. That isn't fair. Now she is all confused and thinks she's crazy. You've seen Allen's face. He is worried she's crazy. None of it makes sense to them. How can the dark souls get away with that?"

"True, they stepped across the line, but they do that. Usually, the living chalk it up to 'lack of oxygen' or fatigue. They rationalize what they don't understand. It's very convenient," said Jacob. He looked around the room in a sweep to scan for disturbances. A shadow was creeping

along the edge of the room building in size. He eyed it and then got up. Walking over to the edge of the wall, he said, "She'll be okay. She has a very pure heart with little malice. Honestly, I am not sure why they are trying so hard. There are easier ones to get." When he got over to the shadow, he stepped on it and it fizzled away.

Ben had learned that often, just the mere recognition of the dark presences was enough to drive them away. They didn't like outright battles. They much preferred to sneak up when no one was looking and quietly pull the living souls to them. Some Protectors were lazy or kept disappearing. It was sad because their assigned soul was always left vulnerable and had little chance for making it. A sitting duck is what they were.

7 - SEEING WITH NEW EYES

She'd been having a nightmare about being pulled to the bottom of the sea by a great squid with long tentacles. The large green eye staring at her terrified her. She tried to scream, but under the water, there was no sound. No one heard. She felt terribly alone as the darkness enclosed around her. Thrashing to get loose, she awoke in the dark night and realized the blanket had twisted around her. She relaxed against the pillow under her head. Allen must have covered her and put a pillow under her head. The room was dark, but she could hear his breathing in the bedroom. She tried to shake off the thoughts of the nightmare, but it was all too real and like what she'd been through.

As her eyes focused in the dark, she saw a movement in the corner of the room. Was it a person? Had someone broken in? Panicking, she cried out, "Allen!" Within seconds, he was beside her, stumbling through the dark.

"Are you okay?" he said checking her over.

"I thought I saw someone, over there!" she said as she pointed to the opposite corner near the table and chairs. He looked immediately. He didn't see anything but got up and went to investigate. He turned on the light. Nothing. He looked back at her with his brows knitted together.

"There's no one here. You're okay. You must have had a nightmare," he said.

"I did. It was awful!" she said thinking back and grimacing. He came back and sat down next to her. "I feel all messed up, Allen. I can't tell what's real and what isn't!" "It's okay. The doctor said that is normal after something traumatic. He gave you the meds to help your

nerves. Do you want one?" he asked.

"Sure. Maybe it will help," she said. He got up and went to the kitchen. She heard him getting her a glass of water, rumpling paper from the pharmacy bag. She looked around the room looking for shadows. She knew something was still wrong. She couldn't see it, but she knew they weren't alone. How could she explain that to him?

He came back in and handed her the pill and then the glass of water. The purposeful look on his face told her it made him feel better to be able to do something to help her. Maybe the meds would take care of it, she hoped. This was just something she would need to work through and then she would be okay. She felt comforted with the thought that maybe he could help her through it.

She drank the last of the water and shrugged back down against the pillow looking at him. "It'll just take time," he said. "It's like a car accident that freaks you out for a while. No big deal."

She wanted to believe him. She really, really wanted that to be true. However, in the back of her mind, she knew it was more than just her head. Well, at least she hoped it was or else she really was losing her mind.

Either there really were beings in the shadows or she was nuts. Neither prospect made her feel good. She'd heard once that the difference between normal and crazy people is that normal people know they are messed up, but crazy people think they are ok. It was highly likely she was crazy.

She started to relax, and her eyes couldn't stay open. She knew it was the meds and she let it take her away into the blissful swirl in her mind. She had a wonderful feeling that none of that mattered, and she could fly across fields of spring flowers. She closed her eyes and rested.

Allen held her close. Her breathing slowed and relaxed into a deep sleep. He waited until she was sound asleep and then a tear formed in the corner of his eye.

"Marie," he whispered, "if only I had caught you!" His faced crumpled with grief and regret. "I'm so sorry. I just want you to be okay. You just need some time to get your head straight. I feel so useless to help you."

Allen held her for a while until he got his emotions back in check and then went back to bed.

***

The next morning, they decided to go into town for breakfast. They got dressed and headed to the car. The morning air was crisp and smelled like pine. Marie breathed deeply. The meds were still having their affect. She felt calm. It was like all that fear was far away and someone else's. As they drove, they didn't say anything. Allen kept glancing at her and scanning the woods as they drove as if he was on high alert for danger. She looked out her window into the trees. The morning light was shining in shafts down to the ground like little spotlights on a stage. Everything seemed so peaceful, but, she knew, even with the meds, it was different. She didn't say anything to Allen. What could she say? There was nothing he could see. Nothing she could put her finger on. It was just a knowledge that there was more around them than she had ever seen.

They parked, got out and were walking inside. She looked across the street and saw the older couple that had been at the diner the other day. They were going in a shoe shop. The lady had an indignant scowl. Marie wondered what she was thinking. The man was looking down as he walked. He held the door for the lady when they got to the store. The lady walked inside like she was the queen of England.

Then Marie saw another young woman follow them in, like she was with them. Maybe that was the lady's daughter. She had never seen her before.

Allen held the door to the Europa Café open for Marie who was still looking across the street. "Whatcha' see?" he asked.

"Oh! Nothing." Marie said as she nearly ran into him. "Just that lady and her husband who were here the other day." She turned and went into the diner. They sat at a booth by the window. They sat silently looking around the diner waiting for the waitress. A lady in her thirties in a ruffled dress with an apron that looked like something Marie would have worn when she was four years old came to the table. Her name badge said, "Peg."

"Welcome to the Europa. What can I get you to drink?" she said without even looking at them. She had her pen ready, hovering over the order pad.

Marie said, "I'll have coffee with cream and sugar." Allen said, "I'd like a Dr. Pepper." The waitress scribbled on the pad and turned on her heel.

It was Sunday. The diner was busy. Some people were dressed in suits and dresses. They must have been at church earlier. Marie and Allen had slept late, and it was after 12:00. Marie looked at one family sitting nearby with two small kids. The mom was wearing a pink linen dress with pearls. The kids were in dress clothes with shiny little patent leather shoes. The mom was talking away about what had been said in her Sunday school group.

Marie had been to church when she was very young. Her parents had dressed her up and she would play with the brick-like blocks with the other kids in the nursery. She never really understood what the point of going was. She knew who Jesus was and his mother Mary and father Joseph. The few times she had sat in big church with her parents, she couldn't understand what they were talking about. They used big words that no one else ever said. Her family moved and life got hectic. Her parents started sleeping in on the weekends. They never went back. Marie had her own ideas about what religion was about, but she really didn't know what she believed. It seemed like a bunch of hocus pocus to her. Maybe aliens had visited earth back when man was still primitive, and legends grew that people thought explained the origins of man. Anything was possible.

One thing was certain, she felt like she had nothing in common with the little family in fresh dress clothes chatting away about "Sunday lessons." Nothing, except that she remembered being little like their little girl all dressed up and eating at a diner after church. She used to look forward to getting chocolate milk with her dinner. She wondered what they learned in "Sunday lessons." Did they learn to tell the truth or be kind? Maybe they learned about saints who lived long ago. Maybe it was all about history.

"We need to gather some bark samples for dendrology today. They are due tomorrow," said

Allen. Marie came out of her thoughts and looked at him. She had forgotten all about the assignment. They were going to see about finding some samples during their hike and that hadn't worked out.

"Ok," she said. "Let's just look around campus when we get back. I am not up for a hike again today!" she laughed. "We just need three each. I need to study for art history, too. I have a test tomorrow."

The waitress brought their drinks and took their order for breakfast. Breakfast was Marie's favorite meal of the day. She got eggs and bacon with hash browns. Allen just got scrambled eggs and toast.

"Sam and Ellen went to his parents' house in San Fran for the weekend. I wonder how that is going. He was introducing Ellen to them for the first time," Allen said. Sam was Allen's roommate at the beginning of the school year. Sam met Ellen and they started dating hot and heavy and he moved into her apartment in Sonora. His family was a bit mafia-like to Marie. Sam never would tell what his parents did for a living, and he seemed very urban. He really didn't fit in with the natural scenery around the college. Marie and Allen really were not sure why he'd chosen to come to Columbia College. Ellen seemed to be a bit of a mismatch with the town, too, so they went well together.

"Probably getting along great! Bet they have been eating dinner at the steakhouse and hanging out in a mansion. That's how I would imagine them," Marie said.

"He's a little odd. So is she. But he does have interesting stories. He went to a private school there. I don't know what he saw in Columbia College. I wonder if he is kind of hiding out here," Allen said. "I wouldn't be surprised if he isn't trying to keep a low profile for a while. He told me once that his parents had told his friends that he was going to college back east."

"Isn't it strange how different some people's lives are?" Marie said. "I would feel like such a fish out of water around his family. He seems like a nice enough guy, but I wonder sometimes what he isn't saying. And then he is never short on cash. He and Ellen are grilling steak and having lobster all the time. The poor "Saf-ay" probably isn't used to staying stocked on the high-end foods!"

The waitress brought their food. Marie looked at her plate like it was Christmas. Everything looked yummy. She picked up the fork and started in. They ate in silence for several minutes. Marie was absently looking at the window and eating bacon when she noticed the lady, her husband and the other lady leave the shoe store. The lady had a bag on her arm. She must have found the shoes she was looking for. The younger woman leaned into the lady's ear and whispered something. The lady shrugged it off. The man trudged along behind them. The younger lady would look back at the man and then whispered in the lady's ear again. The older lady would just look off into the sky. It was really an odd scene. The man seemed to pay no mind to the younger lady like she wasn't even there.

"Allen, do you see those three on the sidewalk across the street?" Marie said.

Allen looked out the window and cocked his head. "I see the man and lady. Did you say three?"

"Yeah, the man and the lady and then a younger lady with dark hair," she said.

"I only see the two," he said.

"Hm," said Marie. Looking at the three people plainly standing next to the car. The man was unlocking the car door. "The younger lady is right

48

there. She is whispering in the older lady's ear. She is wearing a blue sweater."

"Uh, I only see the two." Allen looked at Marie. "So, what about them anyway?"

Marie looked confused and then remembered what she was going to say. "Well, I just thought it was weird the younger lady kept whispering in the lady's ear, but…" Marie trailed off thinking if he couldn't see the younger lady that would make no sense. None of it made sense. How come he couldn't see the younger lady? She wanted to press it, but she felt odd about it. She looked back out at the street just as the car pulled away with the three of them. Maybe she really was losing her mind.

Marie looked around the diner. It seemed even more crowded now. Where did all these people come from? She hadn't noticed them coming in. The booths were packed with four and six people per table. She started feeling dizzy and claustrophobic. She put her hand on her forehead and closed her eyes.

"Are you okay, Marie?" Allen asked with concern.

"I don't feel so good. I need some air!" Marie jumped up and made for the door. She felt like she had to crawl over people. The little bell jingled above the door as she abruptly pushed it open and went out. She leaned against the brick wall outside next to the door panting with her eyes closed. She was afraid to look, afraid to see. Something was off, she knew it.

Allen watched her go out, not knowing what happened. He quickly left a $10 and a $5 on the table and grabbed their coats. As he turned to head out the door, he nearly slammed into Lydia. He managed to stop the forward momentum just before they made contact. She never moved, appearing to almost welcome him crashing into her.

"Trouble in paradise, Allen?" She looked up at

him from under seductive lids that were more of an invitation than a question.

"What?" he said baffled.

"Well, she dashed out of here. I thought maybe there was trouble. Maybe you needed to talk. You're welcome to join me." She smiled and gestured to a table where she was clearly the only guest.

"Uh." Allen was thrown off by her obviously assertive opportunistic suggestion. "No, Lydia. I'm not interested," he put a strong emphasis on the last word and didn't wait for a reply as he strode toward the door, shaking off the unexpected interference.

A minute later he was by her side with his hands on her

arms. "Look at me! Marie! Are you okay?"

"Yes, it just…" she said as she blinked open her eyes. He looked like home. Maybe she could just look into his eyes and stay in this moment forever and it would all be okay. "It's just, I'm dizzy and I felt nauseous. I'm okay. Probably just the lack of oxygen yesterday." She continued to look into his eyes like he was the rope keeping her connected to reality.

8   - THE OTHERS

The next week was a blur for Marie. She tried to concentrate on her classes, but she was constantly distracted by shadows. There were people around that she knew she had never seen before. Some looked like they were foreigners. She had mentioned it a couple times to Allen, and he didn't see them. She stopped asking because he looked at her with such concern. She didn't want to upset him. One thing she knew by now, she could see people that he couldn't. She even asked her friend Kay who she'd been riding with on the tram she drove for the school that afternoon. Marie had seen a young man with Kay. He was talking to her, and she seemed to be nodding. Kay told her no one had taken the tram that afternoon. She'd made her rounds from the school to the parking lot three times without any passengers. It was a long walk from the parking lot to the buildings and the school had purchased an extended golf cart and hired students to drive it in shifts. It was food money for Kay. Sometimes Marie took her shift if Kay had something going on. If there was bad weather, there would be several passengers, but if the weather was nice, it was easy money to sit and wait at the bus stop sipping coffee.

Marie remembered a time when they drove it together to have a chance to visit. It was a cold evening and Kay suggested using the lighter to warm her face. That was when Marie figured out how flammable eyebrows are. In a flash of light, she burned off her eyebrows. Not the best idea for keeping warm, but they did laugh until their bellies hurt waving away the smell of burned hair. She was lucky her whole head didn't catch on fire. It would have if Tom hadn't intervened, but she had no idea.

Kay said she had had no passengers that afternoon, no young man. Kay had been seeing Jack for two years off and on, so Marie felt sure she wasn't seeing someone else, but maybe she was trying to hide a new love interest. Either that, or it was one of the "others." That's what Marie had started calling them. The people she saw that no one else did.

The others never seemed to hurt anyone. They just were there. They walked with people. They would whisper to people. Sometimes it appeared that the people heard, like when she saw Kay nod while the young man talked. Sometimes they just looked the other way defiantly. Sometimes the people seemed truly not to hear them.

It made Marie wonder, were there others around her and Allen. She had never seen them. The only thing she ever saw around them was shadows in the corner of her eye. Mostly when she was watching TV or focused on the professor. She would see a shadow along the edge of the floor or behind a chair from the corner of her eye. As soon as she turned her eyes to look, it would disappear. She wondered if that was a residual visual problem from the drowning. That made sense.

***

One afternoon, after classes were done, Marie and Allen decided to drive to Soulsbyville to look for a shop Kay had mentioned. Kay liked incense and her birthday was coming up. This shop was run by a woman who made her own blends of oils and incense sticks. Kay's comment was that this woman was "Way cool! She had like fifty different blends that she made herself. It's awesome just to stand there and smell the shop!" Kay, with her natural fiber clothes, straight, unisex haircut, and lack of shaving preference, was a bit of a hippie.

When they got to Sunshine Camp, they started looking for the turn off from the Sonora Pass Highway. The directions Kay gave them were pretty good. They found the little shop quickly tucked in a second row off the main road. If you didn't know what you were looking for you never would have seen it. It appeared the shopkeeper had a little apartment above the store in a second story. The whole building looked like it had been there about a hundred years: very cutesy western motif with a big porch with turned posts holding up the roof over the porch. The windows in the upstairs window had ball-fringe curtains. There were crystal sun catchers hanging in the place where the curtain parted. You could see prism rainbows shining on the outward side of the curtains.

Allen smirked a slight frown as he got out of the car.

Clearly this was not his kind of haunt.

"Ohhh! This will be interesting!" Marie said taking in the whole view of the store front. Allen's blond eyebrows shot up as he looked at her. They closed their car doors and started toward the steps to the porch. Allen opened the door for Marie and held it open as she walked into the shop. The rich musky scent of sandalwood stung her nose. She looked back at Allen to gage his response. It looked like it was overwhelming to him. He was discreetly trying to hold his breath and then gave up. Tears formed in the corners of his eyes and Marie could see the struggle he had as he walked in a herky-jerky fashion rubbing his eyes. She hoped that maybe in a few minutes he would become acclimated to the aromatic ambrosia. With selfless dedication to her, he followed Marie to the counter.

"Good day, friends!" came a mellow voice of a sage woman sitting on a stool behind the counter. She was crocheting an intricate pattern that looked like it was going to end up as a hat. She had a perpetual smile on her face. She truly looked like nothing could faze her. Allen's expression clearly showed that he wondered if she was high. Marie had to stifle a laugh.

"What brings you to my world?" the lady asked.

"Our friend Kay has been here to get incense and her birthday is coming up soon. We thought maybe you could help us choose a birthday present for her," said Marie as she looked over a display of woven bracelets on the counter.

"I see!" the woman said with fascinated gusto. "Well, yes. I am sure we can find something. Tell me, what incense did she get before?"

"Hmmm. I don't know. It smelled musky, sort of. But with a little tanginess, too," said Marie.

"Okay," she said slowly drawing out the last syllable as she thought. "You say her birthday is coming up? So, she is a Pisces. Creative, good friend, sense of humor. Hmmm. What color are her shoes?"

"Huh?" Marie looked up.

"Her shoes! What color?" the woman asked. "Blue Vans," Marie said.

The lady thought for a moment and then walked

over to a cabinet in the front corner. She opened the glass door and pulled out an incense holder with inlaid blue stones around the edge and carved designs in swirls. She held it out to Marie.

"Wow! This looks just like something she would like!" said Marie. She turned it over and it was a couple of dollars. The lady handed Marie a box of incense sticks.

"How about $5 and we'll call it even?" said the woman smiling even bigger. "I'll even gift wrap it!" At this the lady seemed giddy. Marie nearly laughed at her enthusiasm.

"It's a deal!" said Marie. She followed the woman back to the counter and watched her pull out a square of wrapping paper that looked hand painted with watercolors. She pawed around under the counter until she found a box that was just the right size. Marie watched her fold the paper around the box in such a purposeful way that it looked like she was making an origami sculpture.

As she watched, she noticed a movement near a wing chair next to a bookcase on the other side of the shop. She turned to look but there was no one there, as usual.

Without even looking up, the shopkeeper said, "You saw her, huh?"

Marie held her breath. "Her?"

"Yeah, my little friend. She follows me everywhere," the
woman said.

Marie looked more closely in that direction. Sure enough, now she could see her standing behind the chair. There was a young woman with long brown hair and fine features. She smiled at Marie. Marie looked at Allen who was still looking around at the displays of unique items. The young woman looked as real as anyone. She wore a long green skirt that looked to be made of wool with a white button-down shirt tucked into the skirt. She wore tiny little brown leather shoes. Her blue eyes stayed a steady gaze on Marie as Marie looked her up and down.

"I have seen her all my life," the woman said. "Funny thing is, she never changes. She looks exactly the same now as she did when I was a little girl. There was only one other person I've known that could see her, too. It was a lady I knew a long time ago."

She didn't say anything else. Marie hated to ask anything else. It seemed like prying. She didn't know the woman well-enough to go poking in her personal affairs. There was just one thing, though, she had to ask.

"Have you seen others, others like your... friend here?"

Marie asked holding her breath.

The woman paused in the gift wrapping. "No. But the lady I knew a long time ago did. She did and more. Odd things she'd tell me about." The woman looked into Marie's eyes searching. "Be careful, my girl. There are things we aren't supposed to be a part of. It's not ours to be about. My friend, well, something happened to her, and she never came back. I miss her."

She tied a cord in a bow around the box and handed it to Marie in a bag. Marie gave her the money. As the woman took it, she clasped Marie's hand and looked at her with concern and said, "Goodbye, dear, and keep love around you, it's the secret you know."

All Marie could say was a nervous, "Thanks." She took the bag and caught up with Allen before she got to the door.

He asked, "Did you find what you were looking for?" "I'm not sure, I guess so," she said. That queasy

feeling
in her stomach was coming back.

9 - THE SHADOWS COME

Marie and Allen were at Ellen's apartment visiting with her and Sam. Sam told them how his parents had loved Ellen, and they all had a great time. Sam had dark black hair. He looked Italian to Marie. His olive complexion and dark eyes made him look exotic. Macho charisma seemed to exude from his pores. He wore designer jeans, an alligator polo, and leather Topsiders with no socks. He seemed to be striking a pose no matter what he was doing. Right then he was reclining on Ellen's wicker sofa, one leg crossed over the other, ankle over knee. His left arm was around Ellen's shoulders as she sat next to him with her feet tucked under her. She was hanging on his every word. Marie almost felt like she was intruding on a private moment. If any girl could worship her boyfriend, it was Ellen. Of course he looked at her like she was a goddess, so they were perfect together. At one point they started kissing rather passionately before they remembered Allen and Marie were still there.

Allen stood up and said he was getting hungry. "Anybody up for a club sandwich at the Europa?" It was getting to be close to the dinner hour.

Sam was looking at Ellen like she was a club sandwich and said, "No, thanks. We'll just fix something here later." Ellen leaned in and put her head on Sam's shoulder and smiled at Marie.

Marie stood up and smoothed her pullover shirt into place and

pulled her jacket on. "Well, we'll see you guys later. Glad you had a nice visit with Sam's parents!"

Allen and Marie let themselves out the door and went down the set of wood stairs outside to the parking lot.

"So, are you hungry?" Allen said.

"Yeah, I am. That sounds great. If we'd stayed any longer, I think we would've seen a show!" Marie said.

"Those two are a bit much. I wonder how that went over with his parents. But then again maybe his parents are like that too! I know what my mother would say about it. "If I ever acted like that with a boy, my daddy would have... blah, blah, blah!"" They both laughed.

"Yeah, I would be way too embarrassed to be with him in front of my parents," Marie said.

They drove around the corner and down the street toward downtown. It was a busy time of day. People were getting off work or heading to the grocery, walking down sidewalks, going in and coming out of stores. Marie spotted the older couple walking on the sidewalk near the Europa Café. The younger woman was with them whispering away. Nearly pleading. This time there was a man with them, too. He was walking beside the husband. Marie saw the pregnant girl ahead of them. She was carrying a department store shopping bag filled with baby clothes. Marie was certain the girl had not been to Nordstrom's lately. It looked like a bag of second-hand clothes.

Allen pulled into the parking lot beside the café, and they got out. As they came around the corner, they could hear the older woman prattling on about the morals of young people today. Just then, the bag of baby clothes the pregnant girl was carrying ripped, and clothes went everywhere. Marie was about to step up and go to her to help when she heard the older woman exclaim to her husband, "If you dare go pick up that tramp's handouts for her little bastard child, I shall not suffer it!"

Her husband looked as surprised as Marie. Marie looked to the girl to see if she had heard the ugly outburst. Apparently, she had. She was starting to tear up as she awkwardly knelt down to pick up the little pastel shirts and onesies. Marie went into overdrive and hustled to her.

"Hey sweetie, Need a hand? These little things are so cute! We need to find a new bag. Allen? Can you see if they have a take-out bag in the café?" said Marie. Allen was a bit dumbstruck by the whole scene, but a look of relief spread across his facing showing he was glad to have been given a job that removed him from the scene temporarily. The older woman's husband found his voice. "My dear, you surprise me! I don't understand what's gotten into you." He turned toward the girl. "Honey, let me help. Pay no mind to my wife. She hasn't been feeling well and it makes her grumpy." He looked back at his wife who looked like she was about to explode. Her elbows hitched up like a line-backer and her eyebrow shot up in shock.

The older woman let out a loud, very annoyed harrumph and turned to cross the street to get as far away from her husband as possible. The younger woman that followed her around was trying to block her from going into the street. The man Marie had noticed was crouched beside her husband with his arm around him.

What happened next was a blur in double time. Just as the older woman's eyes left her husband and the pregnant girl and she stepped off the curb, Marie saw from the corner of her eye that the city garbage truck was barreling down Main Street at a good 30 miles per hour and was about ten feet from the lady. Her husband was looking at the sidewalk to gather up clothes. The young woman tried to pull the older woman's arm with all her strength, but nothing could stop what was set in motion.

The only sound Marie heard was the screeching of brakes and skidding tires as the truck came to an abrupt halt in front of the café. The car behind the garbage truck ran into it, making a terrible crunching metal sound. Everyone looked up in horror. Allen dashed out of the café to Marie's side and shielded both her and the pregnant girl with his body. The husband couldn't move. Marie saw tears in his companion's eyes. It dawned on Marie, the older woman had to have been hit by the truck. She stood up, looked at Allen and crossed to the curb near the front of the truck. Sure enough, there lay the woman. She had a terrible head injury that left no doubt that she was dead. The grotesque scene made Marie catch her breath.

Then, as if the absurdity of it all wasn't enough, she saw the old woman get up. But she wasn't old; she was about Marie's age. She had the same look on her face though, that she did a minute before. It had to be the older woman. She brushed herself off and smoothed her dress. Then she saw it, her older body, crumpled and broken, laying on the ground in front of the garbage truck. People were rushing towards her, but they were kneeling down around the broken dead body scratching their heads and grimacing. Someone took off their jacket and laid it over the older woman's head. The younger version of herself was aghast. She looked at her arms and felt her face. Then her companion, the young lady that Marie always saw with her, put her hand on the woman's shoulder. "It'll be okay. Come with me," she said. This time, Marie could hear her. The woman, like always, looked away. She knew the companion was there, but she turned away from her. The companion looked down sadly. There was nothing she could do now. Marie understood now, piecing together what the shopkeeper told her about her companion who'd been with her all her life. For years this companion had tried to get through to the lady, but she refused to hear,

refused any compassion for others.

The woman stopped and turned back to her companion, "You! You've been with me all my life, haven't you? You saw me being bullied as a child. You saw me wearing rags to school. The other girls were cruel to me." She spat her angry words at the girl.

"Mother neglected me, lost in her bottle. Father in a prison. You did nothing for me! Were you supposed to be helping me? I," she strained the vowel into three syllables, "showed I was just as good as anyone. I worked hard and saved money to buy good clothes and make a good appearance. I," again drawing out the pronoun, "married a husband that was respected. I volunteered at church. I was the one they came to because I got things done. And you, you did nothing for me! Not too late for what? For me to have pity on that hussy? She and her bastard child will pay for her sin. I have no pity for her selfishness now get away

62

from me." She waved her hand to shew her away.

The Protector vanished leaving the younger version of the woman standing in the street alone. She walked a few steps away and then Marie saw the shadows gathering under the cars around the woman. It looked like clouds of car exhaust until they started to take form. They came out from their hiding places and made a ring around the woman. She stopped and spun this way and that. They grew taller and long arms formed from the smoke. Long fingers with claw-like nails. The woman looked horrified as they started to grab at her. Then they changed into people. The smoke faded away. They could have been normal people except they looked drained of life, haggard and worn, dark circles under their eyes. They looked hungry with gaping mouths. They taunted the woman and pulled at her hair, laughing. Then they said horrible things that made Marie wanted to weep for her, "You never were anything and look at you now. You're still nothing. Those fancy clothes can't hide the truth. You're one of us!" Marie shuddered. With that, they circled closer and covered her with their bony arms and claw-like hands. The ground seemed to swallow them all and then there was nothing there at all.

Marie was frozen with fear from seeing how horrifying the whole scene was. Sound came back to her ears. Sirens. Screaming. Crying, the older man's sobbing cries. People were hugging him. Allen was at Marie's side and turning her away from the road.

"Come on. Let's get out of here," he said.

He led her to the car and opened her door. She stiffly got in, still in shock. Allen thought that with what she had been through at the lake, he needed to get her as far away as possible. He took her back to the dorms and they curled up under the covers and cried together.

***

Ben and Jacob were sitting at the kitchen table. Ben had seen the shadows take a soul before. It was so sad. Most of the time it was expected. A person had turned away from compassion and turned bitter or greedy. They had stopped listening to their Protector. It was possible for them to change the course they were on, but unlikely. There was nothing the Protector could do after a certain point. Even at the last minute, the moment after death, there was still a chance. The older woman's Protector could have whisked her to safety within the Gathering place of Protectors. Sadly, there was nothing left to do when the woman turned away. The shadows claim their own. Unfortunately, the woman would be indoctrinated into their ways and would torment people forever. She would never know real peace. Jacob was deep in thought. Something was eating him.

"What's up, Jacob?" Ben said.

"It's just, things are going a new direction. Marie clearly saw everything. I saw her reacting and followed her gaze when it was happening. I'm not sure what will happen next. The live ones usually can't see us at all. They might have a quick glimpse like she did in the lake, but not a full view of someone else's event. We need to talk to Tom." Jacob said.

"Well now I'm worried! If you're uptight, something is

awry!" Ben said.

"I'm going to bop out and find Tom, okay? I'll be right back. And Ben, stay close to her; I mean it." Jacob said. "I will be right back."

Jacob flashed out of sight. Ben got up and went into the bedroom and sat down at a chair by the window. Marie and Allen were asleep. The clock by the bed glowed 2:04 A.M.

***

Jacob appeared at the Gathering. This was a marble portico far away from the world of the living. It was shaped in a circle with Corinthian columns around the edges. Souls were all around. Old souls. The greatest minds from humanity sat around benches and tables and discussed current events. They had the knowledge of all time to draw from. What had worked a thousand years ago was still useful today. There is that saying, 'there's nothing new under the sun' and they knew it to be true. Humanity, and its eccentricities, never really changed. In the center of the Gathering was Lorenzo. He was perfect love. He loved them all as family. Every soul, young and old. He encouraged the Protectors to try harder, never give up until the last opportunity was gone.

The old souls here didn't look like what you would imagine in a museum picture. Their image was the person in their prime of life. They all appeared to be about 20-30 years old. It was deceptive, though. Some had lived hundreds of years of life before lives were shortened, and then had been counselors here for millennia. You couldn't judge by appearances. Even Lorenzo looked like a 25-year- old man. He wore current clothes: jeans and pullover. He was very humble and approachable. The souls that talked to him, though, gave him great respect like you would a king.

Jacob approached a group near the edge and asked,

"Have you seen Tom? Thomas Helm?"

A young woman said, "Yes, he's there talking to Henry." She pointed to a group about 20 feet away.

"Thanks!" Jacob said as he turned that way. He walked over

to Tom and Henry. "Hey, guys! You all got a minute? We have a situation, and I need to ask your advice. Can you both come with me to see Marie and Allen for a minute?"

"Sure thing!" Tom said and nodded at Henry. Henry nodded. They all three flashed away and appeared in Allen's dorm living room.

"So, what's going on?" said Tom.

"Hold on," Jacob said. He went over to bedroom doorway and motioned for Ben to come in. "Henry, do you know Ben?"

"No. I don't think I've had the pleasure," Henry said as he held out his hand to Ben. Ben noticed that Henry had the sweetest smile. He was truly open and friendly in his manner. His strawberry blond hair was cut in close curls around his face. He had freckles across his nose and cheeks. He wasn't a large man but had a presence in the group. He had a gentle confidence and looked as if at any moment he'd find something to laugh about.

Tom said, "Ben, this is Henry, my son that I told you about. He has been a special agent Protector for a long time.

"Ach! Pa!" Henry said and looked at Ben. "He makes it sound like I'm better than anyone else. You guys do the hard work, year in and year out, 24/7. I just bounce around and help."

Tom went on, "Henry died when he was just a little boy. He went to get water from the stream. Natives scalped him. When he didn't come back, I went looking for him. Sweet child that he was, he wouldn't hurt a flea. It nearly killed me right then to find him bleeding on the side of the creek. My anger for the savages nearly consumed me. Henry had barely survived infancy. His mother and I had a soft spot for the child. We found out much later how he had tried to comfort us after he passed. He stayed, refusing to go to the Gathering right away. His mentor got special permission from Lorenzo for Henry to be able to stay. He was inconsolable because he was so worried about us.

"After we learned all this years later, it made sense. Jenny and I were ready to leave Kentucky, to pack it up and forget it. We'd lost so much. We both became useless and bitter. The other children suffered for it. They, poor things, were grieving Henry, too, and now they had lost their parents, as well.

"But we swore we could feel Henry's presence. We'd would hear his soft laughter on the wind and feel his little fingers on our arm. We started to realize that even though we couldn't see him, his spirit lived on, surely. We remembered how much he loved with his whole heart and tried to honor that by loving each other, being kind to each other. Without Henry insisting to stay around us, I'm not sure what would have happened. His spirit and memory gave me strength. Others joined us in Elizabethtown and a town grew. We forged a community in a wilderness and helped each other. It's amazing how much power for good is in one person who chooses to love. The effects ripple to everyone around them for generations."

Henry turned to Ben, "Take note, young fella, at how love can change people. I know you weren't long in this world before you joined us, so you haven't seen much. I was with the team that caught you, though. You saw your mother and dad. And you showed love by wanting to help them like I wanted to help my ma and pa. It's in you. That's what you use to fight the shadows."

"So, what's going on here, Jacob?" said Tom. "What do you need to discuss?"

Jacob motioned for them to sit down at the table. "It's Marie. After you left, she had a little incident and nearly drowned in a reservoir. But it wasn't just an accident, of course. The shadows taunted her. They were hell bent on getting her. Ben did great at beating them back and getting help. Even at the hospital they kept after her in the room, trying to slow her heart and keep her from waking up."

"After that," Jacob went on, "She started seeing more and more protectors. It was like she could see all of us. But the final straw was today. A woman was killed right in front of Marie and the woman turned away from her Protector even with the last chance. The shadows came for her like they do and took her away." Jacob grimaced and frowned.

"Well, we are pretty sure Marie saw them, too. Not just the shadows, but the souls that have gone to evil!" Jacob cried.

Henry and Tom looked shocked. Ben looked from face to face for an explanation.

"This never happens!" said Tom.

"I've seen it once before," said Henry. "It didn't go well. There was a young woman. Similar story. She had had a farm accident of sorts and then began to see more clearly what was around her. It got dicey as the shadows figured out what was going on. They snatched her. Her Protector had left her for a short period, and they just snatched her. Funny thing was there was no body until sometime later. Lorenzo knows but he said it wasn't our concern. Of course, he knows where every soul is.

"We need to act fast. Ben and Jacob, you both stay with Marie and Allen 24/7. Tom and I are going to seek counsel at the Gathering, and we will return. This is very serious. You were right to come get us, Jacob. Good work."

Henry and Tom flashed out. Ben and Jacob looked at each other, and both got up at the same time and headed to the bedroom to watch over Marie and Allen.

***

The shadows kept trying all night. They would creep around the edges of the room. They would linger around the corners of the window. Ben and Jacob were vigilant.

The alarm went off at 7:00, and Marie and Allen stirred, stretching and yawning. They pulled on their clothes, grabbed their backpacks, and headed down to campus for class. They grabbed a coffee and a pack of mini donuts at the commissary on the way. Students were plodding in all directions like sleep-walking zombies. Allen and Marie filed into the classroom and sat down on the far side. Ben and Jacob sat on their desks and looked around the room. It appeared word had gotten out that something was going on. Every Protector was with their assignee. Instead of 30 students and a professor in the room, there were 62 souls. It was very crowded.

Marie started to wake up thanks to the effects of the coffee. She looked around the room and her eyes got very wide. Jacob was watching her. He could tell she could see all that he could. For some reason, she didn't see him or Ben though. Marie closed her eyes and tried to breathe slowly. It was all becoming too much. She wanted to bolt. She wondered what she could do to get away. Maybe the library would be better. One thing was for certain, she could not possibly stay there with 62 people in a tiny classroom.

She turned to Allen and, as calmly as possible, like

nothing was wrong, said, "I need to go to the bathroom. I'll be right back."

"Ok," he said and opened his notebook. Marie got up and walked to the door. Jacob motioned for Ben to go with her.

Outside in the open air, she felt a little better. She headed toward the library. After a short walk, she opened the door into the quiet sanctuary. There were only a few people sitting around, a lady behind the reference desk counter, and a janitor cleaning the glass of a display case full of gold rush artifacts. Marie found an empty cubical by a window in a corner. She sat down and took a big deep breath. From here, she could see the little lake in the center of campus.

The pathways were busy with students, backpacks slung over their shoulders, heading somewhere with purpose.

She realized only half the people had back packs. She looked closely and sure enough, it was not just overly busy, there were twice as many people walking around as usual and half of them were not students. They didn't carry the first book. Half the people seemed to just be following the others around.

She had to come to grips with whatever was going on. She looked around the side of the cubical wall. The woman at the reference desk was busily writing something. There was a man standing behind her, just standing there looking around. He looked like some sort of bodyguard. She noticed that the pairs sitting around the room were not study partners. In every pair, one of them was just looking around. They weren't studying. One girl was asleep in her chair and her study partner was just standing guard.

What on earth? She thought back. It had been about 3 weeks since the drowning. It was right after that when she first started to realize Allen didn't see everything she did. Even in the hospital, who were the two guys there when she woke up that seemed to disappear? The shopkeepers, "friend." The pair with the older couple.

The others seemed to be friendly "guardians." That was all right, she supposed. Maybe she could see guardian angels now. Well, that would be okay. Sort of like a special power. She thought about that a minute as she looked out over the crowds on the sidewalks.

She saw Lydia walking toward the building with another girl. They were talking quietly as they walked and smiling as though they were making secret plans. Marie's face flushed and she clenched her fists. "Hussy!" she thought to herself. Then she saw a shadow behind Lydia as they passed by the library. The shadow clung close to her. It was a smoky figure as tall as she was. Its hands were on her shoulders, and it appeared to be whispering in her ear. After it had leaned in close as though to say something, Lydia smiled like she had just had a great idea and began whispering to her friend. Marie wasn't sure what to feel.

On the one hand she would like to push Lydia off a cliff and on the other hand she felt sorry for her if she was in the clutches of something sinister.

After they passed by, Marie noticed a young man sitting alone on a bench out of the way. He was alone. Where was his guardian angel? He looked sad, hunched over with his elbows on his knees. His hands propping up his chin. Something was bothering him. He was deep in thought. Then she saw a movement behind him. A shadow of the bush moved. It was creeping up closer to him. She watched it slowly uncurl onto the ground of dirt and pine needles behind the bench. It grew larger and taller.

71

Slowly it became about the same size as the young man.

Without realizing it, Marie stood up and put her hands on the window. Her mouth fell open as she watched the shadow take a near human shape of dark smoke. Arms like tentacles pulled out, long branch-like fingers extended and seemed to wrap around his body and head. It was pulling at him. It wanted him to get up. It came around the front of him and started pulling at him. Marie realized it was trying to pull him toward the water. She wished she could scream loud enough that he could hear, but she was too far away and inside the library. He wouldn't hear her.

Looking at that thing, she suddenly saw it! In the water! When she was drowning! The thing she had kept trying to remember and seemed to slip away was what she saw just before she passed out. It wasn't oxygen deprivation making her imagine things! She saw that thing that was trying to pull at the young man. In the water at the bottom of the lake, the shadows turned into horrible demons that wanted her to die!

The terrifying truth made her legs go out from under her. She fell back into the chair of the carrel and closed her eyes. She cried silently. Ben put his arm around her and said soothing words in her ear. He had seen the shadow on the young man and knew she had, too. It was clear that she saw all that he did, but she had no one to explain it to her. It must be so confusing and terrifying. All he could do was hug her.

Marie understood now that there is more to the world that what we can see. There are spirits who help us and spirits who, for whatever reason, want to harm us.

10 - LAST DAY TOGETHER

A whole new world was visible to Marie. It had always been there. She knew that deep inside, but now she could see it with her own eyes. She looked at the Protectors full in the face. She could see the shadows around people. It was both intriguing and terrifying. She couldn't tell anyone, not even Allen. They would call the nut house who would promptly arrive in a little van with a straight jacket and carry her away. Seeing things that aren't there must be a sign of schizophrenia. She knew they were there, though. She could see that they affected what people did.

Recently, Kay decided she should quit smoking. A few days later, she got a phone call from her mother that was stressful. Her mother told her she had no business going to college. She wasn't smart enough and should come home and be sensible. It was more than Kay's resolve could handle and she reached for the pack hidden on top of the refrigerator. Marie watched unnoticed from the couch in Kay's dorm. The young man that followed Kay around was in high gear. He jumped up and covered Kay's hand with his and told her, "You're strong, Kay. This is your mom's issue. She is the one who felt like she wasn't smart enough. You are not her. You are passing your classes. You don't need those nasty cigarettes. You can do this!"

Kay stopped abruptly, listening. A tear formed in the corner of her eye. Almost inaudibly, Marie heard Kay say to herself, "No, mother! I will do this! And I'll take care of you, too." Kay grabbed the pack of cigarettes and threw them in the trash.

Marie knew that without the young man's encouragement, it might have been very different. He leaned back on the counter and looked at Marie. Marie smiled at him.

The shadows were another story. Marie didn't see them as often. They would sneak around the edges of life. Places you would naturally avoid seemed to grow them. Those instincts you have that make you think, "No, don't go in there," seemed to be right on target. Abandoned houses, dark alleys, stores that never seemed to do any business but somehow stayed open, these were places where Marie saw more shadows than anywhere.

Marie remembered seeing Lydia and decided to ask Kay about it. "What is going on with Lydia and her obsession with Allen?

"Oh, yeah, she's crazy, Marie. Just forget it. Allen is nuts for you."

"Yeah, I know. But I don't care for her bumping into him all the time. She is so obvious, she should just make a sign, 'I have the hots for Allen!'" They both laughed and Kay snorted. Then they laughed harder.

"She has issues, Marie. I think her home life was screwed up. Her mom is divorced, and her mom's boyfriends hit on her and then she and her mom argue. It's a mess. You know what they say, 'Hurting people hurt people.'"

"Well, I feel bad for her, but if she doesn't leave Allen alone, I'm gonna hurt her!"

***

It was a Thursday afternoon in April. The semester was winding down. Research papers and projects were on everyone's minds. Marie and Allen had been hanging out in the dorm all afternoon studying and putting together their leaf projects for dendrology. That was their favorite and only class together. But by now, they were both tired of school and books and flattened leaves stuffed in paper towels, smashed flat in heavy books.

Allen sat at the table typing labels for leaf samples. Marie got up and came around behind him. She wrapped her arms around his neck and started kissing his neck and nibbling his ear. He smiled.

"Um. That's very distracting," he said as he tried to keep typing, the click, click, clicking getting slower.

"I should hope I'm more interesting than that old typewriter!" Marie laughed as she ran her fingers through his hair. He stopped typing and reached his arms up to catch her face, bringing her around and down in his lap to kiss her.

He paused briefly to breathe in the scent of her perfume, her hair, even her soft breath. He loved every part of her being. Then he kissed her cheeks, her forehead and then her mouth. Soft, loving kisses.

She got up and pulled him with her to the couch where they snuggled side by side, hugging and pulling each other closer until no space was between them. Their combined warmth and the closeness made Marie relax into a state of bliss. If only she could live in this bubble forever.

"I love you, Marie," said Allen. "I want you in my life forever. I'm so glad you're coming with me back to Kentucky when school is out."

"Me, too! And I love you, too. I don't know how I would have made it after the accident in February. You have helped me so much," she said.

Allen sighed. "Well, I'm just glad all that is past us. We have all our future to look forward to." Marie snuggled in

and tried to block out the other things in her world now. Now, as though it was new, but she knew it had been there all along and only now she could see it.

She thought about a woman she had talked to a long time ago. She was waiting for a doctor's appointment and the woman next to her in the waiting room looked at her and smiled. Marie looked at her and said, "Um, why are you smiling at me?"

The woman laughed a hearty, but quiet laugh. "Because, darlin', you have a beautiful aura. Do you have the gift?"

Marie looked at her in confusion, "Gift?"

"You know, baby. Do they talk to you? I would swear you could hear them, too." The woman looked deeply at Marie making her a little nervous.

"Uh, no. I'm pretty sure I don't know what you're talking about," said Marie.

"Well, maybe one day you will hear them. But when you do, remember, the more open you are to them, the more they will seek you out. Guard yourself or they'll consume you," the woman advised.

"Ohhh. Okay," Marie said, thinking surely this woman had spent too long under the influence of something. Thankfully, the door opened, and the nurse called her name at just that moment.

Was that what was going on now? Were they talking to her? Would they try to consume her? That sounded crazy. Except that they had tried, hadn't they? They lured her over the edge of that lake and then tried to pull her to the bottom. Her head started to hurt, and she let it go. It was too much to think about. She missed the days of blind bliss.

She nestled into Allen's shoulder and hugged him tighter.

***

The sun was just setting when Marie's eyes opened. She yawned and tried to stretch but there was no room with them both on the couch. Allen awoke from the movement and rolled away from her onto his back. After a minute of

letting the sleep go from their minds, they decided they were hungry.

They put on shoes, Allen grabbed his keys and wallet and out they went. The sun was shining low through the trees from the west. The red orange light was brilliant in the crisp mountain sky. By the time they got into town, the light was nearly gone, and headlights and streetlights were on. The little parking lot next to the Europa was full of the square dancers. Allen looped down Main Street and parallel parked in front of a store two doors down.

Marie noticed it was a vacuum repair shop. The open sign was still hanging in the door. A dim fluorescent light was on inside. It was going out and blinked in a random pattern. The store owner was sitting on a stool near a worktable with vacuum parts laying everywhere. There was another man there. He didn't look like a protector or a customer. Marie noticed the store owner was counting money. A lot of money. The other man was behind him with his arm around him. He looked like a hungry carnival con trying to convince someone to see a bearded lady. The store owner rolled up the money and put it in his pocket. The other man smiled wide and then, saw Marie looking at him through the window. His expression took on a new look of interest. He seemed surprised that Marie saw him. Darkness filled his expression and he suddenly disappeared.

Marie was momentarily jolted. What was that? Was it a shadow? But it looked like a person? Not a shadow? And then it looked at her and disappeared! She was bewildered.

Allen put his arm around her, "Ready?" he said.

Marie looked at him blankly and said, "Yes." She glanced back into the vacuum shop as they walked away. The owner was tinkering with a vacuum.

Allen opened the door to the diner and held it for her. She smiled at him as she went through, and he winked back. They found an empty booth near the back. Square

dancers were everywhere. Ruffles on ladies' skirts and men's shirts with colored stitching made the diner look like live decorations were swirling around the room. Laughter and chatter filled the air. This was what Marie loved most about this diner. She wanted to always remember the feeling when it was busy with life and joy.

They scooted in their seats and felt relieved to have their own space in the crowd. It would likely be a few minutes before Peg the waitress would get to them. Marie saw her across the diner busily writing an order and not looking at the guests the whole time.

"So, it'll be a long trip to Kentucky in the Jeep after school is out. It could take us four or five days to get there," Allen said.

"Oh, that'll be an adventure!" Marie said.

"I was thinking we could map out campgrounds along the way at state and national parks. There really isn't a rush to get there. We could visit some places and hike a little."

"I'd love that. The weather should be nice enough

that camping will be fun." Marie said. Marie thought that getting away from any crowds would be a welcome change. Now that the population of the world seems to have doubled. "I would love to see some of the Rockies. Other than driving through them when I was kid, I have never spent any time there exploring."

Peg the waitress finally made it over, working over the gum in her mouth like a grinder. "Welcome to the Europa. What can I getcha?" she said looking at her order pad, pen hovering ready.

Marie said, "I'd like a Coke."

"Dr. Pepper for me," said Allen. "And we know what we want if it'll save you a trip."

"Sure. What would you like?" Still staring at the pad and

scribbling away.

"Two club sandwiches with fries," said Allen.

"Sure thing, kiddos," said Peg as she turned to go and

vanished in the ruffled crowd.

"So, Allen, you said once that you don't believe in guardian angels. What do you think happens to us after we die?" Marie decided to throw it out there. They hadn't talked much about religion, and neither went to church.

"Well, who really knows, you know? The only people that really know are dead and they aren't telling us much about it. So, its all just speculation, isn't it? I like to deal with what I know to be true with my own eyes. I'm not ruling anything out, but I haven't seen much evidence other than the obvious: when our bodies go, we are done." "Yeah, I get that. But I know a lot of people have seen ghosts. They have lived in houses that had a ghost that lived there. They saw something with their own eyes. There must be something more." Marie said.

Allen pursed his lips, and his dimple became more pronounced. "I will agree there are some things that are unexplained. Without more evidence, how can we know anything for certain?"

"So, you don't believe in heaven?" Marie asked. "Or hell?" He added.

"Yeah. I guess they go together."

"Well, I can't say for sure. I guess I'm not convinced or unconvinced. I just rely on what I know to be true with my own eyes," said Allen.

"I suppose that's fair. I would like to think there is a heaven. I would like to think one day I'll see my grandma again. I miss her. She believed in heaven." Marie thought about all the times her grandmother had told her God loved her and sent her little gifts like a cross necklace she kept in her jewelry box.

The waitress brought their drinks, deposited them on the table on coaster napkins and spun away without a word.

"Well," said Marie as she took a draw on the straw in her Coke. "Let's make a pact. If something happens to one

of us, the other will try to contact them. Okay?"

"Sounds fair, I suppose. Although, you might not want me hanging around when you move on and get a new guy. Three's a crowd, you know!" He laughed. "I might think it's a lot of fun to trip him now and then. That'll be your sign!"

They both laughed at that thought.

***

Back at the dorm, they curled up in bed together. Allen had his arm around her waist. She liked the feeling of his warm body against her back.

"I love you, Allen," she said.

"I love you, too. Always and forever," he

answered back.

"Always and forever."

***

Marie closed her eyes and slipped into bliss. Just before dawn, she awoke to a sound. She thought she'd heard something. Rain started pelting the window and she saw the trees being blown by the wind. Allen mumbled in his sleep and turned over. She ran her fingers through his soft blond hair and fell back to sleep.

Ben was leaning against the wall by the window. He waited until she fell back asleep and then went into the living room where Jacob was talking to Tom and Henry.

Henry was talking to them about what he'd heard. "There has been an uptick in activity in this area. The shadows have figured out something is up. We expect them to start poking around to figure out what is going on. We just need to be vigilant. I don't think they'll try anything until they know more."

"Did Lorenzo give any reason why she is seeing everything?" asked Jacob.

"He knows, of course, but he didn't tell us. He is very concerned for her. You know there was another one about 20 years ago that started to see and things didn't go well." Henry added.

Marie was dreaming that she was in a meadow in Yosemite. It was a little meadow near the Yosemite Institute. It was early in the morning and the sun was shining on half the meadow. Dew was on the tall grass and little beetles were crawling up the blades to get a drink. She was sitting inside a sleeping bag having just woke up. The night had been cold. She heard the crunch of grass behind her and twisted around. A young man about twenty in jeans and hoodie was standing there. He came around her and sat cross-legged on the ground.

"Are you the one that stays with me?" Marie asked.

His dark curly hair ruffled in the morning breeze. His hazel green eyes gazed lovingly at her. "Yes, I'm Ben. Do you know how much you're loved?"

She thought that was an odd thing to say, but replied, "Um, yeah. I mean I know Allen and my parents love me." "Use that love they give you to fight. When the time comes, that's what will save you." She looked at him quizzically.

"When what time comes? What's that supposed to mean?" She tried to ask, but he vanished. She was alone in the meadow. Suddenly, it grew dark, like a cloud passed in front of the sun. She looked around and saw the black smoke-like shadows creeping towards her. She stood up and looked around trying to decide which way to run, but it was coming from all sides faster than she would have guessed. Within seconds it was upon her. Long, stick-like arms stretched forward with their bony fingers and claw nails and tried to grasp her. She spun around and jumped back only to find herself enveloped. There was no way out. Blackness was all she could see. She screamed as loud as she could, but in the dorm bedroom, only a whimper was heard. It was just enough to catch Henry's attention.

Henry had been talking to the other protectors and stopped abruptly, holding his hand up to quiet the others as he listened. He raced into the bedroom, but it was too late. He could tell that her spirit was gone. Just a shell of a person was left. She was still alive, but without her spirit, her body was in a coma-like state.

PART TWO

11 - ON THE OTHER SIDE

It was dark and barren. Rocks and boulders were strewn all over the ground. Marie had no idea where she was. It all looked unfamiliar. She was not alone. Shadows were everywhere. There was a slight hissing sound in the air. She sat up and shook her hair out. There was dirt and pebbles encrusted in her hair that fell as she shook. She looked at her clothes and her arms as she sat up and leaned against a large boulder. She had been unconscious, she was sure. She didn't have any cuts or scrapes, surprisingly, because it looked like she had been dragged on the ground. She didn't have long to ponder where she was. The shadows were coming closer.

They'd figured out she woke up and started to circle around her and take shape. Without any fear in their own headquarters, they quickly went from smoky shadows to people. People that, in life, Marie would have avoided. A woman with a very hard, very haughty look on her face came forward looking down her nose at Marie until she stood directly in front of her. She stood looking at Marie with her arms crossed and her feet squared, shoulder-width apart.

"Well, girlie! Welcome to our world, YOUR new world!" she growled while still eyeing Marie without relief. "You don't look near as amazing," she said with a mocking tone, "as your reputation would have me think. But first I have some questions for you. How come you can see us?" This last sentence she nearly demanded.

Marie looked the woman up and down. She seemed to be about 25 with curly dark red hair that wildly fell around her shoulders. She had a dour pinched face and no makeup. Her skin had angry red blemishes on top of freckles. Dark circles were deep under her eyes. Marie thought she looked like she had recently been terribly sick. Terribly sick and very angry about it.

"I have no idea and WHO are you?" said Marie

defiantly.

The woman laughed and said, "Your worst nightmare. Of course you have no idea who I am. You and your stupid line of self-absorbed blithering idiots! For now, I will tell you that I have a score to settle. Something of mine was taken and someone will need to make up for it. In the meantime, get to know my pals. They're bored and need some entertainment."

With that that she swept her right arm out to the side to show the others gathering behind her. Marie thought they would all make perfect zombies. They all looked haggard and tired. Pale, colorless faces with dark circles under their eyes. Some looked angry and some just looked sad. On a bad day, Marie looked like a beauty queen compared to this crowd.

"Where am I?" Marie demanded. "Where is Allen?

What do you want with me?"

The woman smirked, "You don't need to worry about any of that. None of that matters. Your stupid little life is done now." She came forward and grabbed Marie by the hair on top of her head and forced Marie's face up to look into her eyes. "They have moved on and forgotten all about you, just like people like you would do about someone they see as NOTHING!" The hard toned changed to a fake, patronizing croon, "We are your new buddies. We'll never leave you like they did."

"What are you talking about?" Marie was getting more confused by the minute. The woman let go of her and stepped back, clearly done with this conversation.

"You're here now. Get used to it." The woman said and looked Marie up and down with obvious disdain. Then she turned and left. After she left, the others got closer and started picking at her, pulling at her arms and clothes. They didn't talk but just slightly hissed. They pulled at her hair and touched her face. Marie tried to scream and push them away, but now all she could do was hiss as well. They were tormenting her, but why? She had nothing to offer. It was almost like there was nothing else for them to do. Every so often she would hear words in the hisses, "You're ugly! You're so fat! You're nothing!"

This went on for what seemed like hours. She cried. She curled up in a ball. She tried to cover her head, but they never ceased. The picking, pulling and hate-filled words continued no matter what. She couldn't run or even get up. They would trip her and pull her down. In this weird place, there was no time. The sun didn't come up and the weather didn't change. They never got hungry, because although she didn't know it, they didn't have real bodies. They were just the angry, bitter souls that never had compassion, that were always self-absorbed. They wanted to consume her for the peace she had without having to find peace on their own. Others were just jealous and wanted her to feel the pain and torment they did.

Marie tried to retreat in her mind to a safe place and ignore the world from her skin outward. She had no way to get away and save herself. She tried to think of things that made her feel at peace. She thought of lying across the bow of her parents' sailboat staring down into the blue- green depths of ocean as the boat cut through the swells at full sail. The shafts of light moved with her, and flecks sparkled in the water. She remembered the up and down swells and the light shining into the water and it relaxed her. She tried to let that thought supersede what was happening around her.

***

Hester needed time to think. She felt exhilarated and was having trouble containing herself. Now that she had Marie in her clutches, she needed to think about the best way to get her revenge. No need to tip all her hand just yet. She thought about how much she hated that dang Jenny for stealing Tom away. Even though it had been over 200 years, the pain was like yesterday because every day of her miserable existence reflected the immensity of what Jenny did to her, what Tom did to her. She thought about the multiple children and grandchildren she had been able to squash out of existence, causing untold, deliriously satisfying pain for Jenny and Tom. All of this did satisfy her empty, angry heart to some degree, but it never matched the unfairness of her pathetic life. Her life and even her afterlife had been marred and ruined. She'd loved Tom. She waited for him, but he chose Jenny. Hester married Leonard, his brother, to stay close to Tom, hoping he would eventually come to his senses. She had made sure she never carried a child to term so that her first born could be his. All this she sacrificed, and, in the end, it was for nothing. Her life had been ruined because of Jenny coming along and distracting him.

Marie was the first one she had been able to snatch from life who yet lived, now under her control. She had heard from the shadows that Marie had an uncanny ability to rebuff their efforts to overwhelm her. But why? Would Marie still have that strength here, in the other world? Hester thought the best way to finally get her revenge was to somehow get Marie to destroy Jenny, her own grandmother many generations removed, and then Hester could finally have Tom all to herself, even if she had to enslave him to do so.

***

Ben was freaking out. "What happened to her?" he asked Henry as he grabbed at Henry's shirt. Ben's eyes were wild with terror. He was crying as he talked.

"Ben! Calm down. We'll search for her!" Henry said. "Jacob, take Ben into the bedroom and search for any distortion residues that might give us a clue."

Jacob put his arm around Ben and led him from the living room of the dorm. Tom had an alarmed but controlled look on his face.

"Henry, I've never seen anything like this. It's obvious they snatched her but how? How did they take her right under our noses? And where? Is she alive? If she is in the middle of their lair, how can we get her? Why did they even try this? It's very bold. Lorenzo will not be happy at all."

"Yeah, all good questions. All I can figure is that when they noticed she could see them, they took it as an invitation that she wanted to join them. Either that or she just intrigued them, and they wanted to add her to their collection. Who knows what they think?

"My guess is that they did take her to their lair. That's the safest place for them. They must know we will search for her. At least there they have numbers on their side. We do need to tell Lorenzo immediately."

They flashed out to the Gathering and walked across the marble portico. As they approached Lorenzo, he looked up. He already knew. Sadness permeated from his face. A tear fell down his cheek.

"Lorenzo! Marie has been taken," Henry said redundantly, his strawberry blond waves blowing in the soft breeze. His usually joyful expression replaced with a look like he was about to cry.

Lorenzo and Henry embraced and grimaced with the pain of worry for Marie. Lorenzo embraced Tom next and the three paused to think before speaking. Lorenzo had his

hands on his hips and studied the floor.

"I know where she is. They have her in their lair. They are tormenting her. She'll break before long and become bitter like them. When the anger comes, she'll fight back and want to destroy them just like they want to destroy her. Then we may never reach her." lamented Lorenzo. "It's happened before, but we didn't get there in time. It all depends on her."

"But Lorenzo, what can we do? We must do something.

You can do something! Can't we rescue her?" said Tom.

Lorenzo paused and sighed. "Not there. That is the shadows' domain. It's not just a physical place. It's a choice. I have already provided a way, long ago. She must choose to stay or go, and they know that. The only way they can control her is to break her down until she becomes as dead as they are. Right now, it could go either way. If she chooses love, the bonds that hold her there will weaken."

Ben appeared at the edge of the portico. He ran toward Lorenzo, Tom, and Henry.

"Ben!" said Lorenzo as he caught him in an anguished embrace and hugged him.

"I have an idea!" said Ben.

"Let's hear it!" answered Lorenzo looking eagerly in Ben's eyes.

"You can do anything, Lorenzo. I know you can." Ben

stated with authority. Lorenzo frowned slightly.

"I can do many things, sweet Ben," Lorenzo lovingly put his hand on the side of Ben's neck, "but I cannot make choices for another."

"Yes! I know, but could you make a way for us to get her a message before she was snatched?" Ben excitedly searched Lorenzo's face for acknowledgement. Lorenzo turned and looked out over the crowds on the portico. After what seemed like minutes, he turned at the waist and looked at Ben with a slight grin.

"Yes! Yes, Ben! I can do that with your help." Lorenzo put his hands on Ben's shoulders. "There is a way, but what would you say? What message would you give her?"

"Just like I told my mom not to worry," Ben pleaded, "I could tell Marie the one thing that the Shadows can't overcome. Love, she needs to use love! She doesn't know and it will take too long for her to discover on her own!"

"That's true. She knows it innately, but this is all out of her context. The Shadows know that too. Their plan is to torture her until she goes mad." Lorenzo shuddered as though he could see it happening. Tom thought maybe he really could.

Marie could feel stinging pain all over her body. It was like she was being bitten by fire ants. She cried out and no relief came. Then the pain turned to bruising punches on her back and sides. She heard cracking of bones and felt the white-hot pain. She wondered if she could survive. Cold air blew against her skin, icy and frost-biting cold. She could feel the burning freeze in her hands, and she shivered. Next it was water. Water rose around her, first inches and then feet. She found her leg was chained to the ground as the water rose and carried her up with it until her leg held her down. She tried to hold her breath but eventually her lungs convulsed in sharp pain, and she sucked in the water. Terror seized her as she jerked her leg against the shackle to no avail. She started seeing spots in her vision and encroaching darkness. Then just as quickly, the water receded, and she was on the muddy ground.

Panting and gasping, she looked around the dark landscape. The savage people were gone. She cried pitiful tears in the respite. Why did they want her and what did they think she would do? They could have killed her and yet they always stopped just short. Somehow any sign of their attack was gone. It was all trickery. There were no cuts or broken bones. It was all in her mind. Even so, it was so believable, she couldn't help but react.

She felt a presence in front of her and looked up. It was the woman again.

"Having fun yet?" the woman mocked.

"What do you want with me?" Marie screamed at her. "Let me go!"

The woman laughed a throaty laugh. "Funny. No. You get to stay now. There is no going back. There is no way for you to get back. This is your own fault.

Everyone here made their own destiny to be here just like you. Make nice and make friends!"

"What are you talking about?" Marie yelled.

"Ah, good. Somebody is getting mad! You are making progress!" The woman spoke in riddles. "Perhaps you are ready for the next phase," the woman said as she circled Marie.

With that, she vanished leaving Marie as confused as ever. Marie hugged herself and rocked trying to make sense of all this. Suddenly in front of her was a fire pit with a huge, wooded stake in the middle. Allen was tied to it. Flames erupted in the thick woven branches around the stake. Marie leapt to her feet and looked for a way to get to him, but the wood and flames were too wide to cross. The flames were hotter than she could imagine fire ever being. She screamed as she helplessly watched Allen burn, his skin melting as he yelled a grotesque plea for help. Within seconds he was nothing but a charred clump against the stake. Marie sobbed with grief. Then it was gone.

Right on the horrible vision's heals was the next scene, all her friends from high school were on a boat in the sea that appeared before her. Sharks circle the boat. Marie could see it was listing to the side and taking in water. They scrambled for life jackets and screamed for her to save them. There was no one else to help. Marie was alone with no boat to get to them. In a matter of seconds, the boat slipped below the surface leaving her friends bobbing in the water. They yelled to her for help but what could she do? Just as she was about to jump in the water to swim out to them, as if that would help, the sharks attacked with horrific strength. The sharks thrashed them around in the water and soon there was nothing but stillness and a large pool of red.

Marie was panting and close to passing out. She was on her hands and knees gasping for air. After a minute of this, she stood up and looked around. It was just the dirt and boulder dark landscape again.

Thoughts raced through her head. This was a dream, maybe. It had to be something in her head. It had to be not real. Maybe she could just wake up.

"WHAT do you want?" she screamed at the sky. No answer. She walked. Maybe she could find a town or a house. She tried to make sense of things. It seemed so real, but it couldn't be.

She saw something on the ground. It looked like a dead cat. Mangled and hideous. Suddenly it jumped up and started hissing at her. Then, horrifyingly, it started to talk to her.

"You don't remember me, hiss? You ran over me 2 years ago. Remember that thump that night? I have been looking, hiss, for you. Want to pet my head, NOW?" With that it jumped on her with claws bared. Marie screamed.

"Get off me!" Marie cried as she batted it away. The stench of death was all around her. The cat leapt away and looked back at her, "Don't you get it? You're dead!" It smirked and turned away and ran off.

"What? What on earth? How can I be dead?" I didn't die. I was asleep." She thought for a minute and then sat on a smooth boulder. "Maybe I am dead. Maybe this is it. But I'm not done! What about Allen? No! I don't want to be dead!" She got angry. "This isn't fair! And why am I here? This doesn't seem like any heaven I have ever heard of!"

Laughter filtered in behind her. "Very good, little learner! That's right, you are dead, and this isn't heaven!"

The woman pealed laughter now. "Now you just

93

get to enjoy hell for eternity with us! Sound like fun? Huh? Too bad!"

"This is crazy! How can I be dead? I don't remember dying!" Marie hissed at her.

"Silly girl! I could care less what you remember. People die in their sleep all the time. Now get with the program." The woman vanished again like this was some cat and mouse game.

Marie thought that none of this made sense. But just as she was about to start looking for a way back home, the tormentors came again and covered her. Like a shadow on the horizon, they swiftly came to her and consumed her with their violence. They hissed evil words of defeat and told her how worthless her life had been. There was no escaping their torment day and night.

No meditation or mind tricks would help in the long run. It became a matter of just surviving. That was it, they wanted her to fight back and be evil like them. She refused, but she also couldn't make them stop.

12   - SAFE AT THE GATHERING

Allen woke first in the morning. He looked at Marie lying next to him. She looked so peaceful. The rhythmic rise and fall of her side as she lay with her back to him was beautiful. He touched her brown wavy hair as the morning sunlight began to shine on her making her hair look like liquid gold. The curving swoop of her waist and hip with the sheet twisted against her looked like a goddess reclining. He breathed deep and turned and went into the kitchen to make breakfast for them.

As he cooked, he thought of what they might do today. It might be a good day to go out and gather samples in the forest for a project. The eggs popped and sizzled in the pan. The warm smell of toast wafted past his nose. He turned and grabbed the toast as it popped up in the toaster. He put one slice each on a plate and then deftly scooped scrambled eggs out of the little skillet and divided them into two servings on the separate plates. He opened a drawer and selected two forks and added them. With the ease of a master chef, he stacked the plates on his left arm and grabbed a cup of coffee with his right hand and made his way across the room. He set the coffee and plates on the night table and sat on the side of the bed with her facing

him, still sleeping. He nibbled her ear. She didn't move.

He whispered in her ear, "Wake up, Marie." No response. He was surprised she was sleeping soundly and shook her shoulder. No response. This time he shook more vigorously.

When there was no response still, his fear started to

overtake him. "Marie! Marie! Wake up!"

He stood up, knowing this wasn't right. Something is wrong. He shook her one more time, both hands on her shoulders. Her limp body rocking back and forth with his effort. He checked her pulse, and it was there beating away proving life was still here, but he could not rouse her. Now terrified, he ran to the phone and dialed 9-1-1.

***

At the hospital, Allen hovered in the waiting room hoping for good news. He clenched his fists in his pockets. He held back tears. What could have caused this? How long had she been unconscious? The doctor came out to talk to him.

"Mr. McCracken, you share an apartment with Marie, right?" said the doctor.

"Uh, sort of, she has her own dorm, but yeah, she stays with me a lot." Allen stammered.

"It's okay, Mr. McCracken,"

"Just call me Allen," Allen interrupted.

"Sure, Allen. I just have a few questions. Did she hit her head recently?"

"No, not that I know of." Allen thought back trying to

remember anything out of the ordinary.

"Did she drink any alcohol last night?"

"No. She doesn't drink at all. We just had dinner at the Europa Café. Then we went back to the college and went to sleep." Allen waved his arms helplessly as he talked.

"Okay. Have you contacted her parents? We will need someone who is next of kin here to make decisions for her."

"Um, no. I guess I need to do that. Doctor, is she going to be okay?" Allen had a pleading look on his face.

The doctor looked at him earnestly, "I hope so, son, we are doing everything we can. She is in a type of coma for some reason. She could come out at any time … unless there is some reason we haven't found yet why she can't. We'll keep you posted. Call her parents and you can see her shortly."

Allen was trying to process what that all meant. *"Some reason they haven't found yet?"* he thought to himself. His insides started churning and cramping.

He pulled his wallet out of his back pocket and took out a folded scrap of paper. Marie had given it to him a while back in case of emergency. She'd written her parents' phone number on it. He went to the pay phone to make a difficult phone call.

***

Marie went into a small place in her mind. She tried to tell herself that her nerves were not giving her accurate information. She is not being burned or broken. It's just in her head. She just must try to survive until she can find a way to get away. She focused on Allen, but the thoughts of him being burned alive come to her mind and she had to push the thoughts away. She thought of hiking with Allen. In her mind, she is holding his hand. He smiles at her, and his dimple shows. Just one dimple in his cheek. She smiles back. They come into a meadow. Its early morning. Then she freezes.

The dream. She remembered a strange dream. Why had she not thought of it before now? It was almost like she didn't have that memory until just now. She tried to focus on the dream, but it was fuzzy. It was just before they took her. She was in a meadow in the early morning. A man was there, but a man she had never seen before. He told her something. It was important. Yes, about love. He said to remember that I am loved, and that will save me when the time comes.

She thought about Allen and his warm brown eyes. She thought about the way they crinkle when he smiles at her.

She remembered when she met him. She'd seen him moving in. She noticed the Kentucky tags on his Jeep. She was curious since she was born in Kentucky but had few memories of it since her family moved when she was very young. She'd went for a walk after that, down to the lake on campus. The water glistened in the sunset. She had sat on a bench near where the lake overflow poured over round stones into a little bubbling stream. The sound of the rushing water had been so soothing. She remembered closing her eyes and soaking in the warm sunlight and listening to the sound of the water. When she'd opened her eyes, he was there leaning against a tree watching her. She unconsciously smiled at him because he seemed as natural in her life as if he had always been there. He smiled back and his dimple puckered. His eyes crinkled and she knew he was finally here. He was the one she would love forever.

He sat down next to her and looked out over the lake. "I'm Allen," he said. "Anywhere good to eat around here?" He turned his head and looked in her eyes and smiled. She melted in the warmth of his smile.

"Well, I heard there's a café downtown where the locals eat. Wanna check it out?" she demurely blinked and smiled a coy smile.

She didn't know it, but he was done. He'd found her. No sense looking further. She was all he would ever want again.

Marie stayed in this daydream a little longer and then realized the pain from the torturers was less than it was before. She searched for another memory and thought about last Christmas in the dorm. It was too expensive for Allen to fly home, so she stayed with him. The snow fell outside, and they decorated a little tabletop tree with lights. They put Christmas music on the radio and danced around the living room of his dorm. They exchanged silly gifts like an apple and a pair of socks and laughed. He told her he loved her more than anything and she told him she loved him, too. He said, "I hope you don't mind, but I'm going to marry you one day." She just smiled and thinking that sounded wonderful.

"Marie! Get up!" Marie was called out of her reverie by a voice she didn't recognize. She blinked open her eyes. The torturers were still there but barely moving. She easily shoved them away and stood up.

"Who are you?" she said.

He smiled. "I am called many things by many people. I've come to help you out of here. Your choice to remember love set you free. Follow me." He held out his hand.

She looked at him. Was this another trick? He looked different, not like the dead people there. She reached out and put her hand in his. She felt her body pulled against space like squeezing past inflated walls close together. She closed her eyes and held tightly to his hand, although it seemed like nothing could ever pull his hand from hers. In an instant they were somewhere completely different. It was a Roman portico, like a large porch, with a marble floor and marble columns. There were various levels with steps and marble railings with turned marble balusters holding up the railings. Many people were there, possibly hundreds. They were all talking amongst themselves, but she noticed that as soon as they arrived, they all stopped and looked at her and the man. Then joy broke loose with cheering and applause. A small group of three men ran towards them. One was the man in her dream. He was waving his arms and smiling and laughing. When the group reached them, Ben hugged her, and she hugged back awkwardly.

"You're okay!" said Ben.

"Yeah!" She said and sighed a breath of relief as she realized that wherever this was, it was safe. Whoever these people were, they would protect her. She felt instant relief. "So, who are you guys? Where am I?"

"It's a long story. And it's going to be hard to swallow."

Lorenzo said.

Marie looked quizzically at the group around her. "Ok.

Well, let's start with where am I? I don't think I've ever been here."

Tom laughed. "Probably not! At least since you're still alive!"

"I'm alive? But the woman, she said…" she faltered.

"She lied. They do that." Tom said exhaling, "You are alive, at least for now. Although, your actual body is lying in a hospital bed right now, your spirit is here, in a place between life and eternity. All makes sense now?" He laughed a bit and then stifled himself.

Marie looked dumbfounded. "Huh?"

Ben chimed in, "Look, you have seen things lately, right? Things that only you could?"

"Yeah," she looked at Ben.

"You were seeing bits of this world bleeding into yours. You were seeing us, the Protectors, and them, the dark Shadows. They have been after you for some time."

"Looks like they finally got me!" Marie huffed.

"Yes. That is what happened," said Tom.

"So, you all are Protectors? What does that mean?"

Marie asked, looking from face to face.

"We are like guardian angels. I have been with you since birth, Marie." Tom smiled softly. "I have protected you from the dark shadows for a long time. Ben here joined our forces a little bit ago and he has been helping, too." Ben bristled with guilt.

"Joined you?" she looked at Ben, "How does one *join* you?" said Marie.

Tom paused, "Well there is life, where you live, normally," he added, "and then there is afterlife. There are a few avenues of afterlife. Specifically, life eternal and life in hell. Some in the life eternal choose to become Protectors before moving on to heaven."

"So, this isn't heaven?" Marie asked looking around slightly agreeing that she thought it should look more sparkly or something.

Lorenzo laughed. "No, it gets better. We call this the gathering. This isn't bad, though, right? I'd like to say we have a great espresso bar, but spirits don't drink coffee."

Marie didn't laugh, so he continued.

"Anyway, we are a great army whose purpose is to

102

protect the living and give them a chance to choose. Without the help of the Protectors, evil would take over before people could decide for themselves the way they want to go."

"I see," said Marie. She looked at Tom. "You've been with me always?"

"Yes, since you were born," Tom said softly. His smiled like an adoring father looking at his daughter.

"But everyone here looks young. Did they all die young?" Marie asked.

"No. All spirits have their own image that doesn't age. It's the image of us in the prime of our life. I lived to be an old man. Ben here never lived a day. But don't let that fool you. He doesn't act like he was born yesterday!" Tom laughed. Sorry, couldn't help myself."

Ben glowered.

"So how do I get back? I can't stay here!" Marie said, realizing this was all wrong.

They were all quiet and then Lorenzo spoke. "We don't know exactly. You aren't the first to be in two dimensions at once, but so far, you are the only one to survive it.

The dark Shadows took you for some reason. They snatched you. You have a gift that allows you to be in both places. This gift allowed you to see the others while you were in your world. So, I am thinking that this gift will help get you back. We will help you in any way we can," Lorenzo said, smiling gently. "But how it works will be up to you."

"I need to think," Marie said. "Give me a little time." Lorenzo nodded that he understood.

She looked around for a place to be alone. She walked to a step off to the side and sat down with her back to them. Lorenzo, Tom and Ben looked at her wishing they could fix this for her.

Ben and Tom looked at Lorenzo. "Guys, even if I whisked her back into her body, the Shadows would be on her again. We have to figure out why they want her, and she has to learn how to use this gift," Lorenzo said.

***

In the hospital, Allen sat beside Marie's bed drawing imaginary circles on her arm with his finger. It had been a week. Marie's parents came and were staying at a local hotel. They all took turns sitting with her in case there was some change. They wanted someone she knew to be there when she woke up.

He thought of that night over and over trying to figure out if there was something he missed. Their conversation had taken a spiritual tone, and she asked if he believed in an afterlife. They had agreed they would try to contact each other if anything ever happened, but she wasn't dead. Her body was just perpetually sleeping. The doctor said there was brain activity. She was thinking away in there somewhere, or at least dreaming. He hoped she was having dreams of them being together.

He breathed deeply and picked up his textbook and opened it. He tried to read, but it was hard to concentrate.

13 - JENNY

"By and by, have you got the girl all in fits?" A female voice like a songbird, a loud songbird, rang in Marie's ears. She looked up to see a spitfire small woman with her chestnut hair pulled up and back on her head. She wore a beautiful off-the-shoulder gown of light blue satin that went all the way to the floor. The cut reminded Marie of one she had seen in a museum.

The woman marched right up to Marie and held out a tiny delicate hand, "I'm Jenny, Jenny Helm. Tom is my husband. Nice to meet you. Heard all about you. Have they got you confused and scared to death yet?"

Marie shook her hand lightly. Jenny looked to be only a couple of years older than her. She had the same pale blue- gray eyes that Marie's grandmother had.

"Um, no, I don't know, uh…" Marie stammered.

"I'll take that as a yes," she shook her head as she said it. "Darlin' it'll be okay. Don't you fret. We must figure something out. Have they taken you to go visit your kinfolk yet, or maybe that beau?"

"What? I don't think…" Marie trailed off confused.

"Good lawdy, a-mighty! TOM!" she hollered

over her

shoulder. Tom strode over.

"Tom! Do you think it might help her to see something she knows? Let's take her to see her people so she at least feels better."

"Well, Jenny, now, that might not be so good for her to see them all upset," said Tom.

"Well, I don't reckon she is going to expect them to be having a party with her being ill, but at least she can sooth herself some."

Tom nodded that Jenny had a point.

"Ok. That makes sense. Marie, what do you think?"

Tom asked.

"I can see Allen and my parents?" she said excitedly.

Jenny winked at Tom.

"Yes, that's easy to do," Tom said. "Well, let's go!" Marie exclaimed.

"But now, honey, remember that they can't see or hear you, okay?" Jenny took Marie's hand and patted her arm as she said it.

Marie deflated a notch but was still glad to get to go.

"So, I'm basically a ghost."

Jenny nodded and smiled a motherly smile at her. Tom took Marie's hand, paused briefly, and gave her a smile of sympathy before the two of them flashed away.

***

In the hospital room, Allen was asleep, hunched over Marie's bed with his arms crossed under his head. The beep of the IV was droning on in hopes anyone might hear it. It was surreal to Marie to see herself lying in the bed and yet be standing in the shadow in the corner. She looked at Tom as if for

106

permission to move. Tom nodded.

She walked over to Allen and ruffled her fingers through his light brown hair. Her hand didn't encounter his hair though. It was just air. She couldn't really touch him. Her hand went right through him, and it was disconcerting. Being here made everything that she couldn't see before clear now. She was outside of real life, at least her mind was. Her body reclined on a bed. Her hair had been brushed to the right and she never brushed her hair that way, or maybe, she had just never looked at herself from another person's eyes. It was like hearing your voice on a recording. It seemed foreign. Even though she would have thought it was like looking in a mirror, it was like looking at a stranger. What if this body woke up and walked away and left her in this other world unattached to reality. Worse yet, could some other spirit claim her body? *'Oh no, they won't!'* She thought with a flash of anger.

Allen said something in his sleep. Marie turned to look at him. He was getting restless. She knelt beside him and tried to put her arms around him. There was nothing solid to hold. Not even the chair or the bed was solid to her. She was just floating in this parallel world. She wasn't even really standing on the floor.

"No! Marie!" Allen grumbled in his sleep.

"I'm right here, Allen! I love you! It'll be okay!" Marie tried to sooth him. He did calm down and breathe easier. Marie looked at Tom quizzically.

"Can he hear me?" she asked Tom.

Tom moved forward a step. "To some degree. We have been able to make suggestions to the new ones, that's what we call you all. And we can tell that you think about it and either choose to follow the suggestion or not. So, talk to him. He will likely understand somewhere in his mind. Oddly, that is just what the doctors have been telling him about you."

Marie looked back at Allen. "Allen, I'm okay. I'm not sure how to fix this, but I know it'll be okay. I need you to be strong for me. Don't give up! I love you and I need you!"

Allen's eyes opened. He looked at Marie in the bed. He had a look of hope in his eyes, but then he grimaced. "It was just a dream!" he muttered. He sighed and looked at her lying on the bed.

"Marie, what happened to you? Where are you in there?

Can you even hear me? I feel so stupid talking to you like this. The doctor said it would help, that they have seen it bring people out of this. I just wish I knew what was wrong. How did this happen?" He sighed and rubbed his eyes, and then continued.

"Your mom and dad are here in town. They will be here soon. Your mom looks at me like this is my fault. I have wracked my brain thinking about that day, if there was anything that happened, and I can't think of any reason for this. I think your mom thinks I hurt you or something. I love you, Marie! Why can't she see that?"

There was desperation in his voice. Marie thought that he must feel so alone. She had never seen him like this, and it broke her heart. She wanted so much to hug him. She looked at Tom for a suggestion.

He let out a large sigh. "Such is the dilemma of our kind. We feel so much for the ones we protect, and we can do so little. It's up to them to find their own strength. I have watched you cry. Once in high school, you were so upset, and I really worried about you. Your friend had turned on you. I just stayed with you and talked. I tried to remind you of things you find beautiful. And, well, we also fight the shadows that try to take the very life right out of you."

"Oh! I forgot they are here, too! I've seen them slithering around people! Are they here now?" she asked and looked around. She saw a movement in the corner of her eye and saw a handsome, tall man with dark hair and piercing dark eyes intensely fixed on her step out from the shadows. He smiled warmly. "Hello, Marie. I'm Jacob. So nice to be able to have a conversation with you. I won't say meet you because I have known you for some time now." He smiled warmly again, putting her at ease.

Marie stood up and walked over to him, looking him up and down. She looked at Tom who nodded that Jacob was safe.

"Jacob. You are Allen's Protector?" she asked.

"At your service, my dear." He stated gallantly and bowed holding a pretend hat.

"Hm. So you, and Tom, have been with me and Allen all this year that we have known each other?" she asked curiously.

Jacob answered, "That's correct. And Ben, I trust you have met Ben."

"Yes, I have." She absently answered and thought back to all the time she has been with Allen. "So, that day, at the reservoir, Tom, when I fell in, you all were there?"

Jacob looked at Tom, who answered, "I was away on assignment, but Ben was your Protector and he rescued you with great skill. Allen jumped into the water and the shadows tried to pull him under, too, and Jacob pulled Allen out."

"I see," she said as she tried to piece this new

information into her memory.

In a quick burst of movement, Marie saw Jacob quickly move behind Allen. As soon as Marie turned to look a shadow formed and grew behind Allen and materialized into a haggard man with deep creases in his face. His hair was stringy and wild. He lunged at Allen, who sat completely unaware of anything. Jacob leapt forward and swiped at the figure. Tom joined Jacob while Marie watched them both with horror. She could do nothing to protect Allen.

It was a 'distract and attack' move, though, a shadow crept along the floor near Marie's foot. She felt the cool mist around her foot and leapt away. The shadow grew and kept moving toward her. She screamed.

Almost on cue, a nurse came in the room, but Marie instantly realized the nurse could not see any of this battle.

The nurse convulsed and shivered. "Oh! There's a chill in here!" She pulled the blanket up higher on Marie's body in the bed. She asked Allen if he had seen any changes.

The hand-to-hand combat around the bedside continued. Marie tried to stomp on the shadow which did nothing. Jacob and Tom fought the Dark Shadow man on the other side near Allen.

The nurse paused and looked around, seeming to sense something, but shook it off. Marie caught sight of something odd on the woman's shoulders, a shadow crept around her neck. The woman's expression changed, and she looked sideways at Allen.

"You young people will never learn!" the nurse hissed oddly. Allen looked at her horrified and confused. Then the nurse did something that Marie couldn't imagine. She took a syringe from her pocket, uncapped it, and smiled a ghoulish grin. Allen was about to leap to cover Marie, thinking surely the nurse was about to kill her. The nurse registered his thoughts and laughed a deep guttural laugh. Marie saw the shadow around the nurse's neck tighten and then in swift movement, the nurse jabbed the syringe in her own arm and pushed the plunger. Everyone in the room turned to see the nurse fall dead in front of Allen.

Dark shadows seeped up through the floor and surrounded the fallen nurse whose spirit stood up looking rather surprised. She looked at the crowd around her and then the surprised look turned to a knowing smile. The shadows took her spirit away and the fighting in the room continued while Allen ran from the room calling for help.

There was a flash in the room. Marie raised her forearm to protect her eyes. Then she saw Henry, Jenny, and Ben was there, too. The shadows were outnumbered, and they faded from sight.

With a big sigh, Tom said, "Whew! Ok, so the shadows are on a mission. Sheez!"

"Lorenzo told us, and we came right away," said Henry. "We need to do some training with Marie. She is obviously a hot target for them."

Marie looked at Allen with concern, "But why are they going after him and what about that nurse? What in the world?" she asked.

"That's easy! To get to you! They are in a frenzy. The nurse was a sitting duck. She has probably been going their way for some time and the hyped energy in this room sent her careening their way. It's a shame. The shadows probably hoped she would take out Marie's body," said Ben. "They get carried away easily."

"I'm going to stay here with Jacob a while. You all go back to the Gathering and work on some things," said Ben. They all nodded. Tom took Marie's hand. A bright light glowed around her and seemed to

111

consume them.

14 - LIFE IN THE OTHER WORLD

Back at the Gathering, Marie sat by herself again to think. It was becoming clear to her what she was dealing with. Jenny was right, it had helped her to see Allen and to see how she was "different" now. It was also abundantly clear that she and everyone she cared about were in danger. Apparently, the dark Shadows had a great deal of power to get people to fling themselves over the cliff of sanity.

What amazed her most was that she had lived for nineteen years and never realized this whole other world existed right beside her. Not only that it was there, but that the actions of those beings could have a direct impact on her and other people's lives.

Why on earth did they want her? She was just a regular girl. She wasn't out trying to fight for world peace or evangelize the sinners.

Henry had been wracking his brain, as well. He noticed the scowl on Marie's face across the portico and walked over to her.

"There is more to this that you may not know," Henry said as he squatted down beside her.

She looked up at him questioningly. "Go on," she

said.

He sat down on the step beside her. "Have you noticed anything about the group you are hanging around with?" he said.

"Oh, besides the fact that you're all ghosts?" she said

indignantly.

He laughed and said, "Yeah, besides that. Have you noticed that we all have a slight resemblance to each other?"

"Huh?" She looked at them huddled with their heads together a few yards away. "I guess so. I mean, there isn't a lot of diversity there. Jenny reminds me of my grandmother and Ben could be my brother." She paused. "Are you saying we are all related?"

"Bingo! Tom could hash it all out better than I could, but, well, what do you know about your ancestry?" said Henry.

"Well, there's my parents and grandparents. Before that, I have heard stories about a grandmother way back named Sarah Elizabeth. I suppose that's about it." Marie thought hard to think of anything else.

"That's typical. Most people are like that. But you should know, you come from a line of people that were persistent and determined. They had strong ideals and would risk everything for them. Most of all, they loved fiercely." Henry said.

"Henry, are you related to me, too?" Marie inquired. "Yes, not directly. I would be a great uncle way back, before I died as a little boy. But Tom and Jenny were my parents. You are a direct descendant of them through my brother. They were amazing in life just like now. Fighters. They fought for freedom and for what was right. They forged a home in a wilderness that is now a thriving town in Kentucky.

They lost me in the process, and it nearly paralyzed them, but nothing can slow down a heart like theirs for long. Dad was a captain in the Revolutionary war and mom, despite the ball gown, could single-handedly run a fort of settlers. I swear the Indians that attacked the fort were afraid of her. I wouldn't want to be in her path when she's angry." Henry laughed.

"I see. So how does Sarah Elizabeth fit in?" Marie

asked.

"She is later down the line when the land was settled. She stood her ground for love despite her father who vehemently opposed the marriage. But that is just like her and all the rest of us. Our hearts often over-ride reason. I suppose that's why so many of us choose to join the Protectors rather than moving on to the great Destination. We can't let go of those we love."

"Hm, so, could there be something in us that makes the dark Shadows want to take us out?" Marie wondered.

"Maybe. I don't know. Anything is possible," Henry said.

"You'd think that kind of a rift in a family would split it apart. How did Sarah and her dad's relationship change?" she said.

"Well," he paused to think, "it wasn't good, but it wasn't ruined. They didn't talk for a long time. It was a small town so it's not like they were hiding from each other. It grieved him greatly when he heard how they struggled with the crops. Farming can be hit or miss. Sarah's husband only had a small farm that he homesteaded. But he built the house for them. It was cozy. He was a good man and loved Sarah very much. It was a big change for Sarah who had grown up the daughter of a wealthy railroad owner. But nothing could keep her from the love of her life."

Marie thought about and then said, "Allen said that my mom was giving him grief. Sounds like she isn't on his band wagon, either. What if it's a repeat? What if this happens a lot in our family and I am the current player in this repeat performance? I wonder what the cost is to the dark Shadows when we repeatedly choose love over sense or even just over our parents' choices for us," Marie thought out loud.

Lorenzo walked up and sat down next to her. "I can tell you what." He paused and looked into Marie's eyes. Marie felt like she could see all eternity in his eyes. She had never met anyone with such a calm, loving countenance.

He continued, "The dark ones lose everything when you choose love. It's the one thing that trumps them every time. They can work with greed and self-righteousness. They get very powerful with anger. They are nearly unbeatable with hate. Nearly. Love trumps it all."

"So," Marie constructed out loud, "if you disagree with someone and you still show them love, it's more powerful than just loving your mom or your boyfriend that agrees with you?"

"Exactly. Love that is harder to show has more potential energy for good than love that would be expected. Loving someone that does not deserve that love is the most powerful energy in the universe. It's irrational, it has no logic. There is nothing that can explain it or defeat it."

"So, Tom and Jenny's love for me as their child is expected, but Tom choosing to stay in Kentucky after I was murdered made no sense. Sense would have taken him back to Virginia to protect his other children," Henry said. "And Sarah choosing to love her dad even when he cut her off didn't make sense. She had every right to turn her back on him. And her dad had every right to turn his back on her. But they didn't. They still cared about each other and chose love," Marie paused. "I get that they might have it in for my family, but why is this happening now? Why not at some point before now?" she asked.

"Maybe it has more to do with what's to come. The dark shadows are putting two and two together. Allen's family are a passionate bunch as well. Maybe as you both become closer, the Shadows see a potential for the next generation to be even more powerful." said Lorenzo. "Sometimes their choices are not rational. Sometimes they don't see truth as it really is. There isn't any way to predict why they do what they do."

"So, I'm not just fighting for me, or for all of the ancestors, I'm fighting for the generations that don't exist yet." Marie felt overwhelmed. "Lorenzo, why can't you just destroy them?"

He laughed. "I could. But that's not why I'm here. The ones you would have me destroy, I loved like I love you. They made their choice to be what they are. I will not deny them their eternity because I loved them enough to let them be different from me without retribution. I am here for you and anyone who chooses love."

Marie thought for a minute and said, "I need some time."

"Here there is plenty of that. In fact, there is no time, so take all you want. Makes no sense, does it?" said Henry who got up and wandered to the others. After a minute, so did Lorenzo.

***

Marie thought about the ones that attacked her in that barren land. They were spirits just like her. They

117

had had a life. They had made decisions. Things had happened to them. She thought about the woman. In different circumstances, would she have chosen the life she had? All those people had been born and raised by someone. Was there a parade of people who had cried for them when they made bad choices? Were those people here now, fighting for others? Lorenzo said he had loved them, but how could he? Did he still love them now? Could she love them?

She tried to imagine the woman as a normal person, without the dark lines in her face. She tried to imagine her as a teenage girl just looking for someone to notice her and see who she was. Maybe she just had one too many people bully her when she just wanted to be cared about.

Whatever the case, they were warped now and set on a path with no return. Their time for choices was over. Even so, she thought, what if she chose to love them? They could do nothing in return, and it would make no difference in their life. But what if it made a difference in her life?

15   - SOULS IN THE HOSPITAL

Marie stood up and joined the group. They were talking strategy. She had an idea, but she needed to learn some things first.

"Hey, Henry!" she called. "Yes, Ma'am" he called back.

"Would you show me what you do to keep the shadows away," she asked.

"Sure thing, darling. Let's go over here." He motioned

toward an unoccupied spot on the portico.

"First thing, I bet you thought we were fist fighting back in the hospital room, right?" he asked.

"Well, yeah, it looked like that," she said.

"Well, it wasn't. We do use a type of force and we use bursts of it that look like we are hitting. But, since none of us have actual bodies, hand-to-hand combat is useless.

"What we are doing is concentrating emotion, specifically love, into a burst of energy and throwing it at them." He paused, "or stomping it into them."

"You're throwing love at them?" she said perplexed.

119

"Sure, you have heard of a ventriloquist that throws their voice? We throw emotion. In fact, when we are talking to the new ones, we do the same thing, we just don't throw it. We sort of whisper it. Think of how much you love your mom."

"Okay" she said.

"Now 'will' that emotion on to me," he said.

She tried it. It wasn't as hard as she thought. He smiled. "Nice!"

"Now imagine Allen is falling off a cliff and if your love could save him, you'd grab him by the arm and pull him back," he said.

She closed her eyes and imagined the scene. She tried to feel the fear of losing him. It struck her. She reached out in her mind and wrapped that protective love around Henry and yanked. Henry, stout fellow that he was, fell forward to the ground.

He got up and straightened out his clothes, "By Job! You are one tough fighter! Let's go play with some shadows!"

He turned back to the group and called, "Hey, we need to make a trip back to the hospital. Anyone up for it? Joan of Arc here needs some practice!"

They all smiled. They'd all seen her throw down Henry. "Sure," said Tom. "Come on, Ben!" Henry took Marie's

hand and in a flash of light, they were gone.

***

The hospital room was dark. Marie's mom sat in the chair dozing with a light blanket around her shoulders. Marie's body was now on her side facing her mom. Apparently, the nursing staff had changed her position to avoid bed sores. Marie had lost tract of real time.

"How long has it been," she asked Tom.

"Three weeks," he said sadly. "It's starting to wear

120

on them. I talked to Jacob a little while ago. Things aren't going well. Your dad went back home because he had to get back to work or lose his job. Your mom is determined but doesn't know how much longer she can continue at your bedside. She wants to have you moved back to your hometown. Allen is not doing well. As if he wasn't already having a hard time with depression, your being moved seems like you are never coming back to him. He is at a loss.

On top of that, the Shadows have been relentless. They

are all over Allen all the time." "Where is he now?" she asked.

"Back at the dorm. Jacob is with him." Tom said.

Marie started to look around. Sure enough, like roaches crawling along the edge of the floor, a shadow was loaming in the corner. She concentrated on Allen's face in her mind. She thought of his smile as they walked hand in hand. When she had the emotion firmly in her mind, she threw it toward the shadow, mimicking pitching a fast ball with her arm. With a slightly audible hiss, the shadow evaporated! Pleased with herself, she turned to Henry for his approval, which he smiled grandly in return. He mockingly polished his nails on his pretend tux lapel and smiled smugly at Tom.

"Yep! That's my girl!" he crooned.

"Not bad at all for a first timer!" Tom added pleased. "Let's go find some bigger fish." Tom headed toward the door.

They wandered down the hallway of the hospital floor. Marie wondered what he was looking for. He seemed to know it had to be somewhere close. She decided to test her limits in a world with no boundaries and stuck her arm first through a wall, and then feeling confident, stuck her head in. She saw a break

121

room with staff sitting around a table eating fast food sandwiches.

"The family of the man in room 257 is about to get on my last nerve! They all take off their shoes and sit around and when I open the door, I could pass out from the smell of stinky shoes!" Marie giggled and stepped back into the hallway.

"Ah, here we go," Tom said as he motioned for her to go in a room.

"Whose room is this?" she asked.

"Someone who's not very well protected."

The room was quiet and stark. No flowers. No cards. An old man was sleeping on his side, wheezing slightly. The IV dripped away into the line. Marie could sense they were not the only ones there. Sure enough, the shadows were crawling along baseboards and hovering in the curtain folds. Marie stepped toward the man's bed for a closer look. A shadow lay curled in his folded arms. His breathing stopped a minute and then he started a gasping, wheezy cough that sounded like he'd smoked too many cigarettes in his lifetime. He caught his breath and then woke up. Eyes wide, pale, and watery. His mouth gaping as he gasped for air. Shaky stick-like arms shot out and he grabbed for the rails with long bony fingers and pulled himself up. He looked around the room with a scowl on his face.

"Damn hospital!" and then he yelled loudly, "Why does it have to be so cold in here? A man could freeze to death and you all wouldn't care!" He slumped back against the pillow and stared at the ceiling. He looked at his bedside table and groped for his cup of water. He took a sip and screwed up his face.

"NURSE! Nurse! This water is old! I need ice. Can anybody HEAR me?" and then under his breath, "Dang screw-up nurses don't give a rip about anybody. Nobody cares about anybody anymore!"

A very capable looking woman came in the door and crossed her arms. "MISTER Green, how may I help you? Is there a problem?"

"You're dang right there's a problem! This water is so old there's lint in it! I can't drink that! Get me some fresh water, WITH ICE, or so help me, I'll..."

Interrupting, the nurse said, "You'll what, Mr. Green? Report me? You already did that earlier today, remember? I'd be happy to get you fresh water if that will make your stay at Sonora Regional more pleasant!" With that she turned on her heel and was gone in a flash of white uniform, her head held high.

Mr. Green let out a quick sigh and put his head back on the pillow. He grumbled something else under his breath. The shadow crept around his head again. It was small and barely there but it rested right next to his ear. Marie could just make out a hissing voice that said, "No one cares about you. They all abandoned you. That nurse hates your guts. She wishes you would go ahead and die and lighten her patient load. Your son wishes you would die so he could finally have your house. You're a burden on them all, and you always have been."

A tear ran down Mr. Green's cheek. "Damn them all to hell," he whispered to no one.

Tom motioned to Marie to give it a try. Marie closed her eyes and thought of a time when she was laying on the couch with her head on her mother's lap. Her mother was smoothing her hair away from her face. She felt so loved and wanted. With all her strength, she balled up that emotion and then hurled it at the shadow around the man's neck. It hissed and recoiled. It stood up taller and spread out. This was no ordinary shadow. It was used to having this old man for a steady source of negative energy. It grew to

123

the height of a man and stood on the floor and then the dark cloud dissipated until Marie could see a vile, monster of a man. His eyes were bloodshot with dark circles. His pale, pasty skin looked waxy. A smirk was on his mouth as though the confrontation seemed entertaining.

Marie looked at Tom with concern.

"It's okay Marie, give it another shot. I'm right here to help." Tom encouraged.

Marie tried again. She remembered the shadows coming after Allen in the hospital room. A fierce protective emotion came over her. She balled it up and hurled it at the

dark Frankenstein-like fiend. He wavered but didn't budge. Then he let out a guttural gloating laugh that made Marie's hair stand up on the back of her head.

"A little game of tennis, perhaps? I'm game." The ghoul closed his eyes and concentrated. Marie looked at Tom worried and then felt an unmistakable sense of loneliness. Cold loneliness like the bottom of the reservoir. Death. Everything was dead. Marie tried to scream but somehow the air had become water. She could only gargle out a pathetic muffled baby cry. Tom seemed to be receding into the distance at a fast pace like she was being sucked into a whirlpool.

"Marie. Look at me." Tom said calmly. "Remember what Lorenzo told you about the most powerful love of all."

Marie felt like she was losing her grip on conscious thought. "What... who... said?" and then she turned her gaze on the monster. She looked right into his eyes. Sad tired eyes. Why were they sad? What had happened to him? There must have been a young man in there at some point. Then she could see it like he wore his pain on his sleeve. He was a little boy. Same pale eyes, but soft sweet cheeks and a beautiful cherub mouth. He was about 3. There was screaming. His mother was screaming. His father was hitting her. He was too little to help. He just wanted his mommy to hold him and tell him she was ok. He crawled up to her and his father smacked him away. It hurt. He cried and reached out to his mommy, but she turned on him and said, "Stupid brat, this is your fault!"

Marie was horrified. How could anyone be so cruel? They were all so cruel to each other. He was just a baby. A tear slipped down her cheek as she looked at the grown, angry version of that sweet little boy. She wished she could have grabbed up that little boy and loved him. Maybe if someone had loved him, he would have never become so hollow.

Like a whooshing wave of water, the sound came back.

She was free of his grip. He seemed to melt into the floor and vanish. Tom looked at her with great respect.

"You did it, little lady! I think you got the hang of it!" "That was hard. It was so draining, so sad." She

grimaced.

"Yes. That's the thing. Most of the dark shadows have sad stories that affected them. Some are truly just evil, but most of them are just sad and they got swallowed up in their own mess until it consumed them. Eventually they knew no other way than hurting others. Of course, they had shadows sucking the life out of them along the way and so it goes on and on."

"So, there is no hope for them once they cross over?"

she asked.

"No, they are so deep in their own evil by the time

they get with their little friends in nowhere land, that they are unable to feel love when it hits them over the head. In fact, it is repulsive to them. It makes them flee."

"Wow. That's awful." She thought about it a minute. "I want to sit with my mom a little bit. I need my mom."

Tom smiled and stretched out his arm to indicate the way.

***

Marie's mom was still dozing at Marie's bedside. Marie sat in the chair with her mom, overlapping but as close to curling up on her mom's lap as a spirit could get. Marie could hear her mom's steady reassuring breathing. Her mom stirred a little and opened her eyes. She looked around the room and then down at the blanket over her. She looked at Marie's body on the bed, still and serene. Then she hugged herself instinctively. Marie, the spirit, closed her eyes and felt the love her mother had for her. It was a strong resonating energy.

Her mom said, "Marie, I don't know if you can hear me. I am remembering the time when you were little, just three years old, when you drowned in the neighbor's pool. You wandered off. In just few minutes, you'd fallen in. We searched around the house. We ran. There was only one place left, and your father and I realized where you had to be. It was spring and the pool had been half full and the weather had been warm enough that it was green. We couldn't see the bottom. Your father jumped in and went under. He felt around the bottom for you. Sure enough, he found your little body and pulled you up. You were gray. I remember I screamed, 'Dear God! Save her!' I tripped and fell and scraped my knee trying to get to the phone. All I could think about was

126

how I couldn't lose you. We loved you so much! Your father breathed into you and rolled you over to let the water flow out of your lungs. We both willed you to live. You threw up and sputtered and cried." She stopped a minute, and the tears came.

"I can't lose you, Marie. Fight! You must wake up! Come back from wherever you are. You are strong and pure. I know you can find a way." Marie's mother closed her eyes and tears kept streaming down her cheeks. Marie sat curled up in the safety of her mother's lap for a long while.

Some hours later, Marie stood up and looked at Tom who was patiently looking out the window into the starry mountain night. Marie's mother slept soundly, better than she had in weeks.

Tom turned and looked at her. "Look at you!" he said. Marie held her arm in front of her. She glowed an ethereal light like moonlight, but it came from within her.

"What's this?" Marie turned her arms in all directions.

"You newbies would call it a halo."

"What? Like… I'm holy?" she stammered.

Tom laughed. "No, it's love. It's the energy of love all around you. It's powerful in this war. If only there was a way to focus it."

"Yeah, if only…" Marie pondered.

16 - PIECING TOGETHER THE CLUES

Marie looked back at her mother sleeping with her arms crossed under her head leaning on the bed side. She hadn't noticed her before, but a woman stood a few feet behind her. She was short and had black hair pulled back in a neat bun. Her gray eyes took in everything. She stood with her elbow leaning on the counter behind her and she seemed to be kneading her hands, absently rubbing her thumbs over the tops of her hands. Marie realized she was her mother's Protector, some distant relative of theirs, as she had come to understand that was the way of things. Marie smiled a tentative smile at her, and the woman closed her eyes and nodded briefly in approval. Marie realized this woman must have known Marie all her life as well, since she was always with her mother. She was meeting parts of her family that had always been separated from her, parts of the other side of a mirror. They were not frightening or spooky, but rather family she'd never met. Marie felt such a rush of relief.

The woman's expression changed to one of determined disapproval as she straightened and walked over to Marie's mother. Marie turned and saw a shadow growing on her mother's shoulder. She could hear quiet words forming and hissing.

The Shadow said, "Marie hates your meddling. If she wakes

up and finds you here, she'll be angry. You've never been a good

mother, you know that. She wishes you would just leave her alone."

The Protector made a noise, "Tsk tsk! Good gracious!" and flicked the back of her hand toward the shadow. The dark distortion immediately dissipated. "There, there. You are wonderful mother, Nancy. You would do anything for that child. Don't you listen to that talk." She ran her hand across Marie's mother's hair as if to smooth it down and then looked up at Marie and smiled again.

"Who are you?" Marie asked.

"Oh, baby. I go way back," she said. "You can call me Lucinda, but you just need to know how much your mother loves you. She worries about you so much. But look at you," she reached out to take Marie's hand. "You are so grown up and beautiful. You'll find a way to get back. And when you do, don't forget what you've seen."

"I won't. Who could ever forget all this? It's the craziest thing I've ever seen!" Marie laughed at the absurdity of it all.

The Protector smiled and laughed a light little, "Ha, ha.

I'm certain it is. Isn't that the truth?" she commented.

Tom stepped forward, "Marie, I saw Allen pull into the parking lot. Let's go for a little walk and see if we can find him. Sometimes he sits alone in a little solarium to think." "Ok," Marie nodded to Tom. "It was nice meeting you, Lucinda."

Lucinda smiled. She had known Marie all her life but understood Marie's point of view.

***

In the hallway, Marie noticed more around her than she did before. There was the usual nursing staff, occasional doctors, and visitors. Most all of them had someone following them that she knew was either a Protector or a Shadow. She could hear their one-sided conversations. Protectors were encouraging and suggesting. Shadows were spinning lies and making suggestions that would not benefit anyone but themselves. There was a man standing outside the door of a room. The nurses must have been doing a procedure inside. The Shadow behind his back was telling him he should go home and see his neighbor. She was home now, and he needed someone to remind him he was a man. Surely, she would make him feel like a man again now that his wife was no longer whole. The man stepped over to a pay phone, put in a dime and started to dial. Then he stopped.

He struggled with want he knew was right and the thoughts in his head.

Marie and Tom turned a corner and started down a long wide hallway. There were benches along the sides and windows above the benches. The morning sun was beginning to clear the mountain mist and shine sleepy yellow rays across the floor. Marie saw a woman curled up on a bench clutching a thin beige blanket around her shoulders. She was just beginning to wake up and appeared to be regretting it.

The Shadow woman sitting next to her looked at Marie with hollow dark eyes and smiled a ghastly lipless grin creasing the pasty white skin of her face.

She leaned down and continued the barrage of words that hung like tar in the air, "He'll probably die today. Then you'll be all alone. Within 3 days you'll be putting him in the ground. All alone. Just you and all those bills. Kind of makes you wish you could die with him, doesn't it?"

A tear fell from the woman's eye onto the bench.

It dawned on Marie how much we don't see in life. People struggling with tormenting thoughts and sometimes fighting them off and sometimes being pulled under by them. We never see the struggles; the battle being fought. We just see how they act and think we know better. They came to an archway across from a wall where the windows extended out onto a corner of the lawn. The landscaping on one side of the solarium included a water feature with a babbling brook that ended in a three-foot waterfall before it disappeared in a pile of smooth stones. Sitting with his chair facing the waterfall, Allen stared absently at it. His legs were crossed in a wide L and his chin was propped on the palm of his hand with his fingers curling up his cheek.

Jacob stepped beside them, "He comes here often and sits. I'm getting worried about him. I have been diligent, but I find Shadows creeping around telling him it's his fault, that he should

have known. That particular shadow," he nodded toward the corner of the alcove, "seems to go back and forth between him and Nancy with the same story: that it's their fault."

"What? That's crazy! There is no way he could have known. He couldn't have prevented this. Thinking something like that will put him in a spiraling depression!" exclaimed Marie.

Marie walked over to him and knelt on the floor

in front of him. "This isn't your fault! I'm alive!" Then she looked away, "I just need to figure out how to get back."

"Allen feels hollow inside. Helpless. He couldn't do anything to help you." Jacob said. "He thinks you are going to slip away and be gone, just when you were beginning to start a life together. He was going to propose this summer. He tries to push all that aside and to focus, but the thought keeps coming back to him."

"There's just nothing I can do," Allen quietly said aloud. Marie was stunned. She knew he probably felt this way, but the way he said it held so much defeat. She, too, felt powerless as she watched him seemingly give up hope. She stood up weakly.

"Tom? Something is wrong. I know he loves me, but right now it seems like his despair is making me weaker!"

"That's right, Marie, the living don't really realize how much power they have. Let me show you something." He motioned for her to follow him.

They walked farther down the hall until they came to a door marked, "Chapel." Tom went in and she followed. There was a man there, praying. Marie stepped back as she looked at him. He glowed like she did earlier that morning after she had been curled up on her mother's lap most of the night, only more so.

"It's the love. He's praying for his father. Praying for the pain to go away so his father can rest. When the new ones take the time to think of another, to wish them well, to encourage them, or to pray for them, great power is created. That is what the Shadows hope to destroy. This power is far stronger than what they can accomplish." Tom explained.

"Well, since I am not actually dead, don't I have still have this capacity to fight for another?" Marie asked.

Tom looked at her, "Of course you do. That's why the Shadows want you. Imagine if they can wear you down until you despair and then you were to wish ill on others. They would have a weapon of great power. I would say that they are trying very hard to wear down anyone who would be able to help you so that you are weak enough to capture."

Marie looked horrified. "Oh, my gosh! They are still out there conniving!"

"Oh, yes. Don't ever underestimate how long they will keep trying. They are nothing if not persistent. What else have they got to do?"

Marie thought for a minute. She thought about the woman back at that desolate place. She must be seething mad that Marie got away. The woman had wanted Marie for something and had an ax to grind for something. What had she said? Something about how Allen wouldn't look for her.

Marie froze in her tracks. "That's it! Allen! She'll try to find me through Allen!" She turned to Tom, "She knows I'll be near Allen if I can be."

"Jacob would have noticed if someone was waiting," Tom said.

"He mentioned that Shadow that is going between mom and Allen. I wonder if that one is a look out," said Marie.

"Well, there hasn't been a Shadow waiting, but…"
"What? What, Tom? Tell me!"

"Just a girl, that girl Lydia. She has been coming around the dorm and trying to be sympathetic."

"What?" Marie nearly screamed.

"It's okay! Allen is on to her ways. He gets rid of her."

"Holy cow! That tramp! I'm in the hospital and she tries to move in! What a peach! Where is she? Can

133

I mess with her? There must be some advantage to being a stupid ghost!"

Tom laughed out loud, "Relax, rookie. You have other things to worry about."

A bright flash appeared, and Henry was standing next to them. "Hello Tom. Hello Marie," he said.

"Hello," they said in unison and Marie looked at Tom as if to say, *"We'll talk about this later."* Then Tom added, "What's new?"

Henry said, "Lorenzo and I have been talking. He said I should talk to Marie about the time before she was rescued." He turned to Marie.

"Well, it was a weird place. It looked like the moon. There were Shadow people everywhere. They tortured me constantly, picking at me and trying to hurt me. They said horrible things to me trying to get me to give up hope.

There was a woman there, too. She seemed like a leader of sorts. The other Shadows had less intelligent things on their mind. She made a comment," Marie paused remembering. "Yes, she made a comment like: 'Now that I've got you…something or another.' Oh, and she said I was legendary with the Shadows?"

Tom and Henry looked at each other.

Henry said, "What did she look like?"

"The usual hag-look of the Shadows. But she had long, crazy, red hair. Kind of a sour puss expression. But, you know, she could have been normal looking if she wasn't so, so…" Marie groped for the word.

"Evil?" said Tom.

"Well, yeah." She pondered that thought.

"Marie, did she tell you why she wanted you?" said Henry.

"No. Not really, said Marie."

"What do you think, Henry?" said Tom.

"I don't know. There was once a woman that

trailed you and mom for a long time that had long curly red hair. That was a long time ago, back when I was a new Protector. I'd see her around my brothers and sisters sometimes, but she'd always vanish. Then I didn't see her again. Who do you think she might be?" said Henry.

Tom said, "I don't know, Henry. I can't think of anyone that would dislike like us enough to follow our line around. Maybe we should ask Jenny."

"Good idea. Mom never forgets a face. She's with a new assignment, but we can go there. She got a new one, a little baby boy in Louisville. Join hands and I'll lead the way."

The three of them joined hands and Henry closed his eyes and visualized Jenny's face. In an instant they were standing in a nursery on the second floor of a home. Sunlight was streaming in the window. Outside, pink and white dogwood flowers dotted the sky like confetti frozen in mid-air. A white, shabby chic crib with blue plaid bedding was against the wall. Marie tip-toed forward to peak at the sleeping cherubic form. He was just a few weeks old and swaddled in a receiving blanket.

"Oh! He's beautiful!" Marie exclaimed in a whisper. "Yes. He is perfect. He's my grandson through my son Charles." Jenny beamed proudly as she caressed the child's tiny forehead. "So, to what do I owe the honor of this little visit?" Jenny leaned toward Tom and gave him a peck on the cheek and smiled at him.

Henry said, "Well, mom, we are trying to figure out what we are dealing with. Marie says that a woman, a Shadow, was there after she was kidnapped. Marie got out of there before she could hatch whatever plan she had, but we are trying to figure out who she is. Do you ever remember a woman with crazy, long red hair and sour puss expression?"

Jenny thought for a minute. "There is only one other person I know that might fit that description." Henry and Tom smiled knowing that Jenny would have the answer.

Jenny continued, "I'm surprised you don't remember, Tom, you knew her longer than I did. Your brother Leonard's first wife, Hester Farr. The one the Indians killed and dragged away."

Tom thought a minute. He pursed his lips searching his memories. "Ah, yes. I do recall Hester. A rather odd girl. She was married to Leonard for about 10 years before she disappeared, apparently killed by savages. Leonard was a bit relieved, I daresay. Apparently, it was not wedded bliss there. But why on earth would she care about us?"

"Well, she did seem a bit sweet on you, Tom," Jenny

said giving Tom a sidelong glance.

"What? I don't recall that?" Tom looked confused.

Marie's eyes got as big as saucers.

"I'm just saying. She would get flustered when you talked to her. She didn't get that way when I talked to her. In fact, she had no use for me at all. I don't know what I ever did to make her dislike me. It's not like I stole you away from her!" Jenny laughed.

"Uh huh! What were we just talking about, Tom?"

Marie looked at him knowingly.

"No, no. She was just a silly girl." Tom attempted to

reassure both Jenny and Marie.

"Wait a minute," said Henry, "Dad when did you meet Hester?

"Well, I was a young lad. Probably 18 or so. She

136

was much older than me. Older than Leonard even. She must have been 24 or 25. She came into Prince William County looking for work as a wash maid or a nanny. I remember she asked if I wanted to have a picnic down by the creek, but I was trying to finish my education as a lawyer. I wanted to be a judge like my father. I had no use for a woman at that time. It would have slowed me down. And besides, she was a little odd. She was scrawny and rough. Frankly, she scared me if I recall correctly. Next thing I knew, Leonard was bawling saying he'd have to marry her because she was with child. His child! Dad insisted he do the right thing and make an honest woman of her. He married her, but no child ever came. Leonard figured out he was duped, but it was too late. In fact, she never did bear any children. At least, none that survived. I was busy with school and the war and then along came Jenny and I never talked to Hester again."

"It doesn't make any sense," said Marie. "This can't be the same person. This Hester person doesn't seem to have any reason to follow your descendants for generations. Did you ever have an argument?"

Jenny sucked in her breath and thought, "There was a time she had words with me. I was just beginning to show with our first child, little Tom, Jr. Sweet boy, but always having mishaps. Falling out of trees or slipping into a river. No girl would stay around him long enough for him to marry them. They'd just up and refuse to speak to him. It was all very odd. He died a bachelor. Drowned in his bathtub alone. They said the look on his face was like he'd seen a ghost. His eyes were wide open." Jenny shook herself and rubbed her arms.

"Anyway, it was when I was expecting Tom, Jr., not too long before she disappeared because I recall she was already gone by the time I was delivered. She came to me out in the garden one afternoon. I remember the sun was so hot that day. Her crazy red hair was all loose from its bun. She looked like a mad woman. She told me such an odd thing, 'Hold your babies close, Jenny Pope! For all the good it'll do you, it's an evil world and remember we must pay for our sins!'"

Jenny continued, "I just felt pity for her. I was aware that she was barren and figured she felt like it was her sins that kept her from having children."

"Jenny Pope?" said Marie.

"Yes, my maiden name. Tom and I had been married for a year already. But she always called me Jenny Pope."

"Hm. Almost like she really never accepted that you and Tom were married," said Marie.

"I suppose. She was an odd one. I usually tried not to talk to her if I could avoid it. I think everyone was a little relieved when she was gone. That's awful to say, isn't it?" said Jenny.

"Mom, we need to do some checking on this, but be careful. This Hester sounds like a wild card, and we don't have very much to go on. Please watch your back." Henry looked down into the crib at the tiny boy sleeping, "and keep a good eye on that little guy. He's a cutie!"

Jenny laughed and said, "Oh Henry, it takes a lot to scare me."

Just then the door opened, and a young woman came in the room and peered over the edge of the crib rail. She picked up the baby and held it close to her under her chin. She stopped and looked around as though she could sense someone there.

She cautiously started, "My mother told me our ancestors come to see new babies. If anyone is there, I just want to thank you for the visit and for watching over little George." She then went out of the room as though nothing unusual had happened.

"Well, my, my!" said Jenny. "Such a nice girl! I think we'll get along just fine. Her mother sounds very smart, too!"

Tom, Marie, and Henry smiled.

"Well, mom, we need to go. See you soon." Henry said and leaned in and kissed his mother's cheek. In a flash the three disappeared.

17   - HESTER

Ben and Jacob were sitting on the couch at Allen's dorm watching him eat take out from the Europa Café. Marie, Tom, and Henry appeared in the middle of the room. They'd gone back to the Gathering to talk and agreed with Marie that Hester would likely be watching Allen to find her.

"Hi Ben! Hey Jacob!" said Marie. "How's it going here?"

Ben looked up and smiled. "Pretty quiet. He's been depressed for a while now."

Henry stepped forward, "Have you seen anything strange with the Shadows?"

Ben looked at Jacob, who then answered, "Not that you could put your finger on. There has been a definite uptick in incidents. Just Shadows tailing him all the time. It's like they won't leave him alone.

"That's what we came to talk to you about," Henry said. "We have a couple of ideas about what might be going on. From what we have figured out, there is a common thread. There seems to be some woman named Hester Farr from Tom and Jenny's past that may be the root of this. From what Jenny said, she was not a very friendly person and may have it out for them, but they don't really know why. Have you ever seen a woman with long curly red hair, a little scary looking, around Allen or Marie?"

Ben thought for a minute, "Yeah right after the drowning in the reservoir. When we were back here, a woman materialized near Marie and was taunting me. She matched that description."

Marie felt a shiver run down her spine. She wondered about the person she saw at the bottom of the reservoir. Could that have been Hester even then? She realized this person was persistent.

"She said I was legendary among the Shadows. Why would she say that? What would make me any different?" Marie asked.

"Well," said Henry, "In my work, I usually track souls like Hester. They are an interesting breed. They usually have an ax to grind, and they are attracted to something they want."

"Okay. So, what do I have that she wants?"

"I can think of one thing," said Tom, "For as long as I can remember, you have had an incredible ability to shake off suggestions by the shadows. You're like Teflon to them. It has made it incredibly easy to be your Protector. Usually, I just keep you from falling out of third story windows when you hang out of them. You're more a danger to yourself than they are to you. Most souls that end up being Shadows in the 'other' world seem to be bad luck magnets. Besides being accident prone, they are very easily influenced by the Shadows around them.

If Hester sees that you have some ability for good luck, never putting two and two together that avoiding suggestions by the Shadows may be what helps you, she may very well be curious."

"Curious, I could understand, but she seems bent

on getting Marie. It doesn't add up," said Henry as he pondered this thought. "Could it be that Marie has more than crazy skills for deflecting dark suggestion? Maybe there really is something about her, something we have taken for granted. A special gift?"

Marie listened to their conversation with half-hearted ears. She was more concerned for Allen. She drifted toward him at the table. He was picking at French fries. He'd had two bites of the club sandwich. She sat down in the chair next to him at the table. She watched him sigh and pick at his food. What is he thinking? He was staring at the food in its white Styrofoam take-out box. A deep sadness emanated from him.

Marie moved and sat in his chair, sharing the same space, the two of them as close as she could get. She couldn't feel him at all, but she could feel the sadness. She wrapped her arms around herself and closed her eyes hoping he could feel the hug, the love. He put his head in his hands and started to cry quietly.

"Oh, Marie. I miss you so much," he sobbed gently.

Marie slipped down onto the floor next to him and wished so much she could touch him. She tried to put her arm around him, but it slid through the nothingness of her world.

"Allen. I'm with you. I'll figure this out. I love you. Don't give up. Please don't give up. I need you." She closed her eyes and cried with him. Then she wondered, if the same energy she used to repel the Shadows might get through to him.

She stood up and closed her eyes. She balled up her fists at her sides. She concentrated on Allen and how much she missed him. She thought of them laughing and walking hand in hand down a trail. His eyes were filled with joy when he looked at her. She thought about how much she had to get back to her world, her place with him, and then she held her arms toward Allen and threw all that love at him. With the will of her soul, she threw every part of herself at him, hoping he would feel it.

He sighed and then got up and went to the bedroom. It seemed to make no difference. She followed him and watched him shake off his shorts, get under the covers and close his eyes. There was no epiphany, no sudden change, not really anything. The chasm between them was too great and the evil working on him was too strong. Her love alone would not save him.

She watched him fall asleep and then turned to go back into the living room. She crashed into Hester whose expression was anything but sympathy. Marie took a step backwards, surprised to meet a solid object. Hester looked different than before at the Shadow's Lair. A glowing red aura surrounded her. Not only her, but it seemed to now engulf the entire room. Marie screamed for Tom, but her voice seemed like she was screaming into a vacuum of space. It was like the dorm bedroom was now somewhere else. Horrified, Marie looked quickly at Allen who lay sleeping obliviously on the bed and then back at Hester.

"You're a tough one to track down, running off with those creeps all the time. I figured eventually you'd remember poor old Allen," she said with a mocking tone. "What do you WANT?" Marie finally found her voice. "Leave us alone!"

"Oh no, pretty girl. Leaving you alone is the last thing I want. And this time you're coming with me, or he is. He would be a smaller consolation prize, but there is some satisfaction in that still. Yes, there is an amount of reciprocity in that." Hester trailed off weighing this in her mind.

"What? What are you talking about?" Marie stepped between Allen and Hester.

Hester laughed. "Oh, you all are such a dull bunch. So amazingly self-absorbed, just like you have been for over 200 years. How would you like to throw your whole life away, strangle your own newborns, lose your youth and any dreams of a nice life? That's what I did for that idiot Thomas Helm. I loved him. I loved him from the moment I saw him, but he didn't care. So, I waited and waited. I was tied to his dullard brother Leonard who never cared about me. Time after time my belly grew from that hideous man's seed. But I would never let his offspring have the breath of life. No, my firstborn would be Tom's. Tom's firstborn would be my child. I saved that for him if I couldn't save my maidenhood. No, that was long gone thanks to the vile human that bought me as an indentured servant. I was just a little girl."

Her voice sounded far away, and she smiled a silly giddy smile. "Daddy! Daddy! I'm here! Yes, mommy! Daddy is our hero. He'll make life all better in the New World." She paused and her face contorted to its natural evil self.

"But then they were gone. Buried in the sea. The illness took half the ship. I don't know why I survived. I wish I had died with them. A miller took me as an indentured servant, and I served that family for 12 years. His wife hated me. Their brats thought they were better than me. And the miller used me."

"But then I met Tom. Beautiful, sweet Tom. He was perfect. So smart and strong. I knew he would restore me to love. He would love me." At that moment Marie wondered if anyone could have loved Hester. Her red hair had a mind of its own. Her face was freckled and pocked. Her dark green eyes looked more threatening than anything. She was missing several teeth. No doubt the miller had never got her dental care or even bothered to make her brush her teeth as a child. Marie wondered if they even had toothbrushes 200 years ago, but surely someone had thought of something that would work.

Hester's eyes focused on Marie, "But then that infernal Jenny came along and ruined everything. She gave Tom his firstborn. There was nothing I could do short of killing her while her belly swelled. But that wouldn't have worked. Not that I didn't try to think of some way.

So, I told her to watch her babies close. I knew that if I ever had the chance, I'd snatch them right to hell. She and Tom would pay! They would pay and pay until the debt was settled. I managed to get most of them. One at the time. Some sooner and some later. I sent them on to their maker. I watched Jenny and Tom cry for them. Stupid fools! My babies would have lived. Tom would have never had any reason to cry if he'd loved me. He should hate Jenny for what she caused. She is the reason he suffered."

Marie was reeling. *"This woman is crazy!"* she thought.

She watched Hester speak as though all this was normal and reasonable. It dawned on Marie that, as Tom and Jenny's descendant, Hester would gleefully kill her and leave her for Tom to find. She would also hurt Allen and delight in Marie's pain. Clearly the debt had not been paid in full yet.

"Hester, why don't you just talk to Tom about how you feel? Have you ever sat down and just talked to him about all this?" Marie said as she skirted along the wall toward the door.

"Do you think I'm stupid?" laughed Hester. "Why? So, he can humiliate me? No! He had his chance to make this right."

Marie was almost to the door. "But maybe he had feelings for you, too. Maybe he just didn't know how to tell you." Marie continued to distract Hester.

Hester started to answer and then in an instant was inches from Marie's face. "Silly girl. You may have got loose once before, but I won't make that mistake again. Go ahead, try the door. Scream! Yell! Beat on the walls! They won't hear you. I've spent 200 years in the afterlife, and I haven't been twiddling my thumbs. Nothing can get in or out of here until I release it."

Hester had created a force field with her hate that had them caged. "So now I'll ask you again. Are you coming with me, or will dear Allen be my new pet? Of course, he won't likely survive like you did. It'll be a one-way ticket for him."

"So… it's not a one-way ticket for me?" Marie probed.

"Honestly, I'm not sure. I suppose anything is possible, but one thing is for sure, it was my power that pulled you into this world, you'll need my power to get you out. All you must do is one little thing for me."

Marie pondered this. It was Hester that pulled her into the "other world." It had to be some incredible amount of power to do that. No one knew why she survived. Other souls that were taken by the Dark Shadows just died and went on. But one thing was tickling Marie's mind: was it only Hester that could send her back? One thing was for certain, she could not risk Allen's life. For whatever reason, Marie knew Hester was right, Allen would likely die if Hester wanted to take him.

"Ok, what is this 'one thing'?" Marie asked confidently.

Hester smiled. Her gummy, toothy grin made Marie wince. "Nope. You must come with me first. Then I'll tell you."

With no choice left, Marie said, "Alright. Let's go. But you'll help me get back to the living then, right?" Marie knew in the back of her head that making deals with crazy people never worked out, but it was worth a try. She could only hope that Lorenzo had more power than Hester. He had saved her before. Surely, he could save her this time.

"Oh, sure, honey." Hester had a distant look on her face that gave Marie no confidence that she would ever be seen again.

In a flash, they disappeared. The room went to normal. Allen stirred and woke up dazed. Tom, Jacob, and Henry sprang into the room. It was too late. Marie had made a deal with the devil.

18 - ALMOST IN HELL

Hester knew from the last time that Marie would not easily do her bidding. She couldn't make a mistake this time and give Marie a chance to get loose.

In a flash, they appeared in small space that resembled the bottom of a well. Marie blinked and looked around trying to get her bearings. Hester vanished and darkness surrounded Marie. Not darkness as in the absence of light, but darkness because Marie was surrounded by Hester's shadow. Like a vaporless cloud, the shadow covered Marie. If Marie had had a body, the shadow would have filled her lungs as she breathed.

Hate, fear, anger, and sadness pressed in on Marie. All the emotions of 200 years which Hester had lived with poured over Marie. This was another level completely from the torture of the dark Shadows before. This was an inflicted depression. Hester had deposited Marie into a sort of hell to which no one could be immune. Marie tried to block the feelings out, but it was like holding back plastic sheeting from your face under water. It was too much.

Marie tried to scream but there was no sound. She tried

to struggle but there was nowhere to go. She couldn't block

the emotions from her mind. She had the slightest feelings of giving up, being overwhelmed. Hester then laid in a new torture: she began to remind Marie of every slight and hurtful thing Marie had lived through. Hester had been skirting around Marie for years, despite Tom's effort to keep Shadows away. Hester had been watching and waiting for the right time. She had been enjoying all the little prickly moments in Marie's life. There were kids in grade school that said she was weird. There was a boy in middle school that made fun of her acne. There was a time when all her friends were fighting and didn't talk to each other but said things behind each other's backs. There was the young man she was going to marry, and it ended in a hateful argument. There was the times Marie felt alone and ugly and unloved. In Marie's mind, she saw Lydia with her arms around Allen. Lydia whispered in Allen's ear, and he kissed her. Lydia smiled and told him she would never leave him like Marie did. Hester played them for Marie like an afternoon matinee.

A deep depression is like quicksand, and it didn't take long until Marie gave up completely. So lost in her own pain fueled with Hester's anger in her mind, Marie forgot everything. She didn't care about anything anymore. Allen seemed to not exist in this private hell. There was no escape. She just curled up on the cold, rocky ground and tried to sleep, but souls don't sleep. There is no escape for them.

After a period that felt like forever, when Hester could tell that Marie no longer fought against her, the Shadow returned to Hester's shape. Marie lay on the ground motionless. Time was on Hester's side now. She had in her possession a live New Soul completely harnessed.

19 - MARIE, THE DARK SHADOW

"Help me," Marie pleaded, reaching up to Hester.

"Yes, dear. I'm here." Hester crooned. "I'll keep the mean Shadows away."

Marie weakly sat up and looked around. "Can you get me out of here?" she asked.

"Of course I can, but before we go, we need to talk about a few things. You know this is all that nasty Jenny and Tom's fault. They could have saved you, but they didn't. All they care about is themselves. I've seen it many times. They left me for dead. Never came to see if I was okay after the Indians took me."

"Oh. That's awful. You must have been scared."

"Yes, but they are selfish and greedy. We must punish people like that. They hurt you, Marie. They made you all alone here. You'll never get home again. Your life is a waste!"

Marie quietly started tearing up. She had no will to refute Hester or even strength to hope otherwise. The depression stole from her any will to change things.

Hester prodded, "Don't you hate them? They stole everything from you."

"Um. I guess so." Marie couldn't quite remember what exactly they had done but she knew she felt horrible sadness.

"I watched them abandon you. They left you here to suffer. They stole your life. They stole everything. They even left your precious Allen to be swallowed by Shadows so that he'll never love you again. He just thinks you abandoned him. That Lydia already has her hooks in him and is planning to move in with him. They did it to me, too. They stole my chance for love. But you, you can make them pay!"

"What? Make them pay? How? Allen, he must hate me. Is he letting Lydia move in. Did they leave me here? Could they have saved me?" Marie started to piece together the lie into a truth in her mind.

"Yessss. My sweet girl." Hester smoothed Marie's hair back and caressed her cheek. Marie's eyes went black with anger. Now all the anger around Hester felt right. It felt normal to Marie, almost comforting. She and Hester both were victims that had lost everything. Marie felt the searing pain of having the love of your life ripped from you.

"Where are they? I'll tear them apart, starting with that Lydia!" growled Marie, the hatred rising.

"Oh, we must be smart. I have been on their trail a long, long time, but I have a plan and only you can make it work. Let's go."

In a flash, Hester and Marie materialized in the hallway of the home where Jenny was protecting baby George. The door to the nursery was closed. It was dark. Marie didn't know what time it was, but the house was completely silent.

"Now, hon-hee," Hester hissed a bit through her one- toothed mouth. She was nearly giddy and tried to contain herself. She had thought about this for years. If she could just get a New Soul to do her bidding, she would have more power. The New Soul's power was much stronger. Just as a prayer or an encouraging word could smite the efforts of the Shadows, so also could hate and vengeance overtake a Protector. Just as a dark Shadow could be stamped out by a Protector or the prayer of a New Soul, a Protector could be overtaken and even destroyed by the unadulterated power of hate. This was Hester's real plan: she wanted to destroy Jenny and then Tom. If she could do that, then they would have paid the ultimate cost for her pain. She had considered taking Tom for her slave, but decided he was tarnished. He would never love her like she'd wanted. Now she just wanted him obliterated.

"I am going to distract her by going after the baby. You must concentrate. I'll help you." Hester put her hands on Marie's shoulders and let all the dark, vile thoughts from the well fill Marie's head. Marie's expression was like that of a trance. No emotion. Just emptiness. "Now, when she is trying to get to me, you unleash your pain on her. Throw it from your heart to hers. It will weaken her and then I will help you. We'll make her pay."

Marie nodded absently. Her eyes were dark and fixed on the door to the nursery. Hester went first through the door. After about 5 seconds, Marie went through. The nursery was dark, but shadows of the blooming tree outside fell across the floor in the moonlight. Marie darted behind a rocking chair.

Jenny had spotted Hester's shadow near the crib and was trying to stamp it out. The sweet chubby baby, now about two months old slept on its tummy sucking on its fist. Hester was persistent and her shadow was already creeping through the bars of the crib, inching toward baby George. Jenny was feverishly smacking at the shadow.

Marie inched up behind Jenny, her eyes, glazed in the trance. With all her might, Marie threw the hatred onto Jenny. Jenny slumped and fell under the crib. She groped at the floor trying to regain composure, not knowing what had hit her. Hester immediately materialized and joined Marie's effort at dousing any positive energy Jenny could muster. Jenny laid on the floor like a lead blanket held her pinned.

"Help!" Jenny called out; her voice muffled. Little George woke. He could sense the disturbance in his room. As an infant, he had a much closer awareness of the "other world" than adults. His face pinched up and he let out a howl as his baby eyes darted around.

Jenny's image began to become opaquer as she struggled against the weight of the negative energy.

Just then, Henry flashed into the room and was startled to see Marie and this red-headed crazy woman working together. He blasted Marie and Hester with a wash of energy that sent them reeling backwards. Jenny struggled to get to her feet.

Hester grabbed Marie's hand and flashed them both out. They were gone. The door to the nursery opened and a young woman drowsily came into the room in a yellow and white seersucker robe. Her blond hair was bunched up on one side in a frizzy pile. She yawned as she leaned over the crib rail and patted little George on the back.

"What's the matter sweet boy?" she crooned in a sing-song baby dialect. Little George tried his best to turn his head to see her in his face-down position. She lifted him and laid him on her shoulder and patted his back.

"There, there. It's okay. Mommy's here." She said softly. Little George started to make a string of vowel sounds in her ear.

"Henry! Oh, my word! What in tarnation? Was

that Marie? And did you see that woman? If you hadn't come, I'd been done for, for certain!"

George's mother sat in the rocking chair and hummed a lullaby as she rocked. Henry bent down and offered his hand to Jenny who took it and stood up.

"What happened, momma? I got a quick order from Lorenzo to get over here." Henry said.

"I saw a Shadow by the crib. It kept on no matter how hard I went at it. It got closer and closer to the baby," Jenny glanced at the mother and child to satisfy her renewed fear. "Then the next thing I knew, I was on the floor and couldn't move. The most awful sadness and hate covered me. More powerful than any Shadow. I looked up to see Marie, but she didn't look right. It was like she was sleepwalking. And then, that woman joined Marie. Lawsy, Henry! I could feel my grip slipping away!"

Henry put his arm around Jenny, "It's okay, momma. You're okay," he said soothingly. In the amount of time for Jenny to catch her breath, she pulled away and straightened up.

"Well, it looks like we have big problems now," she said.

"Yep. We are going to have to get a stand-in for you with little George. It's obvious, they are after you and not the baby. We can't leave you alone again until we figure this out. I'll be right back."

Henry flashed out and seconds later came back with another Protector for little George. Henry and Jenny left together.

***

Jenny, Henry, Ben, and Jacob sat around Allen's kitchen table. The sun was just starting to shine yellow dusty rays of warmth across the couch where Allen had fallen asleep the night before. He lay

155

motionless on his side, his arms curled around him. His eyebrows scrunched in a fitful snarl reflecting his mood in the dream he was having.

All four Protectors were sitting somberly with their hands clasped on the table and looking down. Only once before had one of the living crossed over but she'd disappeared. And now, a Marie crossed over and had become a pawn of the Shadows. This was bad, indeed. A newbie's power to influence was much stronger than theirs. None of them would be any match for Marie if it came to that. What a horrible thought it was to consider them in a combat situation with Marie. They all loved her. Yet, they had to stop her.

"Any ideas?" said Ben.

No one said anything for a few seconds.

"Well, we have to figure out how deep in it she is," said Henry. "Jenny, tell us again what you saw."

"It was just for a few seconds. And I was a little

distracted!" Jenny raised an eyebrow and glared at Henry. "I know, mom. What was your impression?"

"Well," Jenny paused to remember, "She didn't look normal. Her face was expressionless, and her eyes were dark. She didn't have her usual joyful aura.

Ben chimed in, "Do you think she has been brainwashed, Henry?"

"That would be my guess. She had a tough shell of joy that protected her, but who knows what this Hester is capable of if she's been giving her the third degree.

"So, Henry, what have we done with brain-washed Live

Ones before?" asked Jenny.

Henry sighed. "Nothing really. That's why I mainly stick to ferreting out Shadows. There just isn't anything you can do with Live Ones that completely give themselves up to the Shadows. Even though they never would have outright chosen to be brainwashed, at some point they give up their will and refuse to fight. About the only thing you can do is hope to change their situation enough that they see a viable escape that is more likely than their captor overtaking them again. Usually, they have some fear that the captor has gotten them to internalize, such as the possibility of their loved ones being hurt if they don't agree to be taken."

Jacob piped up, "So that's it then," he nodded toward the couch, "Hester threatened to harm Allen, and Marie believed Allen was in grave danger."

He turned to Henry, "Could Hester have been able to take Allen, even with all of us so close by?"

"Well, she was able to lock us out when she took Marie, so I'd say yes. Hester must be a very powerful Shadow."

Henry said.

"I think we should talk to Lorenzo," said Jenny.

Jacob stayed with Allen and the others flashed away.

20   - DARK TIMES

Hester took Marie back to the dark hole in the ground. Marie had no idea where they were, but really didn't care. The sun never seemed to be shining at the opening. Marie wondered if they were in a hole in the ground inside another cave. But again, she just didn't care. She thought to herself, Hm. You would think this would matter, but I don't care. Nothing matters anymore. I can't think about the past because it's gone. I'm gone.

Marie slumped down and Hester's shadow covered her, pulling the life out of her soul as much as possible. Hester was very agitated that the plan failed. She would have to try another tactic.

    ***

The end of the semester came for Allen. He had two days to pack up and ship out of his dorm per college policies. As if it wasn't bad enough with Marie in the hospital, now he had nowhere to stay here. The only option he could think of was his parents' house in Kentucky. He would rather stay in Sonora, but he wasn't on good terms with Marie's mom. She was always there in the hospital with Marie and Allen felt like an outsider. Nancy resented having to leave so

Allen could stay with Marie. It just wasn't going well.

Allen had no idea how long Marie would continue like this. He'd hoped she would wake up by now. The doctors said there is no guideline. It will just take as long as Marie's mind needs. There was also the possibility her body would give up and she would die. The prognosis was somewhere between not good and maybe. Both Nancy and Allen were struggling with having hope and fighting off grieving for Marie prematurely.

Marie's dad came on weekends. He had to go back to Southern California for the work week. Allen wondered how he managed. He had to be terribly grief-stricken by all this.

Allen finally decided it would be best to see if his parents would help him rent a room in Sonora for the summer. Maybe he could even take a class over the summer to make it worth it to his parents. He had such a hard time managing a full load of classes with all this going on that he wondered about the intelligence of such an idea. Maybe he could find an easy class.

He picked up the phone and started dialing his mom's

phone number.

"Hello," said a woman.

"Hi Mom," said Allen.

"Hi Allen! How is it going there?"

"Well," he paused trying to find the right words, "Marie is still in a coma. I'm done with my classes. The school says everyone must move out by Monday." This pretty much summed up his dilemma, so he stopped talking.

"Well, what are you going to do?" asked Allen's mom.

"I was thinking that maybe I could find a room to

rent

in Sonora for the summer and take a summer class. Then I could also stay here and keep up with Marie's progress." His voice took a slightly imperceptible lower tone with the last sentence.

"Okay, Allen. Look for something and let me and dad know what you need. That's fine with me. And bring Marie

to visit when she gets better, okay?"

"Yeah, Mom, that would be great. Thanks so much.

Love you," he said.

"Love you, too, Allen." His mom added. They both

hung up.

Allen sat here thinking two thoughts: first that his mom was now sitting at the kitchen table replaying all this to his dad and that they would then talk about this phone call in depth for the next two days, and second, the thought of bringing a healthy, vibrant Marie to his house in Kentucky seemed like a pipe dream.

Would she ever wake up? They were supposed to be packing up to drive east right now.

Allen heard his belly rumble and decided it was time for a trip to town to find food. There was a knock at the door. He got up and opened the door to find Lydia in a blue sundress with her long blond hair waving in the gentle breeze. She smiled sweetly, trying not to look too obvious. She had a large basket on her arm.

"What do you want, Lydia?"

"Oh, honey, can I just say I love your Southern accent. That is so sexy." She smiled and waited for the compliment to sink in. He sighed and continued to look down his nose at her.

Lydia's smile faded just a moment and then re-energized. "Well, I just figured with Marie in the hospital," she paused and tried to look around him to see if Marie was in the dorm, "you know, that maybe you needed a little TLC."

"What?" he asked amazed at her brazenness.

"Well, I have a little bit to eat," she pushed the basket forward and pulled back the cloth covering it, "just some sandwiches, roast beef and turkey with bacon, and homemade potato salad, and some chocolate cake, and…"

"Lydia!" Her face fell flat as he spat her name. "Lydia! No! You must go. Go find someone else to share your picnic with!" With that he stepped outside and closed door behind him, causing her to back pedal to avoid being stepped on.

"Allen?" she tried to get his attention as he walked away.

"And besides, I hate potato salad!" he chuckled to himself as he slammed the door to the Jeep and cranked up the engine, leaving Lydia stunned on the sidewalk.

He drove the winding road through the Sierra Nevada foothills to the quiet town. He remembered Marie asking him if he believed in guardian angels. He felt déjà vu of a drive together months ago when everything was wonderful. He remembered the wash of love he'd felt back then. He came around a shady curve where the Ponderosa pines grew close to the road and the sun was blocked by their skyscraper heights. The pine needle forest floor which normally would have made Allen feel like he was in a sheltered place, now felt ominous. He felt like he was not alone in this desolate area, as though someone was watching him. He tried to shake off the odd feeling and turned on the radio. A Crosby, Stills, Nash and Young song blared away the silence. Not satisfied with that, he fumbled with the knob, and They Might Be Giants took over.

They crooned on about Constantinople, but Allen's mind was caught on the thought that a girl could be waiting in Constantinople, but if you only looked in Istanbul, you would never find her. Its silly logic really, they are the same place, but what if that's it. She's here, but not here. Her soul had to be somewhere. What if it was not in her body? What if she had been with him, but he couldn't see her? Allen pondered this. It didn't really make sense in his logical mind, but he knew Marie would have believed such a thing. There had been times he'd think she was there and turn to say something, only to remember she was at the hospital. What if we really were souls that were different from bodies, and she was trapped in a place between here and there? This thought filled him with a new hope. His mind raced with the new thought. She could be stuck, and he hadn't even known it! Now he was more determined than ever to stay in Sonora for the summer.

Although he had no idea how to solve this, he knew he could figure it out.

***

Meanwhile, Hester had plans for Marie. She had waited a long time to get the revenge she sought. Hester's shadow pulled in and the real image of Hester materialized. Marie lay in a trance-like daze on the stony ground. Hester took hold of her hands and started pulling her up.

"Come on, deary," she insisted.

"What?" Marie said confused.

"We have some amusing things to do, girl! Come on! Don't you think it's time we had a little fun?"

"I, I…." Marie's voice faded away and her glazed eyes stared blankly at the wall.

"Well, you aren't exactly a party, young lady. Let's go find some fun. We need to get Tom and Jenny out here in the open, so let's stir up some trouble. I think that baby George would get Jenny's attention. Darn her and her babies! Let's go to Louisville!"

In a flash, Marie was standing on the lawn of a white brick house with Hester. Pink and white dogwoods shaded the left side of the house where the sidewalk came up from the driveway. A large oak tree stood nearby. The windows had an arch design in the brick over the top of them. Two windows to the left of the front door and two windows to the right. There was a second story with two windows flanking a smaller decorative window with an iron faux balcony above the front door. It looked like a French design. Red geraniums had been planted in reddish brown pots around the small front porch.

As Hester and Marie stood in the front yard taking in the scene, a young woman in jeans and a blue gingham plaid shirt came out near the garage and walked down the driveway pushing a stroller. Little George lay in the stroller waving his arms in the air and making gurgling noises punctuated by squeals as the soft breeze rolled over his face.

Marie saw the leaves and the grass softly moving and realized she couldn't feel the breeze.

"I may as well be dead," she thought.

"Now's our chance! Look! Fool took the baby outside!

Jenny's bunch are the dumbest things I have ever seen!"

Hester shook her head.

163

A dog was barking nearby announcing the mother and child. It was inside a fence across the street. The large dog jumped around, springing forward, lunging at the fence.

"There! Go let that dog out!" Hester demanded.

"What? How can I do that?" Marie stammered.

Hester gave a big sigh. "Dear! You get the dog to go mad. Help it figure out how to jump over the fence or get the latch open. Animals are putty in our hands. You do want that dumb Jenny, don't you? It was her that ruined it all for you!"

"Oh!" Marie thought about it. It was getting muddled in her mind because it was Jenny's fault, but she couldn't find anything to argue with Hester about it. She went to the dog and stared at it. She stood there confused and upset because nothing made sense. She could feel the bile rising in her. Her life was over, and Allen was gone. Nothing made sense. She was off balance. She let all the anxiety, fear, depression, anger and rage that swirled in her mind flow out of her and into the dog.

It started growling and ripping up turf with its claws. It threw itself at the fence numerous times until Marie could see a bloody gash on its side. Marie saw a place where a board could be loosened with some exerted pressure and called the dog. The dog immediately responded and began digging at the ground around the board and trying to paw and bite the board. Ordinarily the board would have withstood a dog's abuse, but with the frenzied dog attacking it, it gave way at the bottom. The dog shimmied through the hole between the boards and the ground. It was not really a big enough hole, but the dog, in its crazed state, was determined. It cried a whimper as the wood splinters scratched its hip. It wasn't enough to stop the dog. With Marie's influence, the dog was wild and out of control.

Once free from the fence, the dog made quick time toward the young mother and the stroller. Hester took Marie's hand, and they flashed closer to watch. Marie watched the mother scream and grab up the baby. Leaving the stroller on the side of the road, she ran terrified back toward her house. The dog quickly caught up to her. She tried to kick the dog away with one foot. The dog kept coming at her with teeth bared, trying desperately to get a hold of the flesh of her thigh which she had raised to protect them as well as try to kick the dog away.

The maternal instinct in the mother welled up and a protective bubble of energy exuded from the woman. Marie saw a man, a Protector, step in and try to calm the dog, but was unable to do much. His ability to influence the dog was significantly less than Marie's. The dog, snapping crazily at anything, got hold of a corner of the baby blanket and was yanking, flipping its head left and right. The mother managed to hold the baby and let the blanket go, momentarily sending the dog somersaulting backwards. It was just enough time for her to race to the side door by her garage and get inside. The dog smashed itself, face first, into the door, shook off the blow and started jumping at the door barking rabidly.

Normally Marie would have found the whole seen so disturbing, she would be having trouble breathing. In her trance- like state, she just watched without any regard for either the mother or the child.

"Well, crap!" Hester exclaimed. "Dang Protector! There

he was butting in."

She looked toward the house and at the dog still insanely attacking the side door. The dog stopped jumping and started holding the blanket in its paws and using its teeth to shred the blanket into a frizzy mess of yarn.

"I must have that baby dead! Dang it! And where is that precious Jenny? Taking a coffee break, I suppose. Let's go inside." Hester took Marie by the arm, and they flashed into the kitchen. The young mother was frantically talking to the police clutching baby George in her free arm. George had started crying during the attack and was now at a full wail. His mother's jerky movement and hysterical tone did nothing to calm him.

"We could wait. Eventually she will leave him alone, but we'd need to hide, or the Protector would spot us. Maybe we need to get some help since you can't disappear into shadow." Hester glared at Marie as she said the last part as though Marie was flawed.

Marie watched the mother as Hester jabbered on. The mother's pants leg was ripped and blood from a gash had created an oblong stain on her thigh along the jagged rip. Marie heard sirens in between the barking in the distance. "Well come on, you dope! This isn't going to go anywhere soon. We need to get on with my plan and stop playing around! Everything I try is getting fouled up."

Hester jerked at Marie's arm and frowned. A small bright flash illuminated and the two were gone.

This time they appeared back at the Shadows' Lair, the desolate dirt and rock place where Hester had first taken Marie. As soon as they arrived, Shadows came forward from all directions toward them. As the first ones got close, they tried to pick at Marie and pull on her.

"Quit, you idiots!" Hester slapped and stamped at the Shadows who inched back reluctantly. Hester seemed annoyed with everything now. Within a minute, thousands of haggard-looking souls had materialized. Their faces contorted and they groaned. Marie realized it was not physical pain, but rather a state of anger and sadness combined. They all stood, wavering a bit, as though they might be gone in an instant.

"Now listen to me!" Hester boomed. "We find ourselves in a very fortunate situation. This could tip the scales for us. We have," she cautiously continued looking at Marie, "on our side, this young woman whose body still lives on the other side. We all know the living ones have far greater power than us, but don't know it. Idiots!" she murmured this last word under her breath.

"I have had her out there already creating mayhem with great ease. Even a Protector could not stop what she set in motion." Hester seemed delighted in herself at this, taking full credit.

"What we need to do now is seize the moment in unity. If we all work together at the same time, we can over-throw the Protectors and dominate! We can seek the vengeance we deserve! You can squash the ones that held you down! Some of you have been waiting for centuries for this moment. Now, the sins of the fathers can visit their sons and their sons." Hester was rallying the crowd, and their groans and cheers were rising in one voice. Marie watched with detached interest. None of it mattered to her.

"So, my friends of ages, comrades! Let us go forth now and seek our revenge! Go now!" The Shadows, worked up into a frenzy, started flashing out and soon none were left there but Hester and Marie. Hester turned to Marie and said, "Now darling, your time has come. With them creating mayhem, we will have an easier time. The Protectors will all be distracted. Let's go."

21 - FIGHTING AND CHAOS

Allen pulled into the parking space at the hospital. The small hospital parking lot was full. Allen was lucky to find a space at the far end. He climbed out of the jeep and shut the door, then looked up to the second floor. He could see Marie's window. Every time he crossed the parking lot, he looked up, hoping to see her standing at the window watching for him. As usual, the smoke colored, tinted glass showed nothing but a reflection of the little puffy clouds that randomly dotted the blue sky. It was a warm day for May but still a cool breeze blew through the little canyon in which the hospital was located. The terrain behind the hospital and across the road was covered with new grasses and black oaks with young leaves.

As Allen approached the doorway, he could hear Marie's parents inside talking. Her mom was very animated and annoyed.

"Bill, I cannot just live here in these infernal, backwoods hills forever! We have got to get her transferred closer to home!" Nancy fussed. "I can't get any work done here. I have clients waiting on me and they won't wait forever. It's ridiculous that we are still here. I certainly think we could find a more progressive hospital near LA.

Who knows where they got these doctors!"

"Alright, Sweetheart, I'll see what I can find out when I get back home tomorrow. Just don't worry about it right now. You're going to get yourself all upset." Marie's dad said.

There was a momentary silence. Allen closed his eyes and mustered his strength. He took a breath and went in the room.

"Oh, Allen." Nancy said with a sort of resignation. "How good of you to come by." Allen bit his tongue. He didn't just happen to stop by. He'd put his entire life on hold to stay close to Marie.

"Do you all need anything? I could go get you some lunch?" Allen offered hoping she would eschew any of his suggestions and decide they would leave for a while to get their own food.

"How kind of you to offer, but we just ate." The silence in the room hung like the sky before a tornado, eerily quiet and slightly green.

Seeing no change in Marie, Allen went to the window and leaned against the windowsill. He could see the black top of his Jeep dully reflecting sunlight with wavering smudges of reality cascading down the hood where the heat was radiating off the metal. Never one to not stand his ground, he decided to just confront them.

"So, when I came in, I heard you say you are going to have her transferred to LA?" he said with the same calmness that you'd use to discuss the weather. Inside his mind was reeling, but no hint was showing in his expression.

Nancy didn't move in any way except to move her

170

eyes toward Allen and slightly raise her chin. This was her choice to make, and she was not backing down.

"Yes. There are better medical facilities closer to home." She used just one very logical, irrefutable argument deciding that was all that was necessary.

"That is true. I would expect so. Do you have anyone to stay with her when you are working? I mean, don't you think it's a good idea to have someone with her all the time so if she wakes up, she won't be upset? She won't know where she is." Allen asserted.

"I'm confident a good nursing staff will take that into consideration. There's no need for anyone else." With that she almost turned up the corners of her mouth.

Allen didn't want to play this card, but he felt he had no other choice, "What if she is upset that you pushed me away. I don't think she would like you butting in and running off her fiancé." He hadn't planned to tweak the truth that much, but he was losing his ground. If Nancy and Bill had Marie transferred, it would be very hard for him to follow with no job. LA was a great deal more expensive. He would never talk his parents into funding him while he sat around Marie's hospital room for who knows how long. And, after all, he was going to propose about this time when they were on their cross-country trip. They were just one little yes away from being engaged.

Neither Allen, nor Nancy could see it, but Shadows were creeping into the room like water over the side of a sinking boat. Jacob, Lucinda, and a Protector behind Bill sprang into action, but they were terribly outnumbered. The Shadows immediately transformed into the ghastly forms of the angry souls who possessed them and began hand to hand combat with the Protectors. There were just too many for the three Protectors to subdue. Two evil souls seemed to be contradicting each other over Nancy's head. One was saying that Marie would hate her forever for meddling, and the other was telling her she was entirely in the right for putting that impertinent young man in his place, after all, she knew Marie far longer than he did.

Nancy looked confused for a minute, not sure what to say next. Bill stepped in and stood between Nancy and Allen. "Now look here, we will do anything we want with our daughter. You are perfectly welcome to visit Marie in a hospital in LA just like you are here. Do I make myself clear?" Bill stood up straight with his hands on his hips daring Allen to challenge him.

Allen's eyes never left Bill's as he considered his options, "That's your choice. I will move to LA." After a pause to show he was not being pushed away, Allen said, "Would you do me the courtesy of letting me know prior to her being transferred? I'm sure you understand. You wouldn't care to come here and find an empty room."

Nancy regained her composure enough to speak again, "Of course, if you're around. I hear you have been busy with a girl named... Lydia? She came by looking for you yesterday." Her words lingered on the air falsely maligning Allen.

It was all Allen could take. Trying to regain his composure, he walked over to Marie and caressed back the hair that had fallen on her face. He kissed her forehead.

"Lydia... is delusional," he sternly said to Nancy. Then turned back to Marie, "I love you, Marie. I'll be back later. Stay strong." He breathed a sigh of resignation and left the room.

Jacob left with Allen, looking over his shoulder at the mayhem going on in that room. Lucinda and Bill's Protectors were giving a good fight, but they were completely outnumbered.

As Allen walked down the hallway, Jacob noticed Shadows and evil souls everywhere. The new souls were easily falling prey to their influence. Some were arguing to the point of shoving each other. The hospital staff were either fighting or laying around on hospital beds or in break rooms doing nothing. It was as if everyone had given in to their selfish wants with no consideration for others or responsibility. A patient was crying out in pain, and no one was tending him. The food services staff started throwing trays of food into rooms showing their frustration with the job. The were coaxed, of course, by the evil souls' suggestions. A doctor and a nurse had given in to their lustful desires and let go of all propriety. They stripped off their clothes in an empty patient room with the door wide open.

Jacob watched a Shadow with crazy black hair and wild eyes run up to Allen. He told Allen he should go back there and just kill them. Then he wouldn't have to deal with them anymore.'

"Whoa, whoa, whoa, Buster! What the hell are you doing?" Jacob leapt forward to push the soul away. The man just looked a Jacob and laughed.

"You can't stop us. We have the power now," the evil soul said and took off after another person.

***

Hester thought her plan seemed simple. She had thought about it for a long time. There were two steps. First, she would kill any living descendant of Tom and Jenny. Her list started with Nancy, baby George, and George's mother.

Then, she would need to purge all the deceased

souls of Tom and Jenny's descendants, all the way back to Tom and Jenny, themselves.

She had seen ceremonies in her time performed by witch doctors. She had dabbled in splitting a soul from its body before, but the body usually dies. Just once she was able to take over the body herself for a short time, but it didn't go well.

This was her plan for Marie. At the end, when she no longer needed Marie's power of life, she would purge Marie's soul and steal her body. It would surely work this time because she was smarter now. It would be the perfect avenging of her pain. All of Tom and Jenny and their progeny would be obliterated, and Hester would have a new chance at life and love in a young woman's body. Maybe she would let Allen love her, and she would finally be happy.

22   - OVER THE SIDE

In the parking lot, the pressure in Allen's head was building. He felt angry about their decision. Nancy's accusation of unfaithfulness kept repeating in his thoughts. With a stiff expression, he stomped to his Jeep and got in. He buckled his seat belt and turned on the engine. The radio blared and he didn't even notice. All the words he wished he had said were an argumentative monologue that only he could hear.

He took a deep breath and let it out slowly. He thought of going back to his apartment that he'd just rented with the money his mom had wired him. He liked it and imagined Marie would, too. He planned to just stay at that apartment for the next school year. He'd daydreamed that Marie woke up, and they put all this behind them. The apartment was just two doors down from Sam and Ellen. He wanted to believe he and Marie would enjoy visiting them and going for walks to Main Street.

Now he would need to break the lease and prepare to move six hours away to a huge metropolis. He had never lived in a large town. Even Lexington was barely the size of a suburb of LA. How would he afford it? What if he couldn't find anything right away? How long was this coma going to last anyway?

Then he remembered, maybe Marie was stuck. He couldn't shake the sneaking suspicion that she was stuck and couldn't get home. But what can I do to find her? He needed more information and this was not his area of expertise.

Jacob whispered in his ear.

An image of the incense store came to mind.

Allen thought, "That's it! That bizarre lady at the incense store. She was talking to Marie about some ghost that followed her around. If Marie were here, she would go see her."

Allen put the Jeep in reverse and set out in the direction of Soulsbyville. He didn't have much time.

Along the way, Shadows kept climbing into the Jeep and trying to distract Allen. They would whisper thoughts in his mind, crazy thoughts. Crash into the tree! Hit that pedestrian! Go faster! Allen was having a hard time keeping his thoughts straight. He figured it was fatigue setting in.

Jacob would shove them away or blast them with positive energy, but they kept coming. He noticed that people he passed on the street were also being attacked by several Shadows and the Protectors were in full battle mode. It appeared that the Protectors were outnumbered four to one in almost all the cases.

Allen was making his way outside the city limits of Sonora and, although there was less population around them, the Shadows never let up. Allen was approaching a curve in the road as the mountain went up in elevation. The Shadows were putting images in his mind of Marie fighting for her life, cut, bruised and bleeding. Just for a minute, he lost track of space and time and all he could see was Marie before him. The Jeep continued straight instead of turning in the curve and, before Jacob had a chance to fight off another Shadow and warn Allen, the Jeep careened out into thin air. Allen immediately realized his mistake, but it was too late. It wasn't a terribly high drop, but still the impact of falling straight into the pine forest below would be enough to destroy the vehicle and severely batter Allen.

There was a moment of quiet airborne flying where the Jeep made an arc in the resistance-free space. Allen sat horrified, waiting to see if he would survive. There was nothing he could do to help himself in the face of his unfortunate future. What seemed like minutes to Allen was only a matter of seconds. The Jeep's front grill hit the ground first, jolting Allen forward, straining against the seatbelt that stalwartly held him in place and yet cut into his collar bone so hard it snapped. His head jerked forward with the impact. The forward force of the vehicle and pull of gravity propelled it end over end three times. During the second flip, which was a bit askew and left leaning, Allen hit his head on the side window, and it knocked him unconscious. His body then limply flung in whatever direction the car compelled him. Jacob worked frantically to cushion impacts however he could. It was not an accurate science, but energy could be used to absorb a force.

When the Jeep came to a crashing stop upside down against the trunk of a tree, Allen hung like a bat with his arms hanging. The radio still blared, and the engine hissed steam. Thank goodness his seatbelt was on and had kept him from being thrown. The roll bars had kept him from being crushed even though the black cover was shredded from rolling end over end.

Jacob tried to awaken him, but Allen was out cold. He didn't want to leave Allen with all the shadows looming, but he wondered if anyone had seen the car go over the side.

Ben flashed in at that moment. He knelt and looked inside the Jeep and saw Allen hanging upside down and Jacob squatting on the roof trying to decide what to do.

"Heard you were in a bit of trouble," Ben said studying
the situation.

"Just in time! He is breathing, but I think there are internal injuries. We need to get help!" Jacob stepped out and looked up the hill. Ben followed his gaze to the cut in the hillside where the road must be.

"Woo-wee! What a ride!" Ben let out.

"Uh yeah. A real E-ticket." Jacob said unimpressed, referring to Disney World's ticket to ride the best rides. Ben had no idea what he was talking about but assumed an E-ticket was a great thing.

Jacob continued, "You go up there and tell someone to look down here. I'll stay here. The Shadows have gone crazy for some reason, so I don't want to leave him alone." As he said this, he stomped on a Shadow hovering over the dirt heading toward the Jeep.

"Okay! Be right back." Ben flashed away to the top of the hill. He stood on the side of the road and looked down at the Jeep. It was clearly visible if you were standing there looking over the side. He noted that if you were in a car, you would never see it. Allen would likely be there for days without medical care. The shock alone would kill him if the Shadows didn't. Ben flashed up one side of the road looking for a car. None was in sight. He flashed back the other way. Sure enough, coming out of Sonora, was a telephone truck. The driver was sipping a cola and eating

French fries as he drove. Ben got in close and whispered, "What if a car fell off the road at a curve? A person would be stranded for days. Look here, a curve coming up. Slow down. Pull over. Look over the side to see if there is anything down there."

The man took the suggestions easily. He pulled over, stowed his soda can in the plastic cup holder hanging from his door by the window, and got out, leaving the door ajar. He looked a little confused as though he didn't know why he was doing this. At the edge, he peered over the side and stopped cold. His hunch was dead on. There was a vehicle upside down, engine hissing and radio blaring.

"Oh my god!" He jumped to the left and right trying to figure out what to do first: radio for help or try to shimmy down the hillside to help. He decided to radio first and then head down. He reached in his truck and grabbed the CB radio.

After getting through to the Sonora Fire Department, he started making his way down the hill, sliding as much as crawling. Ben had kept him from completely sliding down the hill. He finally reached the Jeep and nervously peered into the passenger window. Jacob and Ben were watching nearby.

"Ho!" the man said out loud. "Hey buddy? Can you hear me?" The telephone man gingerly reached in and felt for a pulse on Allen's neck. It was faint but there. Not wanting to cause him further injury, he decided it would be best to wait for the paramedics. There didn't seem to be any immediate danger. He turned the ignition key to turn off the car. The radio immediately silenced.

He looked up the hill for signs of help. In the distance he heard sirens. Then he smelled the unmistakable sickly, nose burning smell of gasoline. He darted around the back of the Jeep, Sure enough

179

gasoline had found a way from a busted, crumpled gas tank down the side of the car in the dirt and was puddling under the engine on the passenger side. The engine was still hissing, and an occasional spark snapped from the connections on the battery. He had to get the victim out immediately.

He ran back to the driver-side door and opened it. He had no idea if the victim had back or neck injuries. He figured the best way to get him out without letting him fall to the ground was to crawl under him on his hands and knees and unbuckle him so that he would slump over his back like on a donkey. Hopefully, he could then crawl out the door and ease him to the ground.

It was all working great until Allen's foot got caught on the steering wheel. Now they were both stuck in there and it could explode at any moment. The telephone man was able to reach around and turn the wheel just enough to release Allen's foot. With a sigh of relief, he inched out of the vehicle, careful not to tip his burden too far to one side or the other. Inch by inch in the pine-needled dirt, they moved together, as carefully as was possible. Finally, out from the vehicle, the telephone man lowered his left shoulder slowly and Allen began to slide down to the ground. The man reached behind with his left arm and supported Allen's torso, so he didn't fall all at once. Then he was able to stand on his knees and carefully lay Allen on the ground. At least they were out of the vehicle, but still much too close if it blew up.

The man picked up Allen's feet and pulled him about 20 feet away under the shade of a pine tree. Jacob held Allen's head as straight as he could. The telephone man checked, and Allen was still breathing and had a pulse.

By now the sirens were on top of the hill. Ropes were thrown over the side and rescuers started rappelling down the steep hillside. Ben watched Protectors helping the rescuers get a good footing when they jumped on the loose dirt.

As the first rescuer reached Allen and the telephone man, the Jeep exploded with a crackling boom that sent hundreds of birds into flight. At the first sign of the impending explosion, two rescuers leapt over Allen's body and covered their heads. Metal shrapnel flew in all directions. The carcass of the Jeep was blown completely upside down and now sat up right about five feet away from the men.

The other rescuers on the hillside, momentarily frozen, now moved in double time. A helicopter hovered overhead and lowered an orange and black stretcher down to the ground. Four rescuers picked up Allen and transferred him to the stretcher which promptly hoisted him into the air and into the helicopter where two medics began their work on him.

Within five minutes, Allen was in the Sonora Regional Medical Center ER. Nurses quickly inserted an IV, took blood samples, got vitals, and created charts. The radiology department brought in an X-ray machine. The doctor poured over results, and it was determined Allen had a lacerated liver, broken collar bone, whiplash, and a concussion. All in all, he was lucky. He should have been dead. He most certainly would have been if Jacob hadn't been there, and the telephone man hadn't saved his life and called for help.

Allen was rushed to surgery to stop the hemorrhaging from his liver.

***

In the hallway, Nancy stopped to ask the nurse a

181

question at the nurses' station. There was no one there and so she waited. Two young nurses came around the corner and stopped to talk.

"Yeah, the guy evidently got him out just in time. Joe said as soon as they got there the Jeep blew up right beside them, and he had three pieces of metal in his back from the blast."

"Wow! How did the guy crash?"

"Joe said there were no skid marks. It looks like he just drove straight off the side. What in the world was he thinking? Lucky guy to be alive. No family here either. The Jeep had Kentucky tags. The police will have to track down family."

Nancy's eyes shot up, "Who? Who was it?"

The nurses realized someone was there and stiffened. One answered, "I'm sorry, privacy laws prevent me from discussing patient information."

"No! No, you don't understand! Was it Allen McCracken? He's engaged to my daughter!"

"Would you have information about his next of kin?" the nurse asked.

"I know their names and where they live," Nancy said. "Okay, write that down and I'll get back with you. Where will you be?"

"My daughter Marie is in that room," she said pointing, "Her name is Marie St. Clair." Nancy took a sheet of paper and wrote down as much as she knew and handed it to the nurse. She was wringing her hands when she went back into Marie's room.

"Oh Lord, Bill! I think something's happened to Allen!"

"What? Why do you think that?" Bill asked.

"I heard the nurses talking about a terrible accident. A Jeep that had Kentucky tags just drove off a cliff. There can't be two Jeeps with Kentucky tags running around these hills!"

"What did they say?" he asked with a concerned look. "They are calling his parents. We aren't family so they

wouldn't let me see him. Oh, Bill! What if something happened to him? I never meant to wish him harm. I just wanted to get Marie home." Nancy looked at her daughter in the bed, "She does care about him, and he has no family here. What if something happened to Marie and we were halfway across the country?" Bill put his arms around his wife.

She pulled away, "And what is going on around here? People have been acting crazy. I've heard more fighting and yelling today than I ever have. It must be how these people act around here. We need to get Marie home," she paused, "but maybe we should wait to see if Allen is okay first. This is all just too much."

"I agree," Bill said and put his arms around her again.

Nancy started to cry with her face buried in his shirt.

23 - A NEW ALLIANCE

It was about three hours later when the nurse came into Marie's room. Nancy was reading a book to pass the time but not really knowing what she was reading. Bill was napping on the uncomfortable couch.

"Mrs. St. Clair?" said the nurse.

"Oh! Yes, please come in!" Nancy started to get up.

"It's okay, please sit down. I want to talk to you about Allen."

"Oh? Bill! Bill wake up!" Nancy raised her voice a bit and said, "Bill, it's the nurse about Allen. Wake up!"

Bill sat up and ran a hand over his hair and face.

The nurse began, "We have contacted Allen's parents in Kentucky, and they gave us permission to tell you about Allen. In fact, they asked if you might stand in for them with any decisions until they can get here, which won't be until tomorrow afternoon. It was the fastest flight they could get into Sacramento and then they will have to drive up the foothills."

"I understand! Of course, we will. How is he?" Nancy passionately answered, her concerned tone noticeably different from earlier in the day.

"Well, he is very lucky. Apparently, his vehicle left the road over an edge, fell pretty far, rolled several times and landed upside-down. Luckily, he had on his seatbelt."

"Oh, my lord!" Nancy stopped breathing a minute.

She thought, *"What if that had been Marie?"* She couldn't imagine how his parents felt right now and they were so far from him.

"Then a utility repairman in a truck stopped for really no reason at all on the curve and looked over the side. He said it was just a hunch or a feeling. He saw the vehicle, radioed for help, crawled down a steep slope, and pulled Allen out just before the vehicle exploded."

"What? Good grief! The guardian angels were working overtime today." At that, Lucinda laughed from the corner of the room near the window.

"Then the rescuers put Allen in a stretcher which was lowered from a helicopter and brought him here. In the ER it was determined he had a lacerated liver and was taken immediately to surgery. He also has a broken collar bone, a concussion, and other minor cuts and bruises as you would expect from a car accident. After recovering from surgery, he should be discharged into his private physician's care." The nurse waited a minute to let them process all this.

Nancy tried to understand all of this. After replaying it in her head, she let out a sigh of relief. "So, he'll be okay, then?

"Yes, he should recover and be fine." The nurse said. "Would you like to see him? He is awake now."

"Yes, yes, I would." Nancy looked at Bill.

Bill said, "You go see him. Tell him I will see him after he rests some more. I don't want to overload him. He must still be in shock over it all."

With that Nancy stood up and followed the nurse out into the hallway.

They walked down the hallway zigzagging through medical equipment and cafeteria carts. Nancy caught glimpses of strangers in hospital beds through open doors and felt embarrassed for them for the lack of privacy. It was like peering into people's bedrooms as they were waking up. She wondered what they were here for, how had their lives been turned upside down.

The nurse reached a door on the right and gestured for Nancy to go in. Nancy rapped the door lightly.

"Hello? Allen? It's Nancy." She waited a minute and heard a faint groan and took that as an invitation.

The room was dim with the curtains drawn and just the back light on the wall behind the bed giving enough light to see. Allen looked a wreck. He had bruised cheekbones and swelling on his head. His left arm was in a splint. There was a square of gauze taped to the left side of his head where he hit the window that resulted in the concussion. His blond locks flopped limply over the gauze.

Allen looked as though he was trying to focus his eyes and his head rolled on his shoulders like he was dizzy and might be sick.

"Can I get you anything?" Nancy hesitantly offered trying to be useful. He groaned a sound that resembled, "No."

Nancy sat on the chair by the bed looking at him. The white part of his left eye was completely blood colored, making it hard to see the brown of his eyes.

"Allen, I'm so sorry you were hurt."

Allen tried to push himself up on the bed with just his right arm. "Things happen I guess." He paused, coughed, and continued. "I was going down the road and the next thing I knew, there was no road. I don't know what happened. Glad I'm alive.

Jacob, who was standing behind Allen's right shoulder smiled at Lucinda. Lucinda, who was watching a shadow creep along the floor and stamping it with her foot, looked up at Jacob and winked back.

"Nancy," Allen said. "I want to tell you about something I have been thinking about."

"What is it, Allen?"

"Well, this is going to sound crazy. I am having a hard time even saying it."

He paused and reached his right hand to the tray table for his water cup. He took a brief sip of ice water from the straw and then sat the drink back down.

Nancy wasn't sure what he was going to say next. She braced herself for anything.

"Well, I had this crazy idea."

Lucinda's eyes perked up again and looked at Jacob.

Allen continued, "Marie and I had been talking about guardian angels and the afterlife and stuff like that right before she," Allen struggled with how to say it. "She went in the coma."

"I've never given things like that a lot of thought. It sounds more like fairy tales." Nancy's eyebrow arched but she was listening. "But, well, I get a feeling sometimes like she is near. Sometimes, when I'm alone in the dorm. I brush it off because, you know, she isn't dead, so that doesn't make sense. So," he sighed and then continued very fast to just get it out, "I wonder sometimes if maybe her soul is not with her body. Maybe she is trapped, her soul, I mean, and if she could get back in her body, she would wake up."

He flung his right arm to punctuate his words, but

then just dropped it. "That sounds really stupid and I'm sorry. You must think I'm nuts."

Nancy didn't say anything. She kept her gaze on his bruised face and thought about what he said. She couldn't deny she had felt Marie's spirit as well. But what he was saying didn't make any sense. Marie wasn't dead. How could she have left her body? But what if Allen was right? What could they do, even if he was right?

"So how long have you been thinking about this?" she finally asked.

He looked down at his hands ashamed he had even suggested such a crazy thought. He figured she thought he was ignorant before. He knew she didn't like him. This would certainly seal the deal that she would try harder to get Marie away from him. That's what he would think about a person who would suggest such a thing.

He answered, "I have been thinking about it for a week or so. It's funny, but I know this is something Marie would say. She has such a great imagination." He smiled and realized he never thought she was idiot, maybe just a little too susceptible to wild ideas.

He continued, "I was headed to a lady in Soulsbyville who I thought might have some ideas about all this when I had the accident. She and Marie had talked about souls and ghosts or something. I figured she might give me some sort of direction to prove my theory or maybe an idea. It's just crazy hocus pocus."

Nancy took a deep breath and looked out the window. Unbeknownst to Allen and hesitant to show her cards, she felt inclined to agree with him. If it was true, maybe Marie needed help. She knew she could do something to help if they could figure out what.

Lucinda leaned down to Nancy's ear and said in a

raspy voice, "Sugar, Marie needs you. She's in trouble. You and Bill and Allen can help her if you work together."

Nancy turned back to Allen and spoke before she lost courage, "I believe you. I have felt something similar. Maybe it's a wild goose chase, but I think we need to do some research."

Allen smiled weakly and winced as his shoulder shifted. "Well, how in the world do you research this?" His head started hurting. The doctor had told him not to think about much until his concussion healed.

"Well, you aren't going to be doing much for a few days, so I'll see what I can do in the meantime. Give me the name and address of this lady you were going to see."

"It was a shop. A little place that sells incense and whatnots. A real hippie dive. Marie thought it was wonderful."

"Even better. Maybe I can get her a little whatnot to brighten her hospital room." Nancy smiled, pleased with herself. Allen gave her the information and she wrote it down on a paper from his bedside table and folded it before slipping it in her pocket.

Through the walls, three Shadow souls burst into the room. Allen and Nancy continued to talk about Marie and their experiences of feeling her nearby. Jacob and Lucinda jumped into combat and beat the intruders back, even though the Shadows fought boldly. It helped that a bubble of bright energy was surrounding Allen and Nancy. Their love for Marie strengthened an area of space around them that made it harder for the Shadows to get close to them.

24 - KOE

Hester was trying to remember something she had learned from the tribe of nomadic Indians that she had lived with after she faked her death. She'd discovered them after following a garden thief.

They were an odd group of individuals, not technically an Indian tribe. They were more like a group of outcasts that found each other.

They had lived around her village, hiding and living in the hills and woods nearby. Close enough to steal things they needed during the night, but far enough that most folks had no idea who they were. The group tried to blend in with other natives around that people might see.

The group included some outcast Indians, but there were also some immigrants from Europe that were fleeing the law. There were some runaway slaves from the Caribbean, and other people, like Hester, that just needed to disappear. They tried to blend in and not be seen. No one noticed a few apples missing or a random chicken. They lived off the land and moved around together.

They were not trustworthy. These were people who, for whatever reason, didn't do well in regular society. They had beliefs that didn't follow what you would normally expect. These beliefs, like Hester's, were often shaped by situations around them as they grew up. Even though they were no longer in those situations, they looked at life through the lenses of that broken childhood. Their defense mechanisms to help them cope caused more trouble than they helped.

Koe was a slave from Bermuda that had escaped, found a place to hide on a sailing ship bound for Virginia, and then happened upon the group as he was on the run. They nursed him back to health after he nearly collapsed. He was young, but his back had suffered many lashings and gaping wounds that were in various stages of healing. Infection was about to overtake him. He joined the little tribe about 4 years before Hester.

When Hester was in her late 30s, her home was perfectly clean but lacking any feeling of warmth. No children scampered around. No jovial laughter. No visitors came by to sip iced tea on the porch out back. She spent most of her time alone in the house she shared with Leonard.

Captain Leonard Pope was often out fighting Indians. He was gone for long periods of time. Being a Captain, he provided a comfortable life for Hester that was very different than how she grew up as an indentured servant, but Leonard didn't care about her past.

Hester watched the world from her windows and her garden. She never felt comfortable around the other women around so she kept to herself. She noticed little things because she had nothing else to occupy her. She had never been taught the finer arts of needlepoint or crochet.

One day, when she noticed some of her carrots

had been pulled up, she knew it wasn't rabbits. She knew how the rabbits worked. She would see bits of leaves here or there and just one carrot pulled up at a time. She might lose one carrot a week, but not several. This was something else.

Hester decided to watch her garden at night. She would nap during the day so she could sit up and watch by the light of the moon through her second story window. She was rewarded for her patience after just three nights. She watched a boy about ten years old creep down the path and scamper behind a lilac bush. After a minute of stillness, when she assumed he must be watching to see if anyone was around, he crept out and went straight for the row of carrots near the well.

Hester quickly slipped down the stairs and out the front door. She tiptoed around the house and peered around the corner. The little thief was still hard at work, occasionally looking up to make sure he was still unseen. She figured he'd leave the way he came, and she made for a large oak tree outside the gate and hid behind it.

Sure enough, after another couple of minutes, the boy came out in a full sprint with his tunic bulging and held close with both arms. She followed him as he ran out from the property down toward a small creek. He waded out and climbed into a canoe, dumping his loot onto the bottom of the boat, and felt around for an oar. Hester seized the moment of distraction to leap into the water and grab the back of the canoe, successfully halting the boy's progress.

"ACK!" yelled the startled boy.

"I've got you!" Hester yelled authoritatively. "Now who are you?"

The boy's eyes were wide, and he paused unsure of what to say. "Uh. Uh, I'm Toby," he stammered. His blond curly hair glowed in the moonlight. He looked as though he'd bathed recently, but his clothes were in tatters.

"Okay, Toby," Hester acknowledged, "What are you doing with my carrots?"

"I'm sorry, ma'am, really, I am. I'm just so hungry and my little sister is too. You can have them back." He lurched forward to grab up the carrots.

"I'll tell you what, you show me where your people are, and you can have the carrots. Deal?" Hester was more curious about what sort of people lurked about unseen than she was worried about the carrots.

"Uh, well, you won't turn us in, will you?" he asked afraid.

"No, no. I just want to see if I can help your family." It
was as good a thing to say as anything to get him to agree.

"Well, okay. Get in."

Hester stepped into the canoe with strong steady legs and sat down on the other seat facing Toby. He began to dip the oar into the water and pull long steady strokes. Within a half hour they came to an eddy, and he rowed the canoe onto the shallow bank. They got out and both carried the canoe up onto the bank. Toby pushed it back behind some bushes and came out with his tunic again full of the carrots. He led the way through the forest undergrowth as if he had done it a million times.

After another fifteen minutes of walking, she started to smell smoke and hear quiet murmuring of conversation. She knew it had to be well on three in the morning and wondered who would be out in the woods this late. As they got closer, she started to see makeshift tents and lean-tos. Finally, a man came into view. He was standing in the path waiting as if he knew she would be coming. The whites of his eyes contrasted startlingly with his complexion in the darkness.

"Greetings. I have been waiting for you, missus." His eyes were fixed on her in a way that put her off guard. She expected to catch them off guard and it appeared that this was not the case.

"How-" she stuttered, "how did you know I was coming?"

He smiled broadly showing perfect, straight, white teeth. Then he laughed a hearty laugh, throwing his head back. "Missus, I see many things. You is the most fascinating here lately."

Hester stood there speechless.

"You come and sit. Warm self by the fire? I give you drink." He turned on his heel and darted toward the fire. He picked up a cup carved from wood and ladled an amber liquid from a kettle near the fire. He gestured for her to sit on a tree stump near the fire. Then he sat cross-legged near the stump. Hester noticed others now. They were peeking at her from inside the tents and from behind trees. She assumed they must have scattered when the man started talking.

"I," he said proudly, "am Koe."

"I see," she thought it was a strange name. "I am Hester. Hester Farr."

Koe studied her a moment, as though comparing her to something he already knew. "You live in village a long time?"

"Yes, well, for a few years. My husband and I have a house. He is a captain in the army."

Koe studied her again. "But you not his. Your heart not his. You not give it away."

"I beg your pardon! Who do you think you are?" Hester

played the part of the society wife that she should be.

Koe laughed again, even louder than before. "Oh! You play games. Okay. I play, too. Would you like to dance and hear fine music? Perhaps you prefer some needlepoint?" He was mocking her. She pursed her lips and her face got hot.

"Who the hell are you?" she barked; her pretense gone.

Now Koe's face was serious.

"Ah! Now we see the real Hester Farr. The one I see in my dreams. You is angry. Your anger is big, and it wanders ahead of you. Sometimes it gets caught on the wind and calls out to find what it seeks. Yes, Hester Farr. What is it you seek?"

Hester wondered what kind of trickery this man was about. She had the urge to run. No one had ever so perceptively seen her. She was always very careful to hide her feelings, to push down her reactions. How could he see her soul so clearly and not even know her?

He watched her making her mental somersaults, contemplating whether she should just run back to the creek. She could. She was not afraid and had gone out alone in the woods many times before. Often as a child she would seek the solace of the woods when she was afraid or when she knew the old man would come looking for her.

She could run, but she didn't.

"I seek many things. First and foremost, I seek to know who has been stealing my carrots. Secondly, I seek happiness like anyone else." Hester, a mature woman at this point in her life, looked tired and hard.

"Happiness has eluded you a long time. Happiness is something different for everyone. What would make the devil happy is not the same as what would

195

make a maiden happy, yes?" He had her there. She sat there feeling exposed, naked. Perhaps there was a time when she had the dreams of a young maiden, but now she sought vengeance that would make any devil squirm. She had murdered. She had lied. She could cut your heart out and serve it to you on a plate. The dreams of a young maiden, dreamt on moonlit walks in a forest like this, were long ago snuffed out by the wild horses of hatred that now consumed her.

"Mr. Koe, somehow you seem to know a lot about me. I'm not sure how you know or why you care. Maybe you're just messing with me." She looked him in the eye without flinching, owning up to the truth between them.

"Rest easy, Missus. I am not to judge you. You did not know it when you set out tonight, but you came to me so I could teach you how to use the energy that grows inside you. Yes. There is great power in what you feel." Koe emphasized the word 'you'.

From then on, Koe took Hester under his wing as an apprentice. She learned a great deal about black magic, but the most powerful magic she could hope to use was to conjure the spell of Sempiternal Ruination. It was the evilest spell a witch doctor could invoke, and Koe had been practicing it for some years in Bermuda. It went beyond killing a person. It obliterated their very soul, the part of a person that is supposed to be always eternal, whether in hell or paradise. The person's soul would cease to be.

This was useful if you believed in an afterlife because just killing your enemy would not stop them. They would continue to stalk you from the other side.

"But you must use it sparingly," said Koe, "because it creates an imbalance in the universe. The place where that soul should be is now empty and things you don't want destroyed can fall into that place. When you pull a rock out of a stream, the water around it rushes in."

Hester wasn't sure, at that time, if she believed Koe. After all, how would they even know if it worked? No one would until they died themselves and went on to see what was in the afterlife. But now, two hundred years later, perhaps she could try it and see, and then she would know if Koe's magic was true.

25 - LOVE IS THE ANSWER

Exactly one week after the Jeep drove off the side of the cliff, Allen was discharged. Still very sore from the surgery on his liver, the nurse loaded him into a wheelchair and pushed him out the front door of the hospital. His dad had the car pulled up to the front door and his mom helped him get in. They drove him to the pharmacy to get his prescriptions and then to his apartment in Sonora. Getting up the stairs was a bear. Finally, he settled on the sofa with a pillow.

His parents had a hotel room nearby and had been with him every day as he recovered. They called the insurance company and started the process of getting him a new car. They were very grateful to Nancy for being with him those first two days in the hospital. It was a sad way for them to meet Marie, but they were glad to meet Nancy and Bill.

There was a knock at the door and Allen's mother answered, "Oh hello, Nancy. Please come in. We were just about to go get a hamburger for all of us for supper. Why don't you stay with Allen while we go? We'll bring you back something."

"I'd be happy to stay with Allen, but please don't

get me anything. Bill and I are going to the Europa when I get back." Nancy answered.

"Alright then. We'll be right back." Allen's parents went out and closed the door behind them. Nancy sat on the beige occasional chair next to the couch. The apartment had come furnished with uncomfortable, non-descript furniture.

"I have been doing some checking around town. The lady you said that runs the incense shop has been there for twenty years. She is respected by most people as a business owner. I would assume then that she isn't too crazy of a hippie. At least she has enough sense to run a business." Nancy said.

She continued, "I tried to find it, but couldn't. I think in a day or so when you are feeling better, we should visit her together. Seeing you might jog her memory of Marie." "That sounds like a good idea," said Allen as he winced from the surgery wound.

***

Ben flashed to the Gathering. The level of noise had risen over the last week as the activity of the Shadows had become progressively worse. He saw Lorenzo talking to a group that was waving their arms in dramatic gesticulations and talking over each other. He walked over to the group and tried to get Lorenzo's attention.

Lorenzo apologized and left the group to their squabbling and joined Ben.

"Wow. It's really getting crazy around here," Ben said. "Yes," Lorenzo sighed. "Even we can't shake off the chaos the Shadows are creating. What's going on?"

"The others have gone to stay with Allen and Marie. I just had something on my mind and wanted to ask you about it."

"Anything, Ben," Lorenzo said with a smile that

made you feel like nothing in the world could ever go wrong.

"This Hester that has Marie, how can we defeat her? Can we? I mean, won't she keep coming back? Is there any way to," Ben paused unsure of what Lorenzo's reaction would be. "Can we destroy her?" Ben unconsciously crouched back knowing Lorenzo would not like the question.

Lorenzo's eyebrows creased. He looked at Ben softly and gave a grimaced smile. "Yes, anyone can be destroyed, as you say. But not in the way you think. You can't just fight them until you squash them. That will get them to leave you alone for a while. Some souls are protected with everlasting life because of a choice they made. Some souls have not made the choice, and it is still open to them. Other souls make a choice that precludes them from everlasting life, in other words, it destroys them. Essentially, they are on a path of self-destruction." Lorenzo looked deeply into Ben's eyes with compassion.

Ben thought about it for a moment. It was not the answer he wanted, but it was fair, even just.

***

Three days later, Allen was getting up and around more easily. He still had to take it slow, but he could go out of the apartment for short periods of time before he needed to rest. The Shadows had whispered to him enough that he was a louse for not visiting Marie, or at least the part of Marie he could visit.

His parents were planning their trip home. They would be leaving soon. His mother had been busily washing his clothes and making sure he had three meals a day. His dad had kept him company by discussing every angle of the Cincinnati Reds team this year. It looked very favorable for a World Series win with the Nasty Boys making them nearly impossible to beat.

Nancy told them she needed Allen to join her on an errand for Marie and would be picking him up at 10:00 this morning. She knocked at the door right on time.

Allen's mother opened the door, and Nancy came in. "Good morning, Nancy. Would you like some breakfast?"

"Oh, no! That's nice of you to ask, but I need to get
going with Allen, so he doesn't get tired."

"Here he is," Allen's mother remarked as he came into
the room bracing his right side.

"Hiya, Nancy. You ready? I'll be back soon, mom and dad. Just make yourselves at home."

Allen and Nancy left and closed the door. Allen could hear his mother's irritated tone inside. He was sure his dad was getting an earful. about what she thought of Nancy. His mother doted on him and tried to get along with Nancy, but the differences between California and Kentucky culture made it hard for her not to think Nancy was a bit snobby.

He crept down the stairs, one at a time, leaning heavily on the handrail, and then got into Nancy's blue Crown Victoria. The door was heavy and made a secure latching click when Allen pulled it closed.

Nancy pulled out of the parking lot and headed up the road to Soulsbyville, passing the curve where Allen had wrecked without saying a word. When they were well past this point, she started, "So what should we ask her? We can't just jump in asking about ghosts, or she'll think we are crazy."

"Hm," Allen paused to collect his thoughts, "I will start off by asking if she remembers Marie from the last time we were there. I'll tell her Marie is in the hospital and we wanted to get her something for her hospital room to cheer her up."

Nancy nodded that this was a good start. He continued, "Then I'll introduce you. And after that …" his words faded. "I don't know, after that. What do you think?"

She answered, "After that, I'll tell her that Marie had mentioned her little friend and I'll ask her questions about what 'little friends' do all day. That will get it started. From there, we can wing it."

"Sounds like a plan," Allen smiled at her.

After a while, they pulled into the parking lot and parked in the same spot Allen had before. Nancy took in the scene with as much enthusiasm as Allen had the last time. They climbed the stairs slowly to give Allen time, and then went in the door. A little jingle bell tinkled as they entered.

"Good day, friends!" came a mellow voice from behind the counter. Allen noticed the hat she had been making before now sat perched on a hat stand on the counter with a price tag hanging from the brim. It was $15. Allen thought that was a good return on her investment. It was a pretty hat. Marie would have liked it. He felt the edge of the brim that curled up and was fastened with three crocheted flowers.

"Ah! It's you" the woman proclaimed. "But this is not the same lady." She turned to Nancy and smiled. Allen thought either she has very few customers or a whopping memory.

Nancy stepped forward, "I'm Nancy St. Clair. I think you met my daughter Marie when she came here with Allen recently."

The woman smiled broadly. "Yes! I'm Jasmina. Welcome!" She turned to Allen, "So good to see you. How is Marie?" Allen detected a note of concern on her face as she asked this.

"Marie is in the hospital. That's why we are here. We wanted to get something for her room to cheer her up." Allen said.

Jasmina watched Allen a minute and said, "Uh huh," but it appeared she wasn't talking to Allen. Someone else, perhaps unseen, seemed to have her attention. Then she said, "What happened to her? I'm so sorry to hear this." She never took her eyes off Allen.

"We aren't sure really. She didn't wake up one morning. She is in a coma. Has been for over a month." Allen's faced took a pained look.

"Yes," Jasmina said slowly. "I warned her." "Warned her of what?" Nancy broke in.

"Just to be careful. She was asking questions that worried me. I've seen it before, just once. Just once." With that she turned her back on the two of them and started pushing a pile of receipts into a stack.

Allen looked at Nancy with a knowing gaze. Nancy understood. This woman did have answers. She began, "Jasmina," Nancy said carefully trying to get it right, "tell us about the other time you saw this. We need to know."

Jasmina stopped abruptly as though she was considering if she should say anything. She looked to an empty corner of the shop and shrugged her shoulders. Then she turned back to face them. Nancy thought the woman must be crazy. Perhaps they should leave now, quickly.

Jasmina took a deep breath, "There was another, she was my friend. At least I thought she was." Her eyes darted toward the window. Then she started again, "Her name was Hester. She showed up one day in the shop. Delilah didn't like her. She's my guardian angel if you will. Hester lived here for a year in the spare bedroom. Odd girl. She wasn't from around here, or at least that's what I thought. But I learn from everyone I meet, so I didn't mind. She helped me with the shop. We talked for hours about anything. She knew a great deal of, well, magic. She showed me herbs and spells. I dabble in things like that for a hobby. No harm, you know." She smiled uneasily. Nancy smiled back trying to look non-judgmental.

"Then one day it was the strangest thing. I was looking through the paper. There was an article about a girl that had disappeared. She looked just like Hester, but I knew it couldn't have been her. The girl had lived all her life, just 18 years, on a nearby farm. The stories that Hester told could not have been known by this girl in the paper. Stories of Virginia and Kentucky and a man from Bermuda.

It was the oddest thing. I realized Hester had to have been much older than the body she had. When I asked her about it offhandedly, she was furious and grabbed the paper. She was gone the next morning. I filed a missing person's report. The police thought I was crazy. No body was ever found. Nothing."

Jasmina continued, "She used to say she could see shadows creeping around and would laugh about it. She would jump at Delilah and scare her. I was glad to see her gone, but also sad. She had such knowledge about so many things. It's a pity."

"Yes." Allen said, slightly shocked, "a pity. So, you were worried about Marie?"

"Yes, other than Hester and myself, I never knew anyone that could see Delilah until Marie came along. She seemed so innocent. Like the girl in the photo in the paper. I don't know everything, obviously, but I know that Hester is bad, and it was too much of a coincidence. Nothing is by chance you know. It might be in the wrong order of time, but it's not by chance."

"Well," Allen bolstered his confidence to say something he believed to be absolute hogwash, "what would you say if I thought that maybe Marie's soul is not really in her body? I get an idea sometimes that she is near me when I'm at home." He breathed a deep sigh of relief at having been able to say such a crazy thing.

Jasmina looked at him sadly, "I would say you are probably right, friend. Not all comas are like that. But I believe you can be knocked out of your body and the body is left in a coma-like state. It makes sense."

Allen looked down and whispered to himself, "If you're crazy, it does." He looked back up and calmly said, "Well, if that were true, how could we help her get back into her body?"

Jasmina sat back on her stool and rubbed her hand on her face in thought. She stopped and looked at them. They looked desperate. It was obvious they loved Marie very much. She sighed. "I can only guess. I am certain there is another world around us. An in-between world, between life and the here-after. It's not a permanent place, but I believe souls live there, for whatever reason, before

moving on. Delilah lives there, half in and half out of our world. I don't know why I can see her. But I do think that whatever the reason I can, is why Hester came to me. She was curious." She paused, "I now think Hester was very evil. I often wonder if she hurt the young girl from the farm for her own purposes. When I noticed Marie could see Delilah, I worried for her. Hester or some soul like her could try to get near her. I told Marie that day to remember love, it was the only thing that could save her. I still believe that. Love is the strongest energy in the spiritual universe. It's an atom bomb," she paused before adding, "if you can figure out how to use it."

Allen's face was deadpan. Nancy could see he was struggling. He was teetering on one foot like he was about to bolt. Nancy's eyelashes were batting in rapid fire, and she started to speak but stammered. She licked her lips and started again.

"So," Nancy stumbled, "Love? Love will help her?" Allen looked at Nancy with a worried look. His hands unconsciously started upward as if to catch her if she was going to come unglued.

"Yes! That's it. She must feel your good vibes. When you pray, or even meditate, about someone, they can feel it on the other side. It's not hard to do, but it's the only way to reach them." Jasmina beamed with satisfaction for being heard.

Allen started shaking. He clenched his jaw. His nose flared as he breathed in forcefully. Nancy looked at him with wide eyes that darted back and forth from his face to Jasmina's. She seemed caught between leaping with her heart and calling Jasmina hippy freak.

Allen burst, "What? What are you saying? We should just sit around and think love thoughts and Marie will be fine? Is that it?" He spat out the last sentence in a squeak.

Jasmina sighed and smiled again gently. It was obvious she was used to people thinking she was crazy. "I know it's hard to believe," she nodded. "I can see that it took a great

deal of courage for the two of you to come here and ask these questions." Her smile started to stretch wide, "But you are stretching your minds in ways you never have. Just bear with me a minute."

"If you could put it in more practical terms, maybe it would be easier," Allen was trying.

"All right, Allen, way to try! Well, here's the thing,

the Shadows, the bad souls, try to undo anything love puts together. So, if you are working to create something or cause something and you use love, they will take apart what you are trying to do. And vice-versa!" She smiled as though this made perfect sense.

Allen looked at her, trying to understand how something intangible could create anything tangible.

She continued, "Think of it as a form of motivation. A person is motivated to do something by a feeling, like your coming here today. You came here, which you probably never would have done, because of the motivation to help Marie, right?"

He nodded, "Yeah, but how can a motivation help Marie get back into her body."

Jasmina smiled, "Yes, we are only capable of doing certain things. You can come here, obviously. You can do lots of mortal things. But what can you do that will affect the spirit world?"

Allen and Nancy looked at each other perplexed. Nancy

started, "Can prayer help?"

"I have seen prayer change things, so I would say yes. Prayer can affect the spirit world," Jasmina answered, pleased with them.

"Okay," Allen said, "we need to think about this some.

Thank you, Jasmina. You have been a great help."

"No problem, child. Oh, here," she reached for the hat, "put this on her head. I thought of her a great deal as I made it. It must be hers."

Allen thanked her and took the hat. He rubbed the yarn

between his thumb and index finger and smiled as his brows creased. "Thanks, Jasmina." He and Nancy turned for the door.

"Well, that seemed useless," Allen grumbled,

wincing as he sat down in the car. "How is any of that going to help Marie?"

"I have an idea, but I'll need your help. Are you motivated?" Nancy winked at Allen.

26   - MAKING PLANS

The Gathering was busy. Tom, Henry, Jenny, and Ben were trying to figure out a plan to help Marie. Protectors were flashing in and out. There was a great deal of shouting and running. The Shadows were now working overtime to wreak havoc. An uptick in car crashes everywhere required Protectors to be on high alert. People were arguing on street corners. The police were busy with domestic disputes. The news stations were blaming it on the weather. It had been unseasonably warm throughout the country, so that must be it, they determined.

They were sitting around a table off to one side when Henry noted, "We have not seen Marie in a while."

"Hester must be planning something, and she has her hidden away. All this chaos must be her rallying the Shadows to continue their work," Jenny said. "What can we do to get Marie back?"

Henry started half explaining and half figuring as he talked, "We need to find a way to combine our power. No, amplify it, when we come up against Hester again. As individuals, not one of us is a match for her. Even together, it was difficult to get Jenny out of there."

Henry paused to think and then continued, "I have seen an object used before as a focal point. An object imbued with energy from its owner. Something that had been worn for a long time, maybe even for generations, which could be used to collect and transmit a similar energy. It would amplify our collective energy."

"Wow! That sounds good. But what?" Said Ben.

Tom thought a minute, "Sarah Elizabeth had a watch, a pocket watch, which Nancy now has. I have seen it. I saw her show it to Marie when she was little. I believe Nancy's mother had it before her. If we could find it, then that might be the thing."

"That sounds perfect, Tom!" Jenny said excitedly, "I know that watch! It was a birthday gift from Sarah's father. He cherished her and it broke his heart when she left and married. That gift had love surrounding it then. It was a tie between them that Sarah held onto even when her father seemed distant. She refused to sell it even when she was very poor, which further invested it with love. Then, passing it down, other generations have loved the memories it represents. It's become a symbol of following your heart and loving with all you have, and never turning your back on your family. I think that might work."

"It will be a trick to get it. Moving items in the real world is not our forte'. We will have to hope that its spiritual energy is high enough that we can attach it to ourselves and be able to move it," said Henry.

Tom asked, "But how exactly does that work, using an object? I've never done that."

Henry answered, "Instead of focusing your strength on the Shadow, you concentrate on throwing it at the object. The object then reaches a maximum energy saturation and must explode it out.

Anything around the object in a proximal radius will be blasted with the wave. In this case it will be positive energy, so we are protected, but anything, or anyone, with evil desires will be hit and neutralized.

That's what I have seen before. Use of objects is rare because generally we don't need them. Also, it must be deeply imbued as an energy receptacle. In Hester's case, she is one mean devil. Anything that can help is good."

"What if Hester can do the same thing to us?" Jenny wondered out loud. "What if she has an object imbued with hate?"

"Always a possibility. We just must hope we beat her to the idea." Henry said.

***

Marie felt lost in a fog. She couldn't think straight. She couldn't remember anything. She was laying on the floor of the rocky well in the dark. She tried to think of simple things, like saying the alphabet. She would get to the middle and forget what she was doing. Then she would try to remember the names of faces that would appear in her mind fleetingly. They seemed familiar, but then she couldn't remember who they were. After a time of this, she would give up and try to sleep, but sleep never came. Souls don't sleep. It was an eternal hell.

Hester was nearby. Marie could hear her talking to herself and grumbling. She seemed focused on something and rarely talked to Marie. Hester had assigned Shadows to stay with Marie and continue to cover her with their depression-inducing hypnosis. Hester was saying some kind of strange words and Marie would hear someone else shriek and scream. She decided Hester must be experimenting on one of the Shadows.

211

Marie tried to sit up, propped on one elbow, and peer into the darkness. It was nearly pitch dark in the cave. She could see a green glow coming from around a corner of rock.

The Shadows were not strong enough to hold her still, but followed her, sucking the life out of her. She pulled herself upright and felt along the wall to keep from tripping over rocks on the ground. As she peered around the corner, she could see Hester dancing around a stone table. A strange window of light, oval-shaped, and brightest around the edges floated over the table. She was saying a sing-song chorus of words that was unclear to Marie. The words sounded French. At the end she jumped and shouted, "Sempiternal Ruination!" The unexpected loudness made Marie jump a little.

Marie could see in the window of light; a man was lying on a bed and he would cry out when Hester said her words. The place in the window of light looked very different. It looked open and alive. The colors were vivid. She could see the flowers on the table and the blue and green plaid of his blanket. He seemed whole and alive.

Then Marie realized, it was not Shadows she was practicing on, they were real living people. They probably had no idea what was wrong with them. Marie's head hurt. She knew what Hester was doing was wrong, but she didn't have the strength of mind to fight her. She knew she was lost here and if she fought, someone else would be hurt, someone she really loved. It was all confusing since she couldn't recall exactly who that was, but she knew, it was true. She went back to her spot and sat down. She really didn't have enough energy to care about the man in the window. There was nothing she could do for him anyway. Then she heard Hester shriek with glee.

Marie got up and looked again at the window of light. The man had stopped moving. She saw Shadows overcome him and grab at his spirit before he could get away, just like that woman in the street that had been hit by the truck. With a flash of light, the man's soul appeared near Hester with the Shadows holding him. The man was terrified. Marie watched with a morbid curiosity. She watched as Hester said her sing-song poem again. Again, she ended with "Sempiternal Ruination!" This time even louder. A wind seemed to engulf the man's soul like a small tornado. It ripped at the edges of him, shredding and blurring him. The man started to disappear from the outer edges inward until only a small point of light was visible. Then it vanished and was gone. Hester was giddy, jumping and shrieking.

It appeared that Hester had managed to kill the man's body and then obliterate his soul. Marie gasped at the horror of this. Although she had never gone to church much or studied its teachings, she thought that surely this was not possible. If Hester had found a way to not only kill, which she was more than capable of, but also to obliterate souls, then who could stop her? She could destroy anyone permanently who tried to cross her.

"I've done it! He's gone! Koe was right, that sorry twit. He only speculated that it could be done. He never knew for certain, but I know!" Hester yelled out, slapping her thighs. The Shadows were looking around for the man's soul. They didn't realize what had happened. Marie tried to concentrate about what to do about this, but she was so dazed that it was just a passing thought. It made her head hurt to think about it. The fog in her mind was numbing. She went back to the floor of stone where she had been for days and sat down.

One of the Shadows stepped up to Hester and timidly asked, "Madam Hester, do you need the girl now? Now that you have this power. It's tiring fighting her natural repulsively joyful nature. Why don't you just be done with her, blast her to bits?"

"You idiot! Don't you see? Her body is still alive! I will blast her to bits but not until I'm ready to take her body and have my chance again. I will have my chance! Tom and Jenny stole my dreams away, but now they and all their offspring will pay for my pain. And through their sweet Marie, I will have the life they stole. Imagine what I can do! I have over 200 years of experiences to draw on, including my powers, but I will do it with the life and body of a 19- year-old! I'll take the world by storm."

"Besides," she continued, "I need Marie's power for just a few more things until I am mortal again. Now, I've got some obliterating to do. Let's start with Marie's father." "Oh Marie, dear?" Hester rang out. "Marie? Come dear, we have work to do!" She came around the corner and grabbed Marie by the arm and flashed out.

The Shadow watched them go and then turned to the Shadow next to him, "Do you think anyone will notice the change in Marie's joyful personality when Hester does all that? I mean, Hester is not a barrel of monkeys, and she would be the last person to notice a pretty sunset." The other Shadow just shrugged.
***

Ben, Henry, Jenny, and Tom flashed to Bill and Nancy's house in Southern California. They stood in the living room of the ocean front beach house. It was a two-story home over a garage. The living room had one wall that was all glass overlooking the ocean. It opened onto a wide balcony with chairs and a table. The door was open, and the screen door wavered in wind as it blew in off the water. The rushing white noise of breaking waves filled their ears.

Bill was asleep in a brown leather chair by the window, a cream-colored wool blanket with wide stripes was draped over his lap. His Protector, a woman in a Victorian blouse and long floor-length skirt stood beside him watching the intruders. Her soft brown hair was pulled up in a loose bun on the top of her head. She was very beautiful with porcelain skin and delicate features.

"Good day," she nodded as she spoke with a slight

German accent.

Tom, ever the captain, strode forward and took her hand and kissed the top of it. "Good day, my dear Marguerite. So good to see you again. We are looking for a gold watch that belongs to Nancy."

"As you please, Captain Helm. You won't trouble me." "Would you happen to know of its whereabouts?" Tom

asked.

"Nien. The lady moves it frequently. I can't keep up.

Perhaps Lucinda would know, but, alas, they are not here." "No problem. We'll just be about our business. Thank

you." Tom bowed slightly and turned toward Henry.

Marguerite turned her gaze toward the ocean waves.

"Okay," said Henry, "we need to find the watch. Jenny, you go the bedroom and look through Nancy's things. Tom, you search in here. Ben and I will go through closets."

They split up and used their ability to pass through physical objects to search without touching anything.

Tom passed his head through a bookcase and could look inside every book for one with a false inside compartment. He searched through cabinets the same way.

Jenny walked inside the chest of drawers and peered into them. Due to the density of the contents, it took some time to search every nook and cranny.

Henry went into the walk-in closet. There were several boxes and packages stacked neatly on the shelves. Clothing hung on a rod on the other side of the closet. A shelf for hats and purses was above the clothes and was full of items. He located a large wood jewelry box that was inlaid with wood pieces of various colors. He plunged his head into the space inside the box to look. There were several jewelry pieces, but he did not see the watch. He continued to search.

They all searched for quite a while and could find nothing. They wandered out onto the balcony feeling dejected.

"I can't imagine where else it could be. We searched everywhere," said Ben.

Jenny added, "Maybe Nancy is wearing it?"

"I could flash to Nancy and ask Lucinda. That's all I can figure," suggested Henry.

"Okay, Henry. Do that. We will wait here." Said Tom. A bright light consumed Henry and he was gone. In just a minute or two, the reverse happened. A bright light appeared and seemed to expel Henry.

"Lucinda said the last time she saw it, Nancy hid it in a shoe. A lady's dress shoe." They all headed for the walk-in closet and walked right through the walls. There were several shoe boxes stacked neatly on a shelf. There were shoes in a plastic hanging shoe keeper with pockets where shoes were tucked. Then there were several pairs of shoes on the floor at the end of the closet that looked as though they had been tried on and cast aside.

They split up and started searching shoes by looking into them, passing their heads through boxes and shoes alike. They stopped when they heard a noise in the living room. A scream. It was Marguerite!

27 - SARAH ELIZABETH'S WATCH

The four of them stood motionless in the closet. Henry looked at Tom and said, "It's got to be Hester. You and I will go out there and help Marguerite." He looked at Jenny and Ben, "You two keep looking. The watch is the only thing that can save us." They all nodded, and Tom and Henry darted through the bedroom wall.

In the living room, Hester was hovering over Marguerite who was writhing on the floor trying to fight off the spell. Marie was standing beside Hester in her trance, droopy eyed and expressionless. Hester was reciting her incantation with a horrible grin on her face.

"Marie! Remember your anger! Throw it at her. They took Allen away from you!"

Marie looked at Marguerite with apathy. A tear rolled down her cheek for Allen.

"Yes, that's it, Marie! Remember how it used to be when you were happy, and they all stole it from you! Now give her your anger! They stole your Allen!"

Hester growled.

Marie's face changed to a sadistic scowl, and she raised her arms to focus the blast at the young woman lying on the ground.

Henry lunged forward and placed himself between Marie and Marguerite. Marie's expression changed to one of confusion.

"You idiot!" Hester blasted at Marie. "Destroy them!"

Tom joined Henry and the four of them began attacking, sending waves of positive and negative energy at each other. Marguerite was able to regain her composure and joined the fight. Bill slept peacefully in the chair completely unaware of the war raging around him. The rolling white noise of the waves crashing down on the beach were like a lullaby. Seagulls swooped and turned silently on the breeze. It was a perfect afternoon for a nap.

Beside Bill, both Tom and Henry were throwing waves of blasts at Hester. Any ordinary Shadow would be fleeing already, but she was easily deflecting them. Marguerite, her long skirt swishing around her ankles, was working on Marie with enough success to make it a tie of volleys.

Outside a Shadow that was creeping along the balcony formed into a young man with wild hair and glazed eyes. He inched toward Bill, trying not to be seen by anyone in the room, and whispered to Bill to wake up. Bill stirred, blinked sleepily, and looked around. The room was quiet, and the sea breeze softly caressed his cheek and ruffled his blond hair.

"Call Nancy and tell her how unfair it is that you are here alone working. She sits idly while you toil. There is no need for her to be there and you are here. She is being selfish. You deserve better than this!" The Shadow hissed in his ear while the commotion raged on. The air around Bill wavered as the evil forces permeated him but he saw nothing. The room was still and hollow, not a soul to share his thoughts with. He furrowed his brow and let the feeling sink in.

Bill became agitated and started sighing and shifting his weight in his chair. He sprang up and stomped over to the phone hanging on the kitchen wall and began to dial Marie's room at the hospital. Nancy picked up and you could hear her talking on the other end of the line.

"Hello? Bill? Is that you? Are you okay?"

"No!" he yelled. "Now you are going to come home this minute. There are bills to pay and I am here with all of this on my back. You could be working, too, you know! Marie is fine with the nurses. You come home now, and I mean it!"

"Bill? This isn't like you. What's going on?" Nancy said. "You heard me! I said come home now!" With that he hung up the phone without waiting for a response. He walked into the bedroom fuming. Jenny and Ben were still searching the closet when they saw him stomp into the room with a scowl. The Shadow was still on his trail whispering lies about Nancy.

Bill opened a door on the front of the night table next to the bed. Inside was a shoe box with a pink ribbon tying it closed. Bill tore off the ribbon and threw it on the floor. He swiped at the lid, and it went flying. Inside, wrapped in white tissue paper was a pair of antique slippers. Bill tore off the tissue and let the box fall, holding both slippers with one hand. He opened the drawer next to the bed and pulled out a pair of scissors and started cutting the slippers into shreds. The antique satin material easily gave way to the scissors demands. As he turned them in his hand, the gold watch fell from inside one of them. It hit the carpet, snapped open, bounced under the bed, unnoticed by Bill, whose eyes looked nearly catatonic. He continued to cut the slippers into tiny pieces. Satin and sequins littered the floor on Nancy's side of the bed.

Jenny saw all this happening and her mouth fell open. Bill was generally a very happy, easy-going person. He loved Nancy with all his heart and would never do anything to make her sad. This was not like him at all. Then Jenny saw a gleam of golden light bounce under the edge of the

bedspread on the floor with a gold chain following it like the leash on a lost dog. It silently bounced under the bedcover and out of sight. She flashed across the room and under the bed. There it was.

A glow of gold reflected from the edge. It was etched in thin delicate lines into a graceful pattern of swirls and rosettes. A heavy chain looped through the ribbed pin's link. When it fell, the pin was pressed, and it had snapped open to reveal a white clock face with raised gold numbers. The delicate black minute and hour hand unaffectedly showed the world it was 5:25.

Seeing her lunge, Ben joined Jenny under the bed as they tried to latch onto the energy imbued in the watch to be able to pick it up. Without mortal bodies, energy was all they had.

The yelling and grunting continued in the living room. Bill moved into the closet and began to pull out Nancy's dresses. He cut them into long thin shreds and let the shreds fall to the floor in a colorful heap. The Shadow was delighted smiling his sick smile and clasping his hands together. He continued whispering in Bill's ear.

"Let's both focus a blast into the watch and see if that

does anything. Okay?" said Ben.

"Okay," said Jenny. "One, two, three!" They both concentrated a ray of emotional energy into the pocket watch. At first nothing happened, but then it was as if the energy overflowed the object and poured onto the floor below it, raising it up like a toy boat in a bathtub. It floated.

In a detached, methodical way, trying not to change the energy flow, Ben said, "Okay, let's try to push it out from under the bed." A resonating sound filled the air, like the vibration on a small bell but it didn't quietly dissipate. Instead, the sound seemed to grow in intensity. They moved it by the force of their will with the positive energy into the center of the room and about 3 feet off the ground. The sound of the ringing grew even louder.

Jenny and Ben were concentrating so hard, they did not

notice another soul flash next to them. A short, charming girl with pale blond curls and bright blue eyes crinkled in a perpetual friendly smile. She wore a calico print prairie dress with little blue and white flowers dotting the design. She smiled when she saw the watch.

"Well, looky here! Like a beacon, it called me with the ringing," she stepped closer to it as it floated in the air. "Who're y'all?" she batted her eyelashes and looked at them like unexpected company had arrived on her porch. Jenny managed to split her concentration two ways to keep the watch afloat and sneak side glances at the newcomer.

"I'm Jenny Pope and this fella is Ben. We are trying to get this watch in the other room to use it to defeat one crazy Shadow and release my granddaughter who is still a live one. Makes sense? That's the quick version." And then she added, "And who might you be?"

"Well, I'm Sarah Elizabeth and that is my watch. It called to me."

"Well, doggone, sugar! You're my grandbaby, too!" excitedly added Jenny. "Help us out here and blast some power into the watch."

"What? Oh, yes!" Sarah Elizabeth added her contribution and the watch steadied. The ringing got louder. The watch began to cast a golden glow around it. At the point when it seemed deafening, a sonic burst erupted from the watch and escaped outward in a sphere of golden light. The Shadow that had been tormenting Bill was knocked down. Within a few seconds, it gathered its wits and disappeared.

Bill looked around the closet, turning this way and that and looking at his hands. He vaguely recalled cutting up the dresses and but could not understand why. He turned and saw the slippers in tiny pieces on the carpet. He froze and a horrified expression covered his face. He fell to his knees and carefully scooped up the pile of shredded fabric. "Nancy had cherished these. She'll be heart-broken," he choked out.

"Wow! Did you see that?" asked Ben.

"Yeah!" said Sarah amazed, not paying any attention to Bill. "How did you all figure this out?"

"It was Henry! He is smart, that boy!" said Jenny.

Out in the living room, Hester was gaining ground. Marie had Marguerite and Tom nearly subdued in a crouch on the floor. Her power of destruction as a Live One gave her an upper hand. It was just enough for Hester to hold back Henry with one hand and start her incantation at the same time.

Mon frère, mon foe. Your forever is gone.
I will be here, but you, not so. Sempiternal

As Hester spoke her spell, Marie could hear, far, far away, Allen praying for her. His pleading, weeping voice carried over time and space like a messenger searching for her. The far-away melancholy grief was like a beacon.

"Please, Marie. Be strong.
Come back to me. I'm waiting for you.
I love you more than anything.
We have a life together. Don't give up."

Marie turned to Hester as he said the last three words, her face nearly ashen with horror when she realized it was all a lie. She turned her fury toward Hester. All the white- hot energy of emotion she felt welled inside her like a bubbling volcano. Marie stretched out her left arm toward Hester and, with all her mind could focus, she released that white wave of fury down her arm and released it.

Instead of tearing apart Henry, as Hester had planned, a horrific ripping sound like fabric pulled apart with your bare hands filled the air. Hester was jolted out of her

confident reverie by the turn of events. She realized Marie was much more powerful than she had imagined. They all, Henry, Tom, Marguerite, and Hester, looked around wildly for the source of the sound. A black seam whose center looked to be laced lightening appeared in the air in the middle of the room and began to tear open. The torn edges of reality were flapping like flames of fire. There was a whooshing noise as though the very air in the house was being sucked inside the seam. It widened and they could all feel the pull coming from it. The nothingness inside the rip created a vacuum force that would devour anything close to it.

Tom lunged at Marie to protect her from being pulled in. Henry was the closest to it and, unable to brace himself was pulled inside the void and disappeared. Marguerite had been behind Hester who was losing her footing. Marguerite gracefully lifted her tiny foot and set it squarely on Hester's backside and gave it a shove. Hester screamed and disappeared inside the rip.

Jenny, Ben, and Sarah came in with the watch hanging in the air between them. Its ringing was the only thing louder than the hurricane wind sucking into the rift. Tom looked up to see where the ringing sound was coming from.

"Tom! Help us!" said Jenny. Tom added a blast of energy to the watch. The glowing antique watch made a deafening sound. It was like vibrating glass ringing under your fingertip as you rubbed across the opening of a crystal goblet, only so loud no other sound could now be heard in the room. Marguerite and Marie looked on in awe as they tried to not be carried into the rift.

The ringing reaching a deafening pitch before another sonic boom exploded in the room. The sphere of golden glow expanded, covering everyone and everything.

The rift sealed closed, and Marie fell limp in Tom's
arms. It was over. Hester was gone, but so was Henry.

PART THREE

28 - FREE, BUT LOST

They all collapsed in each other's arms.

"Oh, Tom. We have lost him again. It's happened all over again," Jenny wept. Tom held her and shed a tear as well. His face grimaced and his body hunched. Jenny let out a quiet sob.

"Tom, Jenny. Ben!" Marie started to wake up from the long trance. She looked around. "This is my parent's house!" She got up and ran into the bedroom looking for her mom and dad. Her father was sitting on the side of the bed, still grimacing, holding strips of cut cloth and bits of silk and sequins.

Marie sat by him, but he couldn't see her. "Oh, Daddy!" Tears ran down her cheeks. "I miss you so much. I wish I could just hug you one more time. It'll be okay. It's just stuff." Marie looked around the room. She felt like she had been gone for a very long time. Not just from home, but from everything. The trance Hester had her in was a prison, but now she was free. She felt stronger than she ever had. So much made sense now. All those times when she felt like she wasn't alone growing up, all the times she thought had been serendipitous good fortune, it wasn't just luck or intuition. There was a deep connection between real life and this other world. Now she knew the living have an incredible ability to influence the battle between good and evil and they don't even know it.

Allen's prayer reached her all the way into the time and space between life and the afterlife. Together they defeated Hester: a formidable enemy that wanted to destroy lives and souls with wild abandon. Marie remembered the look on Hester's face just before the rift opened. She had looked right at her. She looked... surprised. Yes, she was surprised, Marie thought. She didn't expect me to be that strong. Hester had spent over 200 years practicing her powers to crush the dreams of those she hated. Marie was a teenager. Nineteen years old and, with the power of love, had surprised old Hester Farr. Marie felt a surge of euphoria. She felt like she could do anything! She stood up and stretched and twirled around the room. It felt so good to be free from the depression and Hester forcing her to do horrible things to people.

She stopped spinning and thought for a minute. Why had Hester been able to force her to do that? She knew she could easily fight off Hester now. What had changed? The only difference she could think of was that she knew it now. She had been unaware before.

"Knowledge really is power!" Marie thought out loud. Like a baby elephant taught she didn't have the strength to break free, she had lived chained up by her own lack of understanding. Before she had been pulled into the other world, she had no idea and bumped weakly through the universe amusing herself. But now, now her eyes were opened to what was most important and how much power is at our fingertips to protect and love.

Bill stood up after gathering all the pieces on the

floor. He put them in the box and sat back on the bed. Tears pooled in his eyes. "How can I fix this? I can't repair them. She loved them."

Marie sat down beside him. "Dad, she loved them because you got them for her. She loved them because they helped her dream that maybe once a young lady wore them in a ballroom in a beautiful gown as a man like yourself waltzed her around in circles as they fell madly in love and nothing else mattered. It's not just these slippers. It's the dream of chivalrous love. It's the daydream of you loving her that matters to her. You and mom are what matters. You all, and Allen." She paused while Bill sat crying hearing none of her words. "Allen! I must see Allen!"

She got up and ran back into the other room. The memories of what happened while she was in the trance were surfacing in her mind at lightning speed.

Sarah Elizabeth was helping Marguerite get her strength back. They used the watch to fill the space with golden light and heal their depleted strength.

"The watch!" Marie said.

Sarah Elizabeth stepped up. "Yes, honey, my watch has touched us all through so many generations. The love and connection we feel is transferred through it and back out again stronger."

"You're Sarah Elizabeth? I have always admired you. You know we talk about you and how true to your heart you were." said Marie.

Sarah laughed a tinkling laugh like little bells. "Oh, my honey, I didn't do anything worth admiring. You just must stay true to who you are. Live with your heart. Listen to your head but live with your heart. It's not always easy, but there's no other way to find true joy."

"Sarah showed up just in time and helped snap you out of that trance Hester had you in. You were quite the charmer a few minutes ago," Tom said making a scowl.

"I'm so sorry. I didn't want to do what she had me do. She told me she would kill Allen if I didn't follow her. She did something to me. I could feel all her emotions, and it was so overwhelming. Then I was powerless to even think." Marie felt so bad.

"It's okay, Marie. That Hester was one mean soul," said Jenny. "Now my Henry is gone again. Oh, I'll miss him."

"What? No! Hester was using that spell to kill souls, not just bodies." Marie said sadly. "What can we do?"

"I need to talk to Lorenzo about all this. Jenny, you come, too," said Tom.

"I have to see Allen. Ben, will you take me?" asked Marie. "Sure, Marie. You're my job." Ben said as he hugged Tom and Jenny.

"Yes, Marie, go to Allen. Follow your heart and you'll be free. Remember that the love will save you. I need to go now," Sarah Elizabeth said.

"I've heard that," Marie said remembering the lady at the incense shop. Marie saw the watch laying on the ground and reached down and picked it up. They all stared at her. It made no sense; she should not have been able to move an object. It was clear she was caught in both worlds.

"It must be because she is still a Live One," said Jenny. "Or maybe she is truly different. Put it on, Marie. Keep it with you. It will protect you if you need it again." Marie opened the loop of chain and ducked her head through. The gold pocket watch glimmered in the light as the sun set over the ocean horizon. Bill had ambled in and was now sitting in the brown chair again. He thought he saw something twinkle in the air, but decided he must be seeing a

230

reflection from outside. He looked out the window searching for the source of the reflection. Not seeing anything, he shrugged and got up. He inspected the air where he saw the glimmer, paused, and then shoving his

fists deep in his pockets, shuffled toward the phone.

After dialing, he sighed and leaned against the wall while it rang. "Hello? Allen is Nancy there?" Then he paused waiting, "Nancy? I just want to say I'm so sorry."

Jenny had seen Bill notice the twinkle of light. "I think the watch has crossed over into our world. It's as though it's invisible to Bill." Her eyebrows furrowed as she tried

to figure out how this could happen. "Marie, you are a horse of a different color. You are here and you shouldn't be. The watch seems to float between both worlds around you. And you can throw a love zap like nobody's business! I can't explain how you do it, but I'm sure proud of you, baby girl!"

Marie hugged Sarah Elizabeth before she flashed away. Then she hugged Jenny and smiled. "I love you, Grandma Jenny." She took hold of Ben's arm, and a silent flash of light carried them all away.

***

"I just don't understand what got into Bill. It really wasn't like him. Maybe all this stress is more than we realize." Nancy was saying to Allen. They were sitting in Marie's hospital room.

"It is hard. I tried doing like Jasmina said. I prayed for Marie, but it seemed so silly. How can a few mumbled words change anything?" Allen shook his head.

"It probably did more good than you know, Allen. Just keep trying. We must keep trying for Marie's sake."

The phone rang. Allen got up to answer it. "Oh, hello, Mr. St. Clair. Yes, sir. She is right here." He stretched the long, tangled phone cord across the room and handed the receiver to Nancy. Nancy smirked as she took it.

Allen went out into the hallway to sit in a waiting area to give them some privacy. His parents had left the day before. They were content that he was recovering well and should be fine. It had been as comforting for Allen to see them as it was for them to see him.

He found a padded bench near a window. The hospital was busy with nurses bustling through the hallway and patients' families coming and going. Some were on pay phones in corners, some were crying quietly, others were pretending to be cheerful. Hospitals are not normal life. It's where life lands when it's turned upside down. It's where you need help just to live, where family clings to hope and each other. You try to act like everything is still normal, so you don't scare anyone because you really want to scream and knock holes in the walls. That won't fix it, though, so you pretend that everything will be fine and try not to lose your mind. Maybe in the quiet of the night you can secretly lose your mind and hope to pull yourself back together before morning.

Allen turned from the people in the hall and stared absently out the window. It was a beautiful June evening. Clear azure skies so blue it nearly hurt his eyes stretched as far as he could see. The sun was just getting low in the western sky making a smear of peachy red on the horizon. The rich green pines and bright new leaves of the oaks waved gently in the mountain breeze. He closed his eyes and imagined he and Marie were hiking somewhere right now and all of this was a bad dream. He could feel the cool air on his face and her laughter as she prattled on about a ludicrous dream she had. A perfect world where things were black and white, there were no lost souls or comas, and they were only concerned about what they might have for lunch. How had things changed so much? How had they been so blind before?

Even though his mind fought him with logic, he was determined to do anything for Marie he could and, right now, that meant praying. He wasn't sure to what or to whom he was praying. He certainly wasn't sure if anyone or anything heard those prayers. All he knew was that was all he had to save her. Part of him believed it would help, a very small, childlike part that believed we really did have a purpose here other than amusing ourselves and deciding lunch possibilities. He knew one thing, he loved Marie, and that made anything possible.

He glanced around to see if anyone was watching and then discreetly bowed his head. Someone might have thought he was dozing.

Quietly so no one near could hear, he prayed, "Marie if you can hear me, listen. I'm here waiting for you. I'll wait forever.

Don't be afraid. I don't know what it's like for you there, but you belong here. You must get back to your body and wake up. I love you. We love you, your mom and dad and me. Even my parents. Find a way, Marie. Find help. Maybe there is someone or something that can help you. Please don't give up. I love you."

29 - WHERE DO I BELONG?

Marie and Ben appeared in Allen's old dorm room. She sucked in a breath as she saw it was empty, deserted. The furniture had been stacked in the corner of the dining area so the maintenance people could shampoo the carpets. The kitchen was bare. No dishes drying on the counter like always. She walked quickly to the bedroom and peered inside. The bed, bare and dismantled, and the wardrobe were pushed to one side. Realizing for certain now he was gone, she walked to the window and looked at the tops of the pines rolling like ocean swells with the breeze moving over them. Loneliness crept up on her and she felt frozen. Her fear of losing him was second only to Hester destroying him.

"He's gone," she choked on the words. "Hester was right. He went on without me." A tear formed in the corner of her eye. She wiped it away before it could fill enough to fall. She turned back to where the bed had been. The last place she had touched him. She remembered tousling his hair in the middle of the night. How precious it was to just be physically next to him, touch him, to feel the warmth of his body from sleep. What would she do now without him? What if she was doomed to forever float alone in this time between worlds. Not alive and not dead.

She felt the weight of the watch hanging from her neck and clasped her right hand around it. She could feel it as a physical object. It felt cool. She had no body to warm it as it hung against her chest. It felt just as though she'd pulled it out of a drawer, the cold metal pressing into her invisible hand. It glowed a soft radiant light even now. She pressed the pin and the cover opened. Tiny, delicate hands floated over an ivory face with roman numerals. She closed the cover and turned it over. There was another side that opened. It was a locket place where you could put a picture or have an inscription. Marie wondered if Sarah Elizabeth once had a picture there of the man she loved.

What would Sarah have done if she had been pulled out of life like this? What if she lost the one person for whom it was worth risking everything? The watch glowed a bit brighter, as if it were hoping to tell Marie something. She traced her finger over some scratches inside the locket compartment. It was not an inscription that a jeweler would make. There were scratches in the gold that looked like letters. They had been worn down as though they had been touched repeatedly. Marie squinted and, holding the watch up close to her eyes, tried to make out what it said.

Love gives life.

Sarah must have written it. She would not have had the money to have a jeweler inscribe it. Marie stared out the window pondering this thought. It was a nice thought, even if a bit pithy. It was something you would see painted on a plate and hung in a kitchen. It was so obvious that it was meaningless.

"But," Marie thought, "that's it. That's the power!'" This watch had an ability to focus power. It wasn't just any power. It didn't help Hester. It was love. Only the power of love in a person's heart seemed to set it in action.

Marie had watched so many things unfold in front of her the past few months. There were clear examples of a tangible consequence of showing love or showing hate.

Hate was a big word for what Hester did, but that was what it was. She had twisted her desire for love into a desire for revenge because, without the love, she was open to hate. Hester had used Marie's fear to change her, to make her tap into hate, to cause pain.

There may have been hope for Hester before she entertained her bitterness, but afterward, when she was only comforted by her own self-pity, love was gone. The lesser satisfaction of revenge was all she could hope for.

Sarah had said to 'follow your heart' but what if your heart's desire is gone? What could Hester have done to find joy when Tom was not going to love her? Marie wondered what she would do if Allen was gone. Is love something you must give away to find life? Or is the greater calling to let love from your heart overflow onto everything you touch without a care who receives it? Can you find life, even alone in a nowhere land between life and death, by just letting love overflow your heart, filling the world from you outward? It is not self-love, nor is it love for others. It is choosing to be a wellspring of love, a conduit for the power of that love to be released on the world.

Tired though she was, she knew she must try. There were things in her life from which she could gather strength: her relationships and her sense of wonder for nature. She closed her eyes and let these things fill her mind. A peaceful contentedness covered her. Like a looping mathematical formula that multiplies, returns, and multiplies again, ever repeating and increasing, Marie could feel the fatigue washing away as the peace increased in the inverse relationship. The antique watch in her hand vibrated and hummed. The golden light radiated out and filled a sphere of space that encompassed Marie. The soft ringing filled the air in a stellar message calling out for anyone to hear and take notice. Marie knew that no matter what happened to her, whether Allen had moved on or not, she was okay. She didn't know what the future held, but she would turn her face toward it, and it would be good. Goodness would be there. She owned that belief.

Ben came up behind her, "He is surely somewhere nearby. We'll find him."

She looked out at the pines. She thought about what he must have had to go through all this time with her in the hospital. She imagined him alone and sad. She could almost imagine she heard him whisper to her.

"Did you hear that?" she asked Ben.

"No. I don't hear anything," he said looking out the

window thinking she must have heard someone outside.

She stood very still and closed her eyes.

Marie, if you can hear me, listen. I'm here waiting for you. I'll wait forever. Don't be afraid. I don't know what it's like for you there, but you belong here. You must get back to your body and wake up. I love you. We love you, your mom and dad and I, even my parents. Find a way, Marie. Find help. Maybe there is someone that can help you. Please don't give up. I love you.

She cried tears of joy. Her heart leapt. "Ben! We

237

must find him! I heard him! He was talking to me! He loves me."

Ben smiled. He knew the precious joy of being remembered. "That's awesome! Sometimes I hear my mom. Every once in a while, she whispers, she says, 'I haven't forgotten you, precious child.' It gives me hope."

"Yes! Hope!" Marie said. "What a gift!" then she paused and tilted her head. "He is close. Maybe he is at the hospital. Let's go." She grabbed his hand and they flashed to her hospital room.

"Hi Lucinda! Nice to see you again." Marie said to Lucinda who was busily whispering in Nancy's ear. She waved a distracted 'hello' at Marie.

Nancy was having an agitated discussion with someone on the phone, whom Marie realized quickly was her father.

They had had some sort of misunderstanding. Marie looked at her empty body on the bed. Her hair was brushed and pulled into a neat ponytail on one side over her shoulder and secured with a pink ribbon. Her mother's work, she assumed. How awful this must be for her, she thought. Gratitude welled in her for the care her mother had taken in sitting with her.

"Bill! I just don't understand you anymore. One minute you're ranting like a crazy man and the next you are crying. Neither makes any sense. Are you sick? Do you have a fever? Poor Allen has been listening to me..." Nancy trailed off and Marie remembered she was looking for Allen and walked straight through her mother and the wall behind her, looking this way and then the other for Allen. "Wasn't there a waiting room near here, Ben?"

"Uh, yes. This way I think," he motioned to the left. They walked right through nurses, visitors, and crash carts. Marie was getting the hang of not having a body. For just a minute she entertained the thought of her running into people and walls if she ever got her life back and how she would have to get re-accustomed to being a solid object.

They came to a wide spot in the hall and saw Jacob sitting next to Allen on a bench. Both were looking out the window. Jacob looked up and acknowledged them.

Twisting around to see them better, Jacob called, "Hey, look who's back from Zombie World!"

"Funny." Marie said deadpan. "So, how's my fella, here?" Marie came around in front of Allen and knelt down in front of him. They were nearly eye to eye. She gave him invisible kisses on his cheek, relieved that he hadn't moved on like Hester said. She closed her eyes and wished for any physical reminder of him like the feel of his breath on her cheek, the warmth of his body, the smell of his skin, but there was nothing. In her world now, there was no sensory input other than sight. Everything that gave her joy in the real world was missing in this half world.

"This just sucks! I am so angry!" she huffed. "I hate this. How am I going to get back to my body and my life? How on earth did this happen anyway?" Marie sat crossed legged on the floor with her face in her hands dealing with escalating feelings of love and anger. The watch hanging from her neck started glowing.

"You're here, aren't you, Marie?" Everyone, including Marie looked at Allen.

"He can feel your presence, Marie." Jacob said in an astounded whisper.

"I can tell." Sucking in his breath, he straightened and searched the air with his eyes. "It's been a while since I felt you nearby. I was worried. Worried you were gone forever. Worried," he paused and slumped, "that you were- just gone." A tear streamed from his eye and fell on his knee as stifled a sob. He sniffed and wiped his cheek with his ring and pinky finger. "God, Marie, I don't know what I'd do if you never came back."

"It's okay, Allen. I love you. It'll be okay." Marie said, knowing he couldn't hear, but at least maybe he could feel her presence. The watch dangled on the chain and started the low continuous ringing. Marie looked down and could see it begin to glow the golden light. Jacob and Ben were looking too.

"Have you ever seen anything like that, Jacob? It must be the combined emotions Marie and Allen are sharing." said Ben. "It's like back at your parents' house, Marie!"

Marie interrupted, "It was doing it at the dorm, too. I wonder if it could always do this, but no one in the living world could see it."

"Possibly but wouldn't Tom or Lucinda or somebody else have noticed?" said Jacob. "Henry knew you could use objects to focus energy. Maybe all this happening has strengthened the watch's ability to be a channel."

Allen heard a faint ringing sound in front of him and fixed his gaze on the empty space between him and window. The ringing was like the ringing in your ears after a loud concert. He thought he could see a golden twinkle of light appearing about two feet in front of him. He gazed at it curiously. Then for a fleeting instant, he could make out Marie, sitting cross-legged on the carpet. His eyes opened widely, and he rubbed them, thinking surely he was seeing things. He smiled a broad smile of joy. Marie did also. She knew he could see her.

It was going to be okay. They could figure this out. She knew it and thought surely Allen must know it, too.

The ringing faded and Allen glanced around suddenly self-aware. People would think he looked crazy smiling giddily at the carpet all alone. Her image faded and he stood up and strode back to Marie's room. "I have to tell Nancy that Marie is okay."

"Wow! That is incredible!" Jacob said. Ben turned to

look him up and down.

"You? Mr. I-Have-Seen-it-All-and-Nothing-Surprises- Me?" mocked Ben. They both got up and followed Allen. Marie sat here a minute thinking about how crazy this all was, but she couldn't help but feel like it was going to be okay. No matter what happened, she was going to be okay.

30   - WHAT COMES AROUND, GOES AROUND

Allen opened the door to Marie's hospital room and stepped in. Nancy was off the phone, but clearly distracted by the conversation she'd had with Bill. She sat in the chair with her back ramrod straight. Her hand was balled up in a fist and propping up her chin with her elbow on the arm of the chair. She looked like she might leap from the chair at any moment.

"Hi, Nancy? What's new?" Allen asked to feel out her

mood.

She gave a harrumph and a sigh and looked at him before speaking, "What has become of the world? Is it just me or are people really losing their minds?"

He was careful to think about his words, knowing what he had to tell her clearly fell into to the category of people losing their mind. "Well, the news did say there has been a lot of bizarre behavior everywhere."

She sighed again and then said, "Evidently Bill lost his mind and cut up several of my dresses and an antique pair of slippers I had. That was after he'd called and was irate because I was here. He seems fine now and really has no explanation. He's fretted about it all night and is very sorry and upset about it." She sighed, "It's hard to be mad at him when he is just as upset about it as I am."

"Hm. Well," Allen was out of his league here and really didn't want to be in this conversation at all. "So, guess what? You'll never believe this?" He hoped to just change the subject.

"Well, I just might after what I just heard on the phone. I might believe anything!"

"Yeah," he paused unsure if now was a good time to throw a real crazy curve ball at her, "Well, I was praying, you know, like Jasmina said." Allen felt like such an idiot for what he was about to say. He imagined himself hearing this from someone else and thinking they must have been on drugs or some zealot.

"Yeah, go on," Nancy prodded.

"Well-, I was praying and, you know talking, like talking to Marie, and, well, I could swear I felt her near me... out there in the waiting room." He thought this was a safe place to start and waited for her reaction.

Allen could tell she switched gears in her mind as she considered this. She shifted her body toward him and pursed her lips in concentration. She looked at Marie in the bed and then back at him. Nancy answered, "Well, we had both agreed we felt that before. So that's good. Is that it?" She had to ask that.

"Nooo," he stretched that out as long as feasible before adding the next part. "I think I could see her for a minute. Her, her spirit. Sitting on the ground in front of me. Just for a second. She smiled at me, too." He held his breath waiting for her reaction this time.

Nancy just looked at him without reacting visibly.

She sat motionless and Allen couldn't tell what she was thinking. Then she tilted her head slightly, still staring at him. "Hm. And you didn't take any of your pain pills this morning?"

He laughed and broke the tension, "No. Seriously. I'm not prone to seeing ghosts or unicorns or anything like that. But I know it was her. We must keep trying."

She settled back in her chair and breathed slowly, "Well. I guess I'm jealous then." She glared at him sarcastically.

He laughed at that and released a long-held breath. "It's weird, she was wearing a necklace I had never seen before. Actually," he paused to remember, "It was a watch on a chain. An old looking watch, like an antique. I noticed because it was- it was glowing."

Nancy's face turned pale as a sheet, and she stared at Allen. After a second, she said, "A what? Did you say a watch? What kind of a watch?"

"Yes. It was a regular pocket watch kind of watch. You know, like people had before wrist watches. It was hard to see it clearly because it was glowing. I saw it, or actually a bright little spot of light, before I saw her."

"Hold on! My watch, I mean, Sarah Elizabeth's watch! It was in one of the shoes that Bill cut up! Let me call him!" She got up and crossed the room to call Bill.

***

Allen sat back in the chair trying to remember anything else. While Nancy was talking excitedly to Bill, totally forgetting her irritation from before, the Protectors were standing around watching like it was a television show unfolding before them. They all jumped in surprise when a loud ripping sound was heard. It was the same sound Marie heard back at her parents. A blinding white line appeared in the air in front of them and the ripping noise grew louder as the light parted into two lines with a black emptiness in between.

While Allen sat there oblivious to anything out of the ordinary, and Nancy chattered away on the phone giving Bill directions to look in different places, the Protectors jumped up and readied themselves for whatever this might be. It was another rift opening. The white line separated into two lines to form an ellipse which continued to widen until, as they gasped in horror, Hester appeared inside the opening and then fell into the room. Henry came through behind her as though washed by a tidal wave. They both landed on the ground and the rift sealed and disappeared with a sound not unlike water being sucked down a drain. The stunned Protectors simultaneously smiled to see Henry and had wide horrified eyes at seeing Hester again. Tom reached for Henry's hand and pulled him up and behind him. Hester took a moment to collect herself and understand where she was. Marie, who had at least felt safe when she thought Hester was gone forever, would have fainted if she breathed air.

Hester, now on her feet started laughing at the absurdity of it all. "Thought I was a goner, huh? Guess I'm not getting any deader!" She looked at Allen in the chair and walked over to him, mockingly caressing his cheek. She sat back in his lap, occupying the same space. He had no reaction at all since he could not see her.

"Get away from him!" Marie yelled with authority.

"Oh, now. I'll take good care of pretty boy. He'll be so happy to see me, or you, that is, when I have your body! Maybe we should just get right down to business." Hester stood up and moved away from Allen, taking a step toward Marie. "With your soul gone, your carcass over there will be free for the taking and guess who wants a do-over?"

"You're crazy. Oh my God! He'll never love you! Isn't that what you really want? Do you really think he won't know it's not me? He'll never love you!"

"Good grief, no! Men are all the same! Bunch of slugs after one thing. He doesn't care about your soul. He just wants something to squeeze at night." Hester spat. "Stop being such a ninny, little girl!" Hester's crazy red hair flew around her face as she jerked her head from Marie to Allen and back.

Marie could see in her eyes, deep behind the evil, there was a little girl who'd been terribly abused and whose dreams of love had been torn to shreds by the evil of others. Just for a minute, Marie felt pity, wishing she could go back in time and rescue that little red-headed freckled girl with sad green eyes.

But it was too late for Hester. Choices had been made too many times taking her farther and farther from the innocent girl she had been on that auction block, sold as an indentured servant to a man who also had made too many wrong choices.

Marie spoke in a controlled tone, "You're wrong, Hester. I wish things had been different for you, but you can't have Allen. Your time is done! And you can't have me, either! I love him and he loves me. No one will keep us apart." Marie stood her ground. Tom and Jenny appeared with Lorenzo behind her.

Tom smiled and said, "Sarah Elizabeth would be proud!"

Lorenzo stepped forward, "Hester, please let me help you."

"You?" She looked him up and down as though it had been a long time since she had seen him. "And where were you all this time? Where were you when I was little? Where were you when no one wanted me? I have no use for you." Hester spat.

She turned to Allen again and put her arm mockingly around his shoulders. Allen felt a chill and convulsed spontaneously. That was it for Marie. She felt the power rise in her. The white ethereal glow of love surrounded her whole being. The watch began to shine like a lighthouse in the fog. Allen saw a twinkle of golden light again.

"There, Nancy! Do you see it?" Allen jumped up. He would he dropped Hester to the floor if she had been on his lap. Nancy turned and gazed fixedly at the golden speck of light. She dropped the phone. Bill's voice could be heard in garbled indistinguishable words. She smiled with her whole face and clasped her hands together. "Marie! Marie, baby! Fight your way back."

"Come on, Marie!" said Allen. "You can do it! We need you! We love you!"

They could not see it, but their love for Marie channeled into the watch as well. The Protectors could see two ribbons of light course from them, through the air and into the watch. The ringing was intense, and the golden glow was even brighter than before. Soon ribbons of light poured out of every soul in the room, except Hester, and into the watch. Now when the object could no longer contain such a build-up of power, a sonic burst lit up the room and washed over everyone. Hester was pushed back and pinned to the ground.

Marie stepped forward and put her foot squarely on Hester's chest. "You are done terrifying my family! Tom never loved you. End of story! You're endless antagonizing is over. You will never hurt anyone I love again, as long as I exist!"

247

Lorenzo knelt down on one knee next to Hester as though speaking to a child. "Hester, I know the sweet girl you used to be so long ago. I never left your side. Tom was not meant for you. There was another I'd planned for you, but you never met him because you wouldn't let go of Tom. You chose to follow your own path without me. That's all so long ago. There is still time though if you will let go and turn from your wicked plans."

Hester looked at him astonished. For just a second, she seemed to consider the possibility of a second chance. Then her eyes tightened, and her mouth pursed. "You lie! It's all lies. I will have my revenge!" She squirmed, but the force of Marie's power would not let her get up.

As crowded as it was, a flash of light showed ten souls appearing around Hester. Young men and women, all Protectors in plain white clothes.

"Who are you?" Hester lay suddenly still as her eyes flew up at them.

One young woman looked around the other nine and calmly said, "We are your children, Hester. You've met us, as infants. Each one of us you killed with your bare hands as we gasped for our first breath. Some you killed even before then, before we ever left the womb, but you saw our broken bodies delivered later. That was a long time ago. We have moved on and now we catch the babies whose time comes much too early. We love them and carry them on."

The young woman turned to Ben and smiled.

She continued, "Your choices have brought you to a place where you can't return. Your spell is just witchcraft, bending time and space for a moment, and has no real power. Your real power is your heart, and you have chosen destruction time and time again.

Now it's time for destruction to visit you."

Lorenzo sadly looked down. A tear fell from his eye. "I have always loved you, Hester. I have always been here waiting for you to come to me. I'm so sad for you."

The faces of Hester's ten children turned grim and horrible as they swooped in and carried Hester away in a cloud of dark smoky shadow. Her screams faded away until the room was silent.

Marie looked up at Lorenzo, "Is she gone forever?"

His downcast eyes looked up and rested on her. "Yes. The spell she thought she could inflict on others was false. Just parlor tricks. The only way a soul can be obliterated is by its own choices."

Marie was both relieved and saddened. She had seen that Hester had once been full of life and love, a long, long time ago, but that person had become twisted and lost.

"I must go," said Lorenzo as he smiled at Marie. "You have grown so much. I'm so proud of you. You have been given a rare gift to see what most must learn by faith."

He looked at Allen who was still searching the air for any sign of Marie. "You have also gotten through to others who now have great faith in what they do not see. You will find a way back. I believe in you."

A brilliant white ring of light appeared around him and consumed him.

Tom and Jenny breathed a huge sigh of relief as they
each grabbed one of Henry's arms and hugged him. "What happened in there when you were inside the rift?

Did you see Hester with you?" Tom asked.

"No," said Henry. "It was just darkness and

silence. I felt very alone. Then, it seemed like no time had passed, and it threw me out onto the floor here."

"Very strange. It must have been a sort of worm hole in space. We thought we lost you, again." He hugged Henry again and started tearing up. "We love you very much, son."

Marie thought how strange the scene looked since they were all the same age in appearance. She noticed Allen was inspecting the area where she was standing. His arm passed through her as he felt the air. His face twisted in frustration.

Marie turned back to the others and said, "I have to figure out how to get back in my body!" She walked over to the bed and tried to mesh the two parts of her, but nothing changed. Her soul was no longer stuck to her body. "Whatever Hester did, I must undo it. But how can I find out what she did?"

Jacob spoke up, "Marie, I heard the woman at the incense shop tell Allen that Hester had somehow taken the body of a woman before and lived at the shop for a while. That was the other case of a person being forcefully pushed to the other world while their body still lived. Maybe there we would find clues? Maybe her Protector at the incense shop knows something."

"Hm." Marie recalled briefly seeing the shopkeeper's Protector. "I suppose it's a start. Ben, are you up for a mystery to solve?"

"Any time, sweet girl. Let's go!" Marie put an invisible kiss on Allen's cheek and took Ben's hand. The bright light flashed, and they were gone.

Nancy and Allen looked at each other.

She said, "Allen, I really have the feeling we are not alone here."

"I know. I never would have believed it before,"

Allen shook his head as he spoke.

Lucinda, Jacob, Tom, Jenny, and Henry chuckled.

31   - ON THE SCENT

Peaceful quiet filled the incense shop as completely as the sweet scent of sandalwood can fill every corner of a room with pleasant fragrance. Jasmina's hands moved in rhythmic undulation as she crocheted brown yarn into a long chain. Marie wondered how the store stayed in business because neither time that she had been there were any customers. Did the storekeeper get lonely? There didn't seem to be anyone else living there.

Marie slowly moved along a display table with shelves made of wooden milk crates. In the open side of the crate, display stands held necklaces and earrings made from beads that looked like little stones. Perhaps they were stones from the nearby creeks. Hats fashioned from wool that had been shaped into feminine, graceful slopes and curves sat on short hat stands on top of the crates. The hats had ribbons of grosgrain or lace around them. They had a slightly homemade, natural look. Marie thought they must have been dyed using plants or natural materials.

She continued to the corner of the shop by the bookcase where she had seen the Protector before, browsing as she went as though she had a real body and might even be a customer. As she passed the glass counter where Jasmina sat perched on a stool, she noticed that Jasmina was wholly unaware of her presence. Marie remembered that Jasmina said she could only see her Protector and decided this must be true. Ben found a chair near the window and plopped down.

The little bell on the door jingled and Marie jumped at the unexpected noise. She turned to see a young woman in a tank top and long flowing pants over sandals come in. She had a wide smile for no apparent reason. The customer walked over the counter, passing right through Marie, and began a conversation about a new store in town that sold yarn. The two of them chit-chatted like two birds without any notion Marie was nearby.

The back of Marie's scalp had that odd sensation of contracting, making the hair stand up and causing a slightly tickling sensation. Someone was watching her. She turned back to the ladies who were oblivious to anything going on around them. Marie casually scanned the room until she noticed a screen with four hinged panels, about five feet tall, sitting in a corner. Various scarves and shawls had been draped over it causing a chaotic mixing of colors and patterns. As Marie investigated closer, tiptoeing around a table, she saw a face peering at her from the side.

"It's okay. I won't hurt you." Marie sensed the girl was afraid. "I'm Marie."

"I know who you are, or, at least who you say you are."

The voice had a slightly Italian dialect.

"I just want to talk to you. I need help."

"I have nothing to say to you. Now leave." The firmness of those last two words made Marie feel like she was about to argue with her wise grandmother.

253

"Why? Are you afraid of me?" The Protector just stood there un-answering. "I just wondered if you could help me, help me get back in my body. I'm not supposed to be here, see?"

The young woman stood motionless at first and then shifted her weight nervously. "I know who you are! You are that devil, Hester! Now get out, I say!" She raised her arms as if to push Marie out of the store, stepping closer to her.

Marie's breathing quickened. "Wait! I'm not Hester! Hester is gone, for good." Marie paused. "She somehow separated me from my body, and I want to go back. I'm still alive. I just thought you might know how Hester did that and maybe I could undo it."

The girl must have believed Marie because she lowered her arms and looked at Marie more closely. Her mouth was a firm line, but her eyes showed concern. She seemed to argue with herself. Finally, she said, "I am Ana."

"Nice to meet you, Ana. Can you help me?"

"That, I do not know. No one is supposed to be here in the other world with a body still living. The soul is what gives the body life. So, what keeps your body alive now?" Ana peered at her daring her to contradict what she knew to be true.

"Um, I don't know."

"Let me explain." She had a European accent that Marie couldn't place. At first it seemed like Italian, but now it seemed a little like Russian. It was nothing like Marie had ever heard. "I was very old when I crossed over. I had lived a long, beautiful life. Of course, you see me at my prime, but I lived to be over 90 years old, which was remarkable in the 1600s. Ah, I don't know." She gestured wildly with her hands, "I only ate what I could grow from the soil. No meats. Maybe that was it.

"I had a wonderful husband." Her eyes shifted to the floor and then slowly back, "He was my life, and I was his. We made many beautiful babies." She winked at Marie and smiled.

"Oh! Was he a lover!" Then she laughed, but quickly the smile faded. "He was older than me by four years. And one day, when his body finally was too old, he took a nap and didn't wake up."

She continued, "Life without him was not life. Even though I had a big family with children and grandchildren and even their children, he was my life. We shared the same life chord with the fates, I suppose. My heart went with him when he died. He was all I thought about. I wondered where he could be. Surely someone as full of life as my Dimitry was not gone forever. I could feel my life seeping away as my heart yearned for him. For all intents, my soul had left my body to search for him. And I died. It was just a month after him. My body ceased living and released me so I could find him."

"Did you? Did you find him?"

"She beamed with delight, "Oh, yes! He was there with me all along. He took my hand as I stepped out of life and into the other world. We were together a long time, centuries! Now, Jasmina is the last of our family. She has no children. I chose to stay with her as her Protector. Dimitry, he is so handsome again, he handles special assignments for Lorenzo. I see him often. When Jasmina has lived her life, together we will go on to paradise. So, do you see? Without the soul, the body wilts away. But not yours, is this so?"

Marie answered, "No. My body is in a coma, at the hospital. I just can't get back in it. I don't stick to it."

"Hm. Very odd. It must have been powerful energy that took you out. I always say, 'You get out what you put in.' Maybe you need powerful energy to fix it."

"So, what happened to the other girl that Hester did this to?"

"Oh, child! Hester is very bad. She sent that girl's soul on and turned right around and planted herself in that girl's body. Then she came here and acted kindly to my Jasmina. Jasmina would trust the big bad wolf, I tell you. I tried to tell her, but she wouldn't listen. Hester knew Jasmina could see me. She figured that Jasmina must be a powerful soul that could help her. I managed to get the newspaper open one day to an article about that poor girl. Her name was Beth. Jasmina saw the picture and the stories didn't match any more than the names. When Jasmina asked Hester about it, Hester flew out of here. Her cover was blown. She threw herself over a bridge and released herself. I was never so glad to see her gone."

"So, you never saw how she did it to the girl in the first place?"

"No. No I didn't. It was too late for Beth for it be fixed, what with Hester running around in her skin. But you, you have a chance."

"Yeah, if I only knew how."

As Marie thought about this, the sound of Jasmina and the customer's voices caught her attention.

Jasmina said, "Well, it helps to have friends. You must have people to help you when you can't help yourself. All the goodness just rains on you and good things happen." Marie thought how Allen would have thought that was the biggest bunch of woo-hoo nonsense he'd ever heard. Even so, maybe she was right, maybe alone she wouldn't be enough to fix this.

32   - DESPAIR

Marie and Ben left the shop. After all she had been through, even with Hester gone, it seemed like nothing was going to restore her back to her body. They went back to the reservoir where it all began for her. It was that reservoir where she first saw the Shadows. Maybe she would find a clue or think of something.

They sat on the edge of the reservoir in the exact place where she fell in, cross-legged on a boulder. The water looked calm, like it should have been that terrible day, but wasn't. The sun shined down in the water making bright green shafts of bubbly light for nearly ten feet. You couldn't see the bottom. Thoughts of the Shadows down there grabbing at her sent shivers up her back. If they were still there, there was no hint of them now.

"Do you want to go down and look? I mean, you don't need air now, so you won't drown. You won't even get wet." Ben asked.

Marie thought a minute. The idea of it terrified her, but a new thought crept into her mind. A fierce strength demanded to be acknowledged, "Yes. I want to go down there. I need to see it again."

"Well okay. Come on." Ben stood up and started

down the side. He stepped into the water, which oddly didn't move. No ripples, no splashes. He didn't even displace any water. He turned and held out his hand to her.

Marie stood and cautiously started down the large rocks on the side fearing she would slip, and it would all happen again. She realized she would not slip. She wasn't a part of the natural world at that moment. She inched into the water without feeling any temperature change, pressure, wetness, nothing. It was no different than air now. She took Ben's hand and the two slipped under the unmoving calm surface. A hiker passing by would have seen nothing at all.

The shafts of green light danced on their faces. Tiny bubbles floated past from plant life giving off oxygen bubbles. In this space below the surface, it was beautiful- a silent garden. Marie looked at the wall of green that encircled them. The realm of unknown was just beyond what her eyes could see.

Ben moved farther down the side of the reservoir until they passed the depth where sunlight easily reached. Now Marie could barely make out Ben in front of her. When she looked up, she could see the light green of the surface. Just a few more steps and she realized they were at the bottom. It sloped a gradual incline toward the center of the reservoir. Memories of Hester and the Shadows seized her, and she nearly panicked. She tugged at Ben's hand to come back.

Ben was next her. "Are you okay?" His words were perfect. Not garbled like the times she'd played games with her friends in a swimming pool trying to send messages underwater. It was surreal.

"I- I'm afraid."

Ben smiled a comforting smile. "I've never been afraid. Not for my safety. I have been afraid for another person. No, sad, really. There is nothing to fear. Your body is not here. The only thing that could hurt your soul is you."

Marie thought about what an amazing reality this was. She really was free. She was the only thing that could hold herself back. Her fear was all that blocked her path. She smiled at Ben. "You would have been an incredible man, Ben."

"Perhaps, but the credit you give me is only because I never learned fear like the living do."

"Maybe, but it's a shame you never lived." "Am I not living now?"

"Yes. You are living now. I'm the one with the handicap. But I am learning not to let it slow me down." She smiled and turned toward the darkness. Ben walked with her holding her hand.

At the center on the reservoir, in the dark forest-green water, Marie sat down cross legged and waited. There was no other sound. No breathing, no water gurgling, no movement, only her mind raced. Fears came into focus, and she bashed them away. They were fears for safety and fears for her future. Fears for Allen and her parents. Fears of loneliness and isolation. Fears of never fulfilling her childhood dreams. Each time she felt the fear grip her; she tossed it aside with the pure understanding that love was all that matters. Loving those around her, having faith that everything else would either come or not matter, and knowing that she had the power within her to make a difference to the people she loved was enough to save humanity. If everyone just knew this and strove to use that power, there would be no more pain. Each of us would be as powerful as we could imagine if we loved instead of feared.

"I think I understand now." Marie stood up and hugged Ben. "Ben, you are a wonderful man. I am so lucky to have you as my Protector." The antique watch glowed softly in the darkness. The circle of light emanated out and created a tangible feeling of warmth for both of them. Ben smiled at Marie.

Marie closed her eyes and bowed her head. "Please let Mom and Dad find love in their hearts for each other. Help them to see each other as the precious mates for each other that they are. Help them not worry about me. Help them figure all this out so they are confident. Help Allen not feel alone. Give him hope and strength. Help him know I am close, whether in person or in spirit. Help them all to know that only love can fix all our hurts. We need each other so much. Help everyone everywhere know that by helping each other, we all win. Help us love the unlovable, as well as the sweetest ones."

Marie opened her eyes and felt so strong. The bright glow of the watch had filled the whole reservoir. There was nothing hidden. The beauty of the underwater world reminded her of a fairy wonderland. Air bubbles in the water sparkled like fairy dust. Instead of a frightening place, she saw only magical beauty. She laughed out loud.

"Come on, Ben! Let's go to the Gathering. I want to talk to Lorenzo more." In a twinkle of light compared to the glow of the watch, they vanished. Only visible to the spirit world, the reservoir continued to glow in the aftermath of such love for quite some time.

33   - LIFTED UP

The following Saturday evening, Bill came to stay with Nancy at the hospital. He had a gift under his arm, a silver- colored shoe box with a red velvet bow. When he came into Marie's room, Nancy stood up and hugged him. He handed her the box.

"This is just something to try and replace what was lost. I'm so sorry. I don't know what happened that day." She smiled a half-smile, half-despairing expression as she took the box.

"You didn't have to do that."

"I know. It's not the same, but, well, maybe you'll like it." She pulled at the ribbon and opened the lid. Inside the smooth white tissue paper, she saw two perfect light blue velvet slippers encrusted with pearls and rhinestones. She gasped.

"Oh, Bill, they are beautiful! Where did you find them?"

"There is an auction house near home, and they were having an estate sale. The auctioneer said the shoes had belonged in the family for generations."

"Oh, if these shoes could talk, I bet they could tell a tale. Thank you, Bill. They're lovely!" She beamed and hugged his neck.

"Anything new about Marie?" Bill looked at

his

daughter seemingly asleep on the bed.

Nancy admired the slippers a moment and then set them on the counter by the bed. "No. No change. Bill, the college is hosting a candlelight vigil tonight for Marie. Allen and I have been thinking of ways to send positive energy her way and I asked the college if they might organize something. It starts in just a few minutes. It's down at the Europa Café. We might be able to see the candle lights from the window. Let's look." She opened the curtains, and they looked out. From the window, they could see a glow of golden light rising from the street in the distance. Nancy took Bill's hand and looked back at Marie.

"Let's pray for her, Bill."

"Okay." He would do anything for his daughter. They held hands, closed their eyes, and prayed for Marie to get well and come back to them.

***

At his apartment, Allen sat alone at the table. He fumbled with a bracelet Marie always wore. The gold chain felt warm in his hands. The warm yellow light of the chandelier reflected off the smooth braided metal. It reminded him of the golden light he saw at the hospital when he'd seen her.

"Marie, please be strong. Come back to us. I love you. I need you here. We have a whole life to live. Please find your way back."

Allen continued to pray as the evening light outside faded.

***

At the Europa, students filled the street holding little candles punched through a paper cup to catch the wax. The waitresses at the Europa joined them. Several Sonora residents who never knew her joined because of the heartfelt plea from the college. In the crowd, a young woman with a baby held a candle, too. Near her was an older man, alone.

A man from the college with a microphone was asking everyone to quiet down. The police had temporarily blocked the street so people could crowd in.

"Ladies and gentlemen, we come here together on behalf of a woman in our community that has been in a coma for several weeks. Her family has been traveling very far to be here with her. Her boyfriend is a fellow student at the college. She is cared about very much by them, and by the college. She is loved very much. It came to our attention, and we arranged this candlelight vigil to remember her and show how much we care. You may not have ever met her, but as people that are all interconnected, we must stand up for each other. Her mother and boyfriend believe that maybe we can help her beat this with our prayers and meditations for her." He held his candle out and an assistant lit his candle. He held it above his head. "Let's let our light shine to light the way for her to find her way to health and life." He held out his candle in front of him and two people lit theirs from his. The golden flickering light passed like a wave from person to person, until all Main Street was a sea of glowing, flickering beacons of hope.

    ***

At this moment, Marie was sitting at the Gathering talking to the others and everyone became silent. A trail of light entered one side of the Gathering, moving quickly like a sunrise on a hillside, it lit a path. Everyone watched it in surprise. Lorenzo stood up and began laughing with joy.

"It's time Marie! Time for you to go back." He reached out his hand to her. She paused briefly, unsure of what was happening. She turned back to the Protectors. Tom, Jenny, and Henry smiled at her. Ben was pleased.

The light reached her and began to pour into the Sarah Elizabeth's gold watch. The ringing was like a chorus of angels and golden, blinding light encircled her and Lorenzo.

"Thank you. I'm so glad I had this time with you." She turned back to Lorenzo and took his hand.

Ben stood up, "I guess this means I'm back on duty."

The others nodded in agreement.

Marie put her hand in Lorenzo's and felt herself pulled away. At the speed of thought, they left the Gathering. They flew over the heads of everyone on Main Street. Marie looked at the hundreds of faces and was overcome as each one prayed for her.

They passed through Allen's apartment, and she saw him praying holding her bracelet. He was crying as he prayed for her. She could just hear, "I love you," as they swooped through on their way through walls to the hospital room.

Pulled by a force she had no control over, a force so powerful you could not resist it, Marie and Lorenzo were drawn to the hospital room where her body lay. Her parents were at the window holding hands and praying for her. The evening sky behind them glowed brightly as the reservoir had. She couldn't tell if it was the candles or the spiritual residue of the love from all the prayers.

"Marie, you have seen far more than any mortal should. It will be hard to go back into the world of pain and hunger and heartbreak. But, every time you can, teach others how much power they must affect good. I love you, Marie. I'm always with you if you call for me." Lorenzo vanished leaving her alone in the room.

Her parents held hands at the window, their eyes still closed.

She walked over to her body and felt a tug. A magnetic pull caught her and pulled her quickly to the center of the bed. Her lungs took a large deep breath and her eyes fluttered open.

Nancy, hearing the shifting of the bed, jerked around, and was filled with joy. Bill turned, too, and they both ran to her side.

"Mom? Dad?"

"Marie!" They exclaimed together and hugged her.

"Oh, it's so good to be back," she said. She sat up in bed. Her body felt stiff and weak. A glint of light caught her eye as she sat up and she looked down. She had the gold watch on.

"Marie!" Her mother gasped, "How did you get this?" Her mother reached out to touch the watch and examine it closely.

"You'd never believe it."

"Well, lately, I just might believe anything!" She laughed

with tears in her eyes.

They exchanged more hugs and smiles and then Nancy pressed the call button for the nurse.

The nurse nearly fell over when she came in the room and saw Marie sitting there chatting away with Bill. Nancy got on the phone and called Allen. Before the evening was out, the whole town was talking about the miracle of the Candlelight Vigil. People laughed and hugged. For a little while, maybe just a couple of days, the Shadows couldn't get in edgewise in Sonora, and peace was felt by everyone.

***

Marie's wheelchair bumped out of the sliding hospital doors as the nurse pushed her. The warm June breeze lifted her hair, and she closed her eyes and sighed. Warm sun caressed her cheeks. She was so glad to have her senses alive again. Lydia came around the corner carrying two carry-out cups of coffee and stopped dead in her tracks when she saw Marie being discharged.

"Oh, Marie. You're- you're better." Lydia said with forced enthusiasm. She looked from side to side as though looking for someone.

"Hi, Lydia. Yes. Thanks to the love and prayers of so many," she smiled at Allen who was sitting in the driver's seat of the car parked at the curb, "I pulled through. I hear you tried hard to take care of Allen while I was… here."

"Uh…, well, just trying to be nice, I guess." Lydia's smile looked strained.

"Right. Lydia, come here." Marie motioned for her to come close. Lydia cautiously stepped closer.

"Yeah?"

"You know, you are an awesome…" Marie touched Lydia's arm, "beautiful girl, capable of bringing such joy if you choose to. I'm going to pray for you to find a man that sees that in you."

Lydia looked at her stunned. "Uh, thanks?" Marie hoped Lydia would take it for what it was, the truth, and not some sort of backhanded insult. Lydia turned and went down the sidewalk as if she was at the hospital with some other intention besides bringing coffee to Allen. Marie watched her go and sighed when she saw the female shape take form next to Lydia, its gnarled hand on her shoulder. Lydia walked through another set of sliding doors without ever noticing her companion.

The nurse pushing Marie's wheelchair said goodbye as Allen jumped out of his new Jeep and ran around to get her door. Marie stood up and hugged him.

"Oh! Look at this! Your new Jeep is awesome! Oh, Allen, I can't believe what you went through without me. I'm so sorry."

"It seems like you went through an awful lot without me there, too," he said.

She climbed up into the seat, and he closed the door. Seconds later he bounded into the driver's seat from the other side, and they drove away.

He asked, "Are you hungry?"

"Yeah! How about a club sandwich at the Europa?"

"Sounds great," he said.

A few minutes later, they pulled up to the parking lot and jumped out. She was still a little wobbly from not using her legs in weeks, but she felt so alive. A soft rain started to fall through the sunlight, splashing large drops of water on them.

"Come on," he said motioning her to hurry.

"No. I just want to feel the wetness." She licked her lips and tasted the sweet soft rain drops. She smiled a broad grin and hugged him.

He clasped his arms around her waist and twirled her in a circle, laughing like a fool. He stopped and bent his head down until his face was nearly touching hers. She could feel the heat of his skin and smell the warm musky aftershave he liked.

"I love you, Marie."

"I love you, Allen."

"Always and forever," she said.

"Yes, Always and forever, he replied."

His lips covered hers and he pulled her so close she felt like surely nothing could ever break them apart.

EPILOGUE

An old woman lay in a hospital bed surrounded by her children. Her soft grey eyes were weak but still crinkled in the corners as she hugged each one.

"It won't be long now. Now you all don't weep for me. I'm going somewhere better. I love each one of you."

The old woman relaxed back into her pillow and her breathing got lighter and lighter. Soon she drifted out of consciousness and all the sound went away.

"Momma? Momma?" She heard a young man's voice say. She opened her eyes and saw a young man with whom she was not familiar. He held is hand out to her. She looked into his hazel eyes and then at his brown wavy hair. His sweet face seemed so soft and unhardened, as though he had never lived in the world, nor had the sun bake down on him.

"You call me Momma?"

He smiled, "It's been a long time, but I told you I would wait for you. I'm Ben. The one you lost."

She smiled and tears streamed down her cheeks. "Oh, son! I never forgot you," she managed to say as her mouth twisted into a crying smile.

"I know, Momma. I heard you telling me often. I

never felt alone because I could hear you." He hugged her and said, "Come on. There are others for you to meet."

She reached out her withered, pale hand and placed it in his.

Ben pulled her out of the bed, and she turned back to see her other children. They embraced each other supportively, and she knew they would be okay.

She turned to go and as she walked away, her image shimmered. Her white tufty hair smoothed and grew longer, sweeping down over her shoulders in a chestnut wave. The wrinkles on her face flattened and disappeared. Her withered arms and legs became strong and muscled, but one thing that didn't change was the expression of eternal joy as she gazed at her fine son leading her.

"I wish you could have met your Daddy," she said. "I already have! In fact, he's waiting to see you, too."

With an easy step, her arm curled around his, they disappeared in a bright flash of light.

THE END

REFERENCES

They Might Be Giants. Istanbul (not Constantinople).
Elektra, 1990. CD.

***

If you enjoyed Between Time, please leave an honest review on Amazon, Goodreads or Smashwords. Reviews help other readers choose to purchase a book and in turn help me as an author. I truly appreciate your feedback. If you would like to let me know your opinion of my books, email me at Carolynbondwriter@outlook.com.

www.ingramcontent.com/pod-product-compliance
Lightning Source LLC
Chambersburg PA
CBHW070748280626
47162CB00018B/2777